THE *Anti-* BOYFRIEND

PENELOPE WARD

First Edition
Copyright © 2020
By Penelope Ward
ISBN-10: 1951045378
ISBN-13: 978-1951045371

This book is a work of fiction. All names, characters, locations, and incidents are products of the author's imagination. Any resemblance to actual persons, things living or dead, locales, or events is entirely coincidental.

Edited by: Jessica Royer Ocken
Proofreading and formatting by: Elaine York
www.allusiongraphics.com
Cover photographer: Nadia von Scotti
Cover design: Letitia Hasser, RBA Designs
www.rbadesigns.com

THE Anti-
BOYFRIEND

ONE

Carys

MONKEY BALLS

The sound of the bed creaking might as well have been nails on a chalkboard. My neighbor, Deacon, didn't always have women over, but when he did—boy, he *really* had them over. Over him. Under him.

Tonight was the loudest one of all, and the noise always seemed to kick up just when I'd nod off. Once something woke me, it took a long time to fall asleep again. They tell mothers to *sleep when your baby sleeps*. Well, that's not possible when the apartment next door is *The Bachelor's* fantasy suite.

My daughter Sunny's room was on the opposite side of our place, so thankfully, the noise coming from 5B didn't wake her. But my room was right on the other side of the wall from Deacon's bedroom. I heard the bed moving, and each and every sound of pleasure was clear as day—every excruciating moan, groan, and shriek. And as a bonus, I could feel the vibrations right behind my headboard. Sadly, this was the closest I'd come to getting action in over a year.

You'd think I'd have the balls to bang on the wall or something, but I felt like I didn't have the right to interrupt.

1

After all, he was a single guy living his best life in his own apartment; he was allowed to have sex. He couldn't help it if the walls were thin.

It wouldn't have been such a big deal if he were quick. But he had so much stamina! Like the Energizer Bunny of cock.

Did I mention that Deacon was hot as hell? I'd only met him a few times in passing, but it was hard not to stare at his sculpted face with its perfectly placed chin scruff over his angular jaw. Knowing what he looked like didn't help this situation, because yes, I was annoyed, but imagining what was happening on the other side of the wall wasn't exactly a hardship. The imagery itself was enough to keep me awake.

So there you have it, my pathetic situation.

Eventually, as always, it stopped. The banging and sounds of sex morphed into muffled laughter and talking.

As I tried once again to fall asleep, I vowed that the next time I ran into Deacon in the hallway, I'd gently make him aware of the situation. Surely he didn't realize our beds were back to back, since he'd never been in my apartment. It would be an uncomfortable conversation, but it had to happen. I needed my sleep. I wasn't working at the moment, but taking care of my six-month-old daughter was a full-time job.

Sunny was the beautiful result of a brief relationship with my former boss, who'd ended up going back to his ex-wife before he realized I was pregnant. He'd wanted nothing to do with me nor the baby once he found out I was carrying his child, so I'd been raising her with virtually no help—aside from some money he'd send me when he felt like it. I should emphasize that he and his wife had been legally separated for over a year when I met him.

I'd always told myself I'd go back to work when Sunny turned six months old, but we'd just reached that milestone, and it hadn't happened yet. I missed getting out of the house and socializing each day, and yearned to go back at least part time. Affording childcare was a lot easier said than done, though. Not to mention, I wasn't totally ready to leave Sunny. But I struggled with the decision, because I was slowly going insane without adult interaction. Would leaving Sunny to go back to work make me a bad mother?

That was the type of question that kept me up at night—that is, when my studly neighbor wasn't the one responsible.

The following day, Sunny was down for her afternoon nap, which usually gave me about an hour and a half, though possibly three hours on rare occasions. That time was pretty much my only guilty pleasure. *Me* time. When she first fell asleep, I would make myself lunch while watching *The Young and the Restless* on low volume. I wasn't really all that into the show, but it reminded me of my childhood and being home sick from school when my grandmother would watch me.

Leaving my sleeping daughter alone even for the one minute it took me to check the mail always made me nervous. So, after lunch I'd run downstairs and open the mailbox as fast as I could before sprinting back up. It probably took me under a minute, and I never left without the baby monitor in hand.

Today, just as I got back to my door, Deacon was exiting his apartment.

"Oh, hey, Carys-Like-Paris. How goes it?" He flashed a wide smile.

When people ask me my name, for some stupid reason, I sometimes answer, "Carys, like Paris," particularly when I'm nervous. That was the case the first time I met Deacon.

A whiff of his amazing smell put my body on alert. He looked handsome as always. Today he wore a camel-colored suede coat with a shearling collar. His blue eyes, which stood out against his tanned skin, glimmered under the fluorescent lights overhead, which also brought out the copper tint to his otherwise medium-brown hair. He was at least six-foot-two—a beanstalk to my five-foot-four self.

This was my opportunity to bring up last night. But now that he was right here, towering over me, his musky smell saturating the air, I seemed to have lost the words. Still, I was determined to speak up now or never.

My heartbeat accelerated. *Here goes.* Still out of breath from my sprint up the stairs, I said, "Well, honestly, in answer to your question... I'd love to say I'm doing great, but I had a hard time getting to sleep last night. So, I've been better."

He frowned. "I'm sorry to hear that."

"Actually, it's sort of your fault."

Deacon's forehead crinkled. "My fault?"

"Yeah. I don't know if you realize this, but your bed is right up against mine, on the opposite side of the wall.

4

Your...*interactions*...last night woke me up, and I had a hard time getting back to sleep."

Boom.

There.

Said it.

Deacon closed his eyes momentarily. "Shit. I'm sorry. I didn't know you were right behind me."

"Yeah. It's basically like I'm...right there."

"Well, that was rude of me. I should've invited you to join."

What? It felt like all my blood rushed to my head.

He held out his palms. "I'm kidding. Bad sense of humor comes out when I feel awkward, I guess."

Slipping a piece of my hair behind my ear, I brushed off his comment. "I know you're kidding."

"Totally kidding." He smiled. "But I'll try to be more considerate now that I know you can hear everything. You should've said something."

I tilted my head. "How exactly would that have worked? Barging in on two naked people? That's why I'm saying something now."

"Solid point. But I take it last night wasn't the first time you overheard things?"

I looked down at my feet. "No, it wasn't."

"You could've banged on the wall or something."

"I'm not one to rudely interrupt someone's...personal happenings. I just wanted you to be aware of the situation. We don't need to discuss it further."

"Maybe we should come up with a code."

"What do you mean?"

"Like, if I'm disturbing your peace, you play a song and crank it up to send me a message." He snapped his

5

fingers. "Something ironic like 'The Sounds of Silence' by Simon and Garfunkel."

"Can't exactly crank up a song when a baby is sleeping."

His smile faded. "See? That goes to show you how clueless I am. Clueless and so sorry, Carys. Truly. I'll try not to let it happen again."

"It better not, fuckboy!" a voice shouted from behind one of the apartment doors.

Deacon and I turned around in unison. I noticed Mrs. Winsbanger's door move across the hall. The old lady must have been listening in. She lived alone, and I often spotted her peeking out her door, spying on people.

Deacon grimaced. "Mrs. Winsbanger loves me."

"Apparently I'm not the only one who overheard things last night," I said.

His face turned red. His embarrassment was a bit surprising. I'd expected him to be more cocky.

"I'll move my bed to the other side of the room. That should help."

"Well, that would be nice, if it's not too much trouble."

"It's not."

Happy to have the conversation over with, I let out a long breath. "Okay, well, I'll let you get going."

He didn't budge and seemed to be examining my face. "You okay?"

"Yeah. Why?"

"You seem frazzled."

Well, yeah. I didn't get good sleep, I'm trying to get things done in possibly the only hour of the day I have free, and we just had the most awkward conversation EVER.

"This is just me—my life. I have what could be barely more than an hour to eat my lunch and have some quiet time before my daughter wakes up from her nap."

"Ah." He scratched his chin. "How old is she now?"

"Six months."

Deacon knew I was a single mom. He'd run into me one day and helped me bring groceries in while I tried to juggle Sunny and her stroller.

I was just about to head back inside my apartment when his voice stopped me.

"Do you need anything?"

I wasn't entirely sure what he meant. "Like what?"

"Something from the store? A...coffee, maybe? I'm just headed out to run a quick errand, but I can stop somewhere on the way back."

"It's the least you can do, monkey balls!" Mrs. Winsbanger chimed in from across the hall.

She was apparently still listening.

"Did she just fucking call me *monkey balls*?" he whispered.

At that moment, I lost it. Laughter got a hold of me, and it took almost a minute before I could even speak. Deacon laughed, too, but I think he was more cracking up at my reaction.

"No idea why she just called you monkey balls. But I haven't laughed this hard in weeks."

After I finally calmed down, Deacon repeated his earlier question.

"Anyway, as I was saying, can I get you a coffee or something?"

His offer gave me pause. It was rare that anyone asked if I needed anything. I had a couple of good friends in the city, but they worked and had busy social lives. It wasn't like they were around in the middle of the day to run to the store for me. And given that it was fall in New York, it was getting chilly out. I had to have a damn good reason to take Sunny out in the cold.

Honestly, I was dying for a latte from Starbucks. Running to the coffee shop was definitely something people without babies took for granted. It wasn't worth having to bundle Sunny up.

"I would love a vanilla latte from Starbucks, if you pass one on your way back," I finally said.

"Done." He smiled. "That's it?"

"Just one pump of vanilla would be great."

"One pump. Got it. Anything else?"

"Isn't that enough? It's hardly a necessity. I shouldn't be taking advantage."

"Take advantage of me. What else do you need? Seriously. It's the least I can do after disturbing your peace last night."

Take advantage of me. Yup. Mind straight in the gutter. "You're not my gopher."

"Carys...." His baritone voice turned serious, and he repeated in a slow and exaggerated manner, "What. Do. You. Need? I could run to the store."

There *was* something else I desperately needed.

"Diapers?" I said hesitantly.

"Okay." He laughed. "You're gonna have to help me out with those. I've never purchased them in my life."

Before I could tell him what size, he handed me his phone. I was all too aware of the brief touch of his hand.

"Enter your digits. I'll text you from the store to make sure I get the right kind."

I did as he said before handing him back the phone, once again enjoying the contact from that brief exchange. Cheap thrills were as good as it got these days.

He put it in his pocket. "Anything else?"

"Not that I can think of."

"Alright. Well, if you change your mind, you can let me know when I text."

"Thank you. I *really* appreciate it."

"Talk to ya in a bit," he said before heading down the hall.

I stood by my door and watched him walk away. The view from the back was just as good as the front. And moreover, it seemed Deacon was just as lovely on the inside as he was on the outside.

"One pump my ass," I heard Mrs. Winsbanger say before she slammed her door.

———————

A text came in about a half-hour later.

> **Deacon: Okay. I'm in the diaper aisle. There are a lot of choices.**

I smiled as I typed. *Bless his heart.* The idea of my hot neighbor standing clueless in the diaper aisle was as adorable as it was funny. Some unsuspecting mama was going to have a heart attack when she went looking for diaper pail bags and found him instead.

> **Carys: Anything in size 2 will be great.**

Deacon: Huggies or Luvs?

Carys: Whichever is cheaper.

Deacon: Which does she prefer?

Carys: LOL. Well, we've never discussed it. She can't exactly tell me.

Deacon: Ah. Right.

Carys: But Mommy prefers whichever is cheapest.

Deacon: Which do you like better?

Carys: I've never really compared. Either one is fine.

He didn't text again, so I assumed he'd chosen something. Then another message came in.

Deacon: Oh...plot twist!

I laughed.

Carys: What?

Deacon: There's Pampers too.

Carys: Just choose one. LOL

Deacon: There are a couple of women coming to my rescue now. They think I need help.

Sure. I bet it's the diapers they're concerned with. I needed to pick a brand to put him out of his misery.

Carys: Luvs will be great.

Deacon: K. Got 'em!

Carys: Thank you.

Deacon: Anything else while I'm here?

I needed some tampons and deodorant, but I wouldn't dare send him for those.

Carys: No. Thanks. That's it.

A few seconds later, another text came in.

Deacon: What's a peepee teepee?

Lord. He needs to get out of the baby aisle. Cracking up, I typed.

Carys: It's a tent for your wee-wee.

Deacon: A tent for MY wee-wee? Are you suggesting I need one after last night?

I couldn't believe he was bringing that up again. I also couldn't believe how hard I was laughing right now. I'd laughed more today than I had in ages. I hoped I wouldn't wake up Sunny.

Carys: It's for baby boys so they don't piss on people.

Deacon: Ah. Then I'm good. I haven't pissed on anyone in a while. ;-)

Holy shit. Where was this conversation going?

Carys: SMH

Deacon: Doesn't look like they have my size anyway.

Oh my God.

Deacon: Okay. Really leaving this time!

And now I was burning up.

———————————

When Deacon returned a half-hour later, Sunny was still sleeping.

He handed me a bag containing the diapers. He also carried two coffees in a cardboard tray.

He lifted mine out. "I got you a venti. Wasn't sure if that was too big."

"No such thing when it comes to coffee." I smiled and took it. "Thank you."

I walked over to my purse and took out my wallet.

He held out his hand. "No way. Everything's on me."

"I can't let you pay."

"Just consider it my apology for keeping you up last night."

"I need to pay for the diapers at least."

"No, you don't."

"Seriously, I can't—"

"Yes, you can. I won't take it. So put your wallet back."

I was never good at accepting charity but conceded. "Well, thank you."

I took the first sip of the hot, foamy latte and closed my eyes. I moaned, perhaps a little too loudly.

"You sound like something coming out of my bedroom last night." He laughed.

I nearly spit out the coffee.

My face must have turned red too, because he added, "Too much?"

"Actually, no. I appreciate you making light of the situation and not pegging me as the bitchy neighbor." I took another sip of my coffee. "This is so good. I haven't had one of these in a while."

"Any time you want one, if you can't leave, just let me know. I'll make a coffee run. It's right down the street."

As tempting as that was, I wouldn't be beckoning Deacon to fetch me coffee anytime soon. If there was one thing I hated, it was appearing needy.

I squinted. "Why do you have to be so nice? It makes it hard to be annoyed at you."

"I didn't realize being annoyed at me was a goal of yours." He smiled and looked around. "Your daughter is still sleeping?"

"Yeah. It's been a couple of hours now—above average, though on occasion, she'll go to about three. I'm loving it. It's rare to get this long of a break."

"Well, I'd better not say *monkey balls* again. Otherwise you'll start laughing and wake her up."

And now I was laughing again. I covered my mouth to dampen the sound. "Oh my God, that was so funny."

"Have I mentioned Mrs. Winsbanger *loves* me?" he asked. "She gives me the stink eye, too."

"Have you actually *seen* her? I normally just notice her door cracked open when she's spying on people in the hallway. I think I've only seen her once or twice."

"One time I tried to help her carry some shit in, but she refused and gave me the dirtiest look. You would've thought I was trying to rob her. I was just trying to help." He grabbed his phone. "Let me look it up."

"Look up what?"

"Monkey balls. Maybe I'm missing something." He typed something and scrolled. "According to this, *monkey balls* is slang for chafing that causes guys to walk like a monkey." He looked up from his phone. "Well, shit. That doesn't sound too pleasant." He returned his eyes to the screen. "Oh! Look at this. Monkey balls are also an inedible fruit used for pest control. They ward off spiders."

"You learn something new every day." I chuckled.

"Thanks to Mrs. Winsbanger." He rolled his eyes, putting his phone down.

Gosh, my cheeks hurt. Having him here made me realize again how much I'd missed adult interaction.

He took his drink out of the tray, and I noticed he had some ink on his left wrist, coming out from under his sleeve. I wondered how much of his arm was covered. Part of the ink was a word, but I couldn't see it clearly aside from "hie" at the end. Was it a name? *Ruthie*? No clue.

He had the biggest, most beautiful hands, too, with prominent veins and rough skin. Long fingers. Deacon was the epitome of masculinity. I forced my eyes away from admiring him, instead focusing on the writing on the side of the cup he held. He seemed to have ordered three shots of espresso straight, no milk. A strong drink to match a strong man.

He noticed me looking at his cup. "They got my name wrong. They wrote *Beekman*. Who the fuck's name is *Beekman*?"

"My dad's actually," I said, forcing a straight face.

"Are you serious?"

Releasing my stoic expression, I shook my head. "No."

"Ah...Carys made a funny. Maybe she's more than just the prude next door."

"Hey!" I laughed.

He winked. "You know I'm kidding."

"Well, I can certainly relate to the name screw-up thing. Normally, they write Paris on mine, even though I sound out the C pretty clearly."

"That's true, *Carys-Like-Paris*."

"Sometimes they write Karen." I shrugged. "Happens all the time."

His eyes lingered on mine. "Carys is a unique name. I like it a lot."

There was something about the way this man looked at you when he spoke. He gave you every shred of his

15

attention. His eyes were two giant spotlights on me that drowned out the rest of the world.

Feeling my cheeks heat up, I said, "Thank you. It's Welsh."

"Are you Welsh?"

"My mother is half Welsh, yes."

"Well, it's a beautiful name."

A shiver ran down my spine, as if he'd complimented me on something much more exciting than my name.

My senses were having a field day between Deacon's amazing scent and the delicious aroma of the espresso—two of my favorite smells blended together. But mostly my body was hyperaware of the gorgeous creature standing in front of me—one who'd made a woman scream in pleasure just last night.

Deacon walked over to the corner of the room. I admired him as he examined the photos displayed on my shelves. Most of them were of Sunny, but he lifted one of me. I braced myself as he looked back and forth from the photo to where I was standing.

"You were a ballet dancer?"

I nodded. "Yeah. I was...for several years. Not anymore, obviously."

"Professionally?"

"Yes. I performed for The Manhattan Ballet as a principal dancer."

If I'd thought his stare was penetrating before, that was nothing compared to the way he looked at me now.

"Wow." He glanced back down at the photo. It showed me in an arabesque. He looked at it for longer than I was comfortable with. "Why did you stop?"

I swallowed, not prepared for this discussion. "I had an injury, and it forced me to retire." Saying the words aloud left a bitter taste in my mouth.

He seemed to freeze, looking almost like it devastated him to hear what had happened to me. "I'm sorry. That had to have been hard to go through."

"It wasn't easy."

Deacon stared at me, and with each second that passed, I felt a little more naked.

"It was the hardest thing I'd been through up to that point," I finally admitted.

"What did you do...after? When you couldn't dance anymore?"

"I took a behind-the-scenes position with the company for a couple of years."

"What happened with that?"

I shrugged. "Sunny happened."

"Ah." He sighed and placed the frame back on the bookshelf. "Of course."

The fact that he seemed genuinely interested gave me a push to open up a bit more. "Well...Sunny happening is the short version, actually. The longer story is that I began a relationship with the director of the ballet. Charles is the son of the long-time owner. He's in his position via nepotism. Charles was legally separated from his wife at the time I was working for him. He left me to go back to her, but not before I got pregnant."

"Shit," Deacon said, taking a few steps toward me.

"Yeah." I exhaled. "Finding out about the baby didn't change anything with us. And honestly, I wouldn't have taken him back anyway. He had two kids already, and while

17

he did tell his ex-wife—now wife again—about Sunny, he's chosen not to tell his children about their half-sister. He asked me to keep his name off the birth certificate."

"He doesn't support her at all?"

"He gives me money under the table. It's a minimal amount, but it helps. I take it because I'm not going to let pride get in the way of caring for my daughter."

"Well, that's really sucky of him not to take more responsibility."

"I'd honestly rather he not be in her life at this point. The only thing that feels worse than not having a father around is feeling rejected by the father you do see from time to time."

He examined my eyes. "You sound like you have personal experience with that."

Somehow this coffee run had turned into a therapy session. Deacon had a certain quality that made me feel like I could tell him anything, like he wouldn't judge.

"You would be correct," I said. "My dad wasn't around for me." I shook my head and looked down. "Anyway, no need to get into my life story. You went for coffee. This is more than you bargained for."

"Are you kidding? I'm the one asking the questions. Sorry for being nosy." He took a sip of his drink. "Anyway, I hope you don't mind me saying, I've always been curious about you—your deal, what happened to your baby's dad. It's none of my business, but I did wonder."

I sighed. "Well, now you know."

"Yeah." He smiled.

Since he didn't seem to be going anywhere, I decided to ask something *I'd* been curious about.

"So, what about you? What's *your* deal, Deacon? Are you from New York?"

"No, actually. I'm from Minnesota originally. I came out to New York from California a few years back because I wanted a change. But I can work from anywhere."

"What do you do?"

"I design interactive games for a company based out of Asia."

"That sounds so cool."

"Definitely not a career I could've predicted, but it's fun. Our app is very popular, and it does well. So that gives me a little job security in the otherwise unpredictable field of entertainment."

"So you never have to go into an office?"

"I work from home the majority of the time. Only have to go to the company's New York office occasionally for meetings. Their headquarters are in Japan."

"That's a great situation."

"It is. But sometimes it's hard to get your shit together at home. I get distracted a lot."

"Yeah. I think I might have heard one of those distractions during the afternoon once." I winked.

"Ouch." He grimaced. "And here I was, thinking I'd done a good job distracting from your initial impression of me." He formed his fingers into an L for *loser* over his forehead. "Fail."

I laughed. "Just teasing." It amazed me how fast I'd grown comfortable around him. I enjoyed his company.

"Anyway," he said. "The good thing about working remotely is that I can work at all hours. So if I'm goofing off during the day, I get my shit done at night."

"It's awesome to have flexibility like that. I'm trying to find a similar type job as we speak. Know of anyone hiring?"

"Not off the top of my head, but I can keep an ear out. What kind of work are you looking for?"

"Well, my experience is pretty much administrative work. So, maybe like a virtual assistant? But I'm open to something new. I have a degree in general studies, but I spent so many years focused on ballet that my resume is limited, aside from the couple of years I worked behind the scenes. I assumed for so long that dancing would be my career."

"Of course." He nodded. "That makes sense."

I fiddled with the green stopper that had come with my latte. "Not having a job has been fine for a while. I always planned to stay home with Sunny initially, but I think it would be good for my mental health to get out of the house a couple of days a week or find something I can do from home. It's hard to find the perfect situation. But I definitely don't want to leave her five days a week."

Deacon let out an exasperated breath, seeming almost overwhelmed. "A kid changes everything, huh?"

"Yeah. It really does. These six months have gone by in a blur. I feel like I've been in my own world. But I wouldn't trade it. My daughter is everything."

"Well, for what it's worth, from the little I've witnessed, I think you're doing a great job. She seems like a happy baby. You're a good mom."

His words made my heart flutter. I don't think anyone had ever said that to me before. And as much as I knew I was trying my hardest every day, it was nice to hear someone acknowledge it.

"Thank you, Deacon. You're very sweet."

"I don't hear that too often, but okay."

Our eyes locked. Then he suddenly looked down at his phone. "Anyway, I'll let you enjoy the last of your quiet time before she wakes up."

I wanted to tell him he didn't have to leave. Instead, I said, "I'm glad you got to know me a little today—so you know I'm more than just the cranky, cockblocking neighbor."

"And hopefully you see me as more than just the manwhore next door."

"Not quite yet." I winked. "But we're getting there."

He chuckled. "Take care, Carys. And if you need anything from the outside world, just say the word."

My brow lifted. "What's the word?"

He scratched his chin. "That would have to be... *monkey balls.*"

I cackled. "Ah. The perfect choice."

As he headed to his apartment, I called after him, "Thanks again for the diapers and coffee."

He turned around to face me, walking backwards and flashing a gorgeous smile that made my heart ache a little. "Diapers and coffee. Can't say I've ever been thanked for that combination before." He winked. "My pleasure."

After I closed the door, I leaned back against it, catching myself mid-swoon.

Really, Carys? You're pathetic.

Don't even go there. He wouldn't touch this situation with a ten-foot pole. Leave it to my starving heart to take a man's charitable gesture and turn it into the beginning of some unrealistic romance.

After I polished off the rest of my coffee, I opened up the bag of diapers he'd brought.

There was more than just the package of Luv's inside.

He'd thrown in a little stuffed Peppa Pig.

And some earplugs.

TWO

Carys

BABY WHISPERER

A couple of weeks later, Sunny had a pediatrician appointment downtown late in the afternoon. Since we were out and about anyway, I took her to meet my friend Simone for an early dinner at a restaurant near the doctor's office.

"How did her appointment go?" Simone asked as she perused the laminated card that listed today's specials.

"Six-month checkup went great. The doctor says her weight is right on target for her age."

"I'm so glad." She looked up from the menu. "And how are you?"

I paused, momentarily stumped as to how to answer that. "Good...good."

There was no point in venting about my day-to-day problems. Simone and I were in two different places in life, and she likely wouldn't understand. As one of the city's top ballet dancers, Simone was where I would have been had I not been injured: an elite principal dancer, performing at night, sleeping in most mornings, and attending rehearsals in the afternoons, in addition to having an active social life. In many ways, I lived vicariously through her. So, instead of admitting that most days I felt lonely or worried about my finances, I just responded with *good*.

"Have you been taking care of yourself?" she asked.

"You mean like...self-care?"

"Yeah. Taking time for yourself."

I looked over at Sunny, who was sitting up in the highchair. Her cheeks were flushed, likely from the vaccine she'd just received. The doctor had warned me she might get a bit feverish.

I placed my hand on her forehead. "I rest when she rests, but I haven't had a chance to go out much or, you know, get a massage or some crap like that. There's just no time."

Our food arrived, and Simone's questions stopped for a bit as we shoveled in our burgers and fries.

"Are you thinking of going back to work at some point?" she asked suddenly.

Wiping the ketchup off the side of my mouth, I answered. "If I can find someone I trust to watch Sunny. But then I'd have to weigh the cost versus benefit."

"It's too bad your mom isn't closer."

What a joke. "Well, not sure she'd be able to handle it anyway."

I loved my mother, but she wasn't capable of taking care of Sunny. She'd had my brother and me pretty young, and had told me she was done raising kids and now was her time to enjoy life. She'd moved from where I grew up in New Jersey to Florida a few years ago. She'd made her position clear to me the couple of times I'd hinted that I'd appreciate it if she visited more.

Simone jumped in her seat a little, looking like she'd had a lightbulb moment. "You know, Cynthia was telling me they're looking to hire a new PR person. I wonder if she'd consider you for the job. I mean, you know the ins and outs of the ballet. You're attractive—when you're not in your mom uniform—and you're personable. I bet you could do a lot of it from home, writing press releases and such. You'd probably only have to go into the office occasionally or show up for special events."

Simone performed for a different ballet company than I had. While I'd never consider going back to work for my old company—since Sunny's estranged father was still the director—a job at a competitor would be ideal.

I perked up at her suggestion. "Really? You think she'd consider me?"

"She's always talking about how much she admires you. And don't take this the wrong way, but we talk about how much of a shame it is that you were injured in the prime of your career. You're legendary in many ways. Everyone wonders what could have been if Carys Kincaid hadn't been taken out."

I felt her words deep in my soul. The agony over never being able to perform professionally again was something I tried to suppress.

"I'd rather still be dancing than be a legend, but it's nice to know I'm respected posthumously."

"Posthumously? You're not dead, Carys!"

"I know, but in the ballet world, I might as well be."

"Look at it this way, if it weren't for your accident, you'd still be dancing, but you might never have gotten close to Charles, and Sunny would never have come to be.

As much as we hate Charles now, he brought you Sunny. Everything happens for a reason."

"Well, I definitely don't regret her, so you're right about that."

I looked over at my daughter. Sunny smiled as if she could understand we were talking about her. I loved her little pumpkin face so much. She had the Peppa Pig Deacon had gotten her from the store in her hand and waved it around.

"That's such a cute toy," Simone said.

"My neighbor bought it for her."

"The old lady across the hall?"

"No. Not crazy Mrs. Winsbanger. The guy in 5B."

Her eyes widened. "The hot one we saw leaving the last time I visited you?"

"Yeah. Deacon."

"*He* bought her a toy?"

I nodded. "He ran to the store for me a couple of weeks ago and bought that as a surprise. And that was *after* I scolded him for fucking someone too loudly the night before."

Simone covered her mouth. "Oh shit. You scolded him?"

"Yeah. Kind of an embarrassing conversation, but he was really cool when I asked him if he could please keep it down."

She leaned back in her chair and crossed her arms. "I bet I know a way around that little problem."

"What's that?"

"He can keep you up in a different way—you know, on *your* side of the wall." She winked. "You can't complain if you're the one getting the action."

"Very funny." I brushed off her joke, but I felt my insides heat up. It wasn't like that hadn't already occurred to me. Before I could explain why it wouldn't be happening, she stood up.

"Anyway, I gotta run. I have a date tonight I have to get ready for. I'll talk to Cynthia about the PR opening and let you know what I find out, okay?"

That gave me as much anxiety as excitement. "Thank you. I really appreciate it." I got up from my seat to hug her and watched as she kissed my daughter on the top of the head.

After Simone left, I fed Sunny a couple of jars of baby food at our table.

Later, as I bundled her up to get going, I spoke to her as I often did, even though she couldn't talk back.

"What do you think? Would you be okay if I went back to work? I don't want to leave you, but I also want to make sure I can take care of us."

She cooed, and I kissed her forehead. "We'll figure it out, right? We always do."

———

That evening, as Sunny and I arrived at our building, we ran into Deacon and "a friend"—a fiery redhead. They were approaching from the opposite end of the block. I wondered if she was the same person from that night two weeks ago.

When Deacon spotted me, he lifted his hand. "Hey, Carys."

"Hey!" I stopped the stroller in front of the entrance.

"Let me get the door for you guys," he said.

Deacon held the door open as I pushed Sunny's stroller through. I normally had to fold it and carry it up to the second floor in one hand, while I held the baby in the other. But as soon as I took her out, Deacon worked to collapse the stroller and carried it up the stairs for me while his date quietly followed.

"Thank you for your help," I said, my voice echoing in the stairwell.

"Of course." He smiled. When we arrived at our floor, he finally said, "This is Kendra."

"Nice to meet you," I said, feeling instantly jealous. I shouldn't have, but I suppose I'd developed a crush on the guy.

"Nice to meet you, too," Kendra said. "Your daughter is adorable."

"Thank you."

Once we got to our respective doors, Deacon leaned the stroller against the wall outside my apartment.

He noticed the toy in Sunny's hand. "She likes the pig, huh?"

"Yeah." I smiled. "That was a good choice. Thank you."

Kendra turned to him and gushed, "Aw...you bought that for her? That's so sweet."

"It was," I said. "And it helped calm her down today."

"What happened today?" Deacon asked, looking concerned.

"She had a doctor's appointment."

His eyes narrowed. "Everything okay? Is she sick?"

"Just a checkup."

"All good?"

"Yes. Thanks for asking. She had to have a shot, so that's always stressful. But it went fine."

"Glad to hear." He smiled. "Well...you guys have a good night. We're just heading inside for a nice, *quiet* evening." He winked. "Maybe play some Parcheesi."

"Ah...well, you have fun with that. I have earplugs now in the event your *Parcheesi* gets rambunctious."

He laughed. "Have a good night, Carys."

"You, too." I waved to Kendra. "Nice meeting you."

"Same." She grinned.

I swallowed my jealousy as I disappeared into my apartment.

Later that night, Sunny was inconsolable. She would not stop crying, and I cursed myself for letting her get that shot today. I'd called a nurse's hotline, and they told me her fever of 102 was normal under the circumstances, and there was no need to take her to an emergency room. They said to monitor her and make sure she was getting enough fluids.

I'd brought her into my bedroom because I couldn't leave her alone like this. I also thought holding her would help, but it didn't seem to matter. Holding her only made *me* feel better.

Her wailing continued as I paced the room and rocked her. I'd never seen her like this before.

There was a knock at the door that I barely heard through her crying.

Shit. Had one of the neighbors complained? I didn't need anyone's wrath on top of this.

I walked over to the door and looked through the peephole.

It was Deacon. Remembering he had that girl over, I cringed. The roles had reversed. Now we were disturbing *his* peace.

When I opened, I started babbling away before he had a chance to say anything. "I know we're disturbing you, but I can't get her to stop crying. I'm really sorry. She has a fever from the shot, I think, and there's nothing I can do. So, if you're going to complain like I did to you, that would only be fair, but I can't do anything about this, so—"

"Carys, calm down. It's okay," he said, placing his hands on my shoulders.

The unexpected contact shot what felt like an electric current through me, which stopped my rambling. I let out a long breath. "I can't calm down. My baby is in pain."

"I didn't come here to complain. I would never do that. She clearly can't help it."

"Then why are you here?"

"I wanted to make sure you're okay."

My heart softened, but I kept myself from getting carried away. "You don't have to check on me, Deacon."

"I know that. I wanted to. There's likely nothing I can do, but I can't listen to a baby screaming for two hours straight and not offer help."

It dawned on me that Deacon had left that chick to come over here. *Kendra*.

"Where's Kendra?"

"She went back to her place."

"She left because of the noise?"

"She...had to get up for work early in the morning, so she went home to sleep."

"Sunny totally cockblocked you tonight. I'm sorry."

I really wasn't.

He waved his hand dismissively. "It's alright."

"When this is over, you can get me back—fuck someone's brains out nice and loud."

I'd expected him to laugh, but instead he looked at me with concern. I immediately wished I could take my crass joke back.

"Did you try giving her a cool bath? I'm no expert, but wouldn't that bring the fever down? I remember my mother doing that for my brother when he was small and had a temperature."

It seemed so obvious, but it hadn't occurred to me— or to the damn nurses I'd talked to apparently. "You know what? That's a good idea. I think I'll go start a bath right now. Do you mind holding her while I run to the bathroom and set it up?"

Deacon looked anxiously around the room. Was he trying to come up with a reason not to take her from me? "Uh...sure," he finally said.

I handed Sunny to him and took a few seconds to admire how cute it was to see Deacon holding her, bouncing her up and down gently.

I rushed to the bathroom, not wanting to freak him out too much. I'd already disrupted his night enough. Running water in the tub, I tested the temperature, so it was cool but not too cold. When I finally shut off the faucet, I noticed something odd: silence.

For the first time all night. Sunny wasn't crying. My first instinct was to be alarmed. *Had she passed out?*

I darted back out to the living room, but before I could utter a word, Deacon held his index finger to his mouth.

"She just fell asleep," he whispered.

Somehow, I was still concerned. "Are you sure she's breathing?"

"I'm positive. I can feel it and hear it." He swayed from side to side. "I'm afraid to stop this motion, because that's how I got her to sleep."

As I watched him rock her back and forth, my ovaries felt like they were about to explode. This man was sexy when he *wasn't* holding a baby. Now? Off the charts.

"I don't get why I couldn't get her to sleep, and then you hold her for five minutes..."

"Can't say I understand it, either." Looking down at her, he said, "I gotta be honest, though. I kinda wanted to run for the hills when you first asked me to take her. But she made it easy." Deacon shrugged. "Not bad for my first time holding a baby, huh?"

My mouth fell agape. "Ever? You're kidding me."

"Nope." He laughed.

"That figures."

She looked so comfy in his big arms. No wonder she'd fallen asleep. It must have been like lying in a warm, king-size bed compared to the usual fold-out cot with uncomfortable springs.

"I think you'll be okay if you stop rocking. Normally, once she's asleep, she stays asleep."

His voice was low. "Should I put her down?"

I'd enjoyed watching him hold her too much to suggest that myself.

"Let's try putting her in the crib, yeah."

Deacon followed me to Sunny's room. He carefully placed her on the mattress, and at first it seemed he'd been successful.

We tiptoed out of the room, seemingly in the clear until we heard rustling.

Shit!

And there was the crying again.

"Damn it," he groaned. "I thought I was careful."

"You were. Not your fault. She somehow sensed it. The same thing's happened to me before. She must be super sensitive tonight because she's sick."

I went in to get her, but once again, she wouldn't stop crying. It was just as it had been before.

"Should I try rocking her again?" he asked.

"I can't make you do that. This is not your—"

"It's no problem, Carys. Honestly."

Deacon held out his hands, and I placed her in his arms again. He walked back out into the living room and this time sat down on the edge of couch, still rocking.

Slowly but surely, over the next several minutes, her crying slowed until it was non-existent. Sunny fell asleep again in her king-size bed.

I shook my head in amazement. "She definitely likes being in your arms."

He smiled down at her. "Anything you want to do, go do it. Because I don't think I'm getting up anytime soon."

"You can't just sit there with her all night."

"Why not?"

"Because it's late. Don't you have to sleep yourself?"

"Sleep is overrated. Plus, don't forget I work from home, so I can sleep in tomorrow if I need to and catch up on work later."

After sweating from nerves all night, I needed a shower badly. I normally bathed each night before bed, but with Sunny being upset, I hadn't been able to. *Would it be terrible if I took him up on his offer?* I hated feeling like a charity case, but if he wasn't going anywhere for a bit, why not take advantage?

"I'm just gonna take a quick shower, if that's okay?"

"Take your time. Don't rush. I'll be here."

Despite his words, I couldn't relax in the shower. So I washed my hair and rubbed the soap over my body swiftly. I did, however, take the time to properly brush through my wet hair after, and I dabbed a bit of concealer under my eyes to get rid of the dark circles. I wanted to look good in front of Deacon, even if that was difficult to admit, and even if nothing would come of it. There was an extremely attractive man in my apartment, and if I had the opportunity not to look my worst, I was going to take it. It wasn't like I'd been planning for him to come over tonight.

Before I ventured back out into the living room, I peeked out my bedroom door so I could properly enjoy the sight of Deacon holding Sunny without him noticing the look of swoon on my face.

THREE

DON'T EVEN THINK ABOUT IT

I was pretty sure my balls had fallen asleep. Or if not fully asleep, they were definitely numb from lack of movement. Not wanting this baby to wake up again, I hadn't moved an inch the entire time Carys was in the shower.

How did I get myself into this situation?

Oh yeah. I'd felt bad for Carys and wanted to show my concern. I never thought I'd actually be able to help. Because shit, what the hell did I know about babies? Absolutely nothing. And I'd always thought it was better that things stayed that way. Such a huge responsibility. The last thing I expected was to be comfortable holding her, or that she'd actually *want* me to. Apparently this little one liked me for some reason.

When Carys came back out, I nearly did a doubletake. Her long, straight, strawberry-blond hair was down and towel-dried. I'd never seen her hair down before. She typically had it tied up, which was also nice because she had a beautiful neck. She wore a short nightgown that clung to her petite frame. Carys was attractive in a graceful way. It had come as no surprise that she'd been a ballet dancer, though normally she didn't show off her body. And why should she? Taking care of her daughter was her priority. It wasn't like she needed to impress anyone.

But damn. It felt kind of wrong to be checking her out under the circumstances. From the moment I met her, I'd thought she was hot. But the fact that she's someone's mother automatically made her off limits.

"Everything okay?" she asked.

"Perfect." I whispered. "Aside from the fact that my ass has that pins-and-needles feeling from not moving. But I'm afraid if I hand her to you, she'll wake up."

She laughed. "You're a saint, Deacon. Feel free to pass her off to me any time, even if she does wake up. You have no responsibility to stay."

Maybe not, but I didn't want Sunny to start crying again. At least one of us—Sunny—was getting sleep in the current situation.

Carys sat across from me on the couch.

She looked down at her baby. "I still can't get over the fact that you hadn't even held a baby before, and you nailed it on your first try."

"Eh. She makes it too easy for me. Unfair advantage."

Carys smiled. It was nice to see that she'd relaxed a bit. She'd seemed really tense earlier tonight when I'd helped her up the stairs, and that was before any of this crying stuff happened. Come to think of it, Carys seemed wound up most of the time. Not that I blamed her. She had her plate full.

She really did have a pretty smile. And I *really* needed to stop noticing that. This girl might as well have had a sign on her face that read: *Don't even think about it.* I wouldn't be dating anyone who had a kid; children were *not* in the cards for me. It would be bad enough to inevitably fuck up a relationship with someone who lived next door, but to have a child involved who might be hurt when you left? No, thank you. No matter how damn cute—or intriguing—Carys was, I wouldn't be going there.

She fascinated me, though. Even before I knew anything about her, I'd had the sense that there was more to her than met the eye. Something in her eyes, maybe—they were always trying to tell a story. For a long time, I couldn't put my finger on it. But when I saw that photo from her ballet days, it started to make sense. Her life as she knew it had been cut short by a traumatic event.

I could relate to that. Maybe I'd somehow sensed we had that in common. Maybe that's why I was drawn to her the moment I looked into her eyes.

I wanted to know more about her past, but I didn't want to pry.

She caught me a bit off guard when she did some prying of her own.

"So...how many women do you date at once? I hear them over at your apartment from time to time, but I don't know if they're the same ones or different people."

"Don't hold back," I said, eyes widening.

She blushed. "Sorry if I'm being nosy. I'm just curious."

"I'm kidding. It's alright." I sighed and shrugged. "I date around. I'm not gonna lie. But I don't sleep with all of them, as you're probably assuming. Contrary to popular belief, it gets a bit exhausting."

She pursed her lips. "Hmm... It's interesting you say that."

"Why?"

"I notice that you... Well..." she hesitated.

What is she getting at? "I what?"

"When I've...overheard things..."

"Yeah?" I prodded.

"I've noticed that you last a long time. I sometimes wonder if that's stamina or—"

"Boredom?" I laughed.

"Yes. I suppose."

I nodded. "Okay. Truth? That *can* be due to a lack of interest sometimes. Humans are not machines. I like sex—love it with the right person. But there are times when I'm not in the mood, or the chemistry wasn't what I thought it was going to be."

"Sorry for all the questions. I'm just living vicariously through someone who actually *has* a sex life."

Maybe it was a dumb question, but I asked anyway. "Why can't you have a sex life?"

"It's kind of hard to go out and meet people when you have a baby. I can barely go to the bathroom."

"Well, not for nothing, but if you put your photo out there, pretty sure you'd find a line of guys willing to make house calls."

She shivered. "That's kind of disturbing. I have to be careful who I bring around her."

"I get that. I was mainly kidding—not about there being a line, but about that being a safe and feasible option for you."

"Anyway, one-night stands are not my thing. I've never actually had one, and don't think now is the right time to start."

My curiosity grew by the second. "Your last relationship was Sunny's father?"

"Yeah." She looked down at her daughter. "He was the older, powerful, authority figure who drew me in with a false sense of security. He was apparently just using me to pass the time until he decided to go back to his ex-wife. It sucks, but it was a big life lesson—be careful who you trust." She looked contemplative. "But, like I always say, I got Sunny out of it. Being a mother so young wasn't something I planned, but I wouldn't trade it."

"How old are you?" I asked.

"Twenty-four."

Damn. She was younger than I thought.

"How old are you?" she asked.

"Twenty-nine."

"Geezer." She smiled. "Just kidding. I was going to guess in that range."

"How old is your ex?"

"Thirty-eight."

I wondered if she liked older men in general, or if that was just a one-off deal. There were a lot of things I wondered about Carys. Things I probably had no business knowing.

The baby seemed deep into sleep now. As I stared down at her sweet little face, those almond-shaped eyes and her pudgy little nose, I got the courage to ask something else I'd always wanted to know. I hoped it didn't offend her.

"When did you find out that Sunny—"

She finished my thought. "When did I realize she had Down syndrome?"

"Yeah. I hope you don't mind my asking."

"Not at all. I like when people ask me about it. They shouldn't be afraid." She looked down at Sunny. "I didn't know until she was born."

My first thought was to say something like, *"That must have been devastating."* But why? Why would it be devastating? Because she's different? I chose to just let Carys continue, because I didn't want to say the wrong thing.

"Of course it was shocking, you know? And at first, I was sad, like there was some kind of loss, but that was only because I was really ignorant about Down syndrome at the time. I was feeding off of other people's reactions, which were to say things like 'I'm sorry.' Can you believe that? In retrospect, they were so wrong, even if they meant well. *I'm sorry* is something you say when someone dies, not when they're born. I hope no one ever says *I'm sorry* to me in the future. Because they'd get an earful."

See? My instinct to shut up was correct. "How long did it take you to realize it wasn't something to fear?"

"I started going online and connecting with other parents of kids with Down's, and it was a totally new world. When you see their kids thriving, happy, communicating, it tells a different story than one based on fear or misinformation."

"Well, I'm definitely learning from this conversation. I've never known anyone with Down syndrome before Sunny. But I can clearly see that she's a healthy, happy baby."

Sunny continued to sleep through our whispered conversation.

"Don't get me wrong," Carys said. "She will definitely face challenges a typical kid wouldn't. But overall, our day-to-day life is the same as if she didn't have Down's." She stared off. "When people ask me, 'what she has' or 'how I feel,' I tell them she was blessed with an extra chromosome and leave it at that."

I loved that. I nodded. "Everything is a matter of outlook."

"That's right. And I don't view her as handicapped. Unique, maybe. But not handicapped." Carys played with some lint on the couch. "They did tell me to expect her speech to be delayed. She started early-intervention services as soon as she was born. Someone comes to the apartment a couple of times a week. She might have to learn sign language before she starts talking, but I'll take that as it comes. I'll line up the best speech therapist. I'll learn everything I can myself. But I already see her trying to communicate with me. Even if the words don't form as clearly or as quickly as other kids, we'll manage."

I'd admired Carys before, but I had even more respect and admiration for her now. *This girl is phenomenal.* If only every kid with challenges was lucky enough to have a parent like her.

But what she said next broke my heart.

"I think the only time it ever really gets to me is when I'm out and about with her in public. You know how sometimes people see a baby and lean in to get a closer look? Well, some people do that to us. And sometimes, I see their faces go from happy to sympathetic when they realize she looks different. That makes me sad—not sad for me, but sad that people look at her as something unfortunate, something that would warrant a sympathetic look." Her eyes watered, and she quickly wiped them. "I hate it, Deacon. Sorry. I don't talk about this stuff often."

41

"Thank you for sharing all this with me." This conversation had changed the way I viewed people with special needs.

She stared into my eyes. "Thank you for not being afraid to ask."

I looked down at Sunny's sweet face with a newly acquired sense of hope. "You think it might be worth trying to put her down again?"

"Yeah, I do."

I carefully lifted myself off the couch. It felt good to stretch my legs and take the pressure off my numb ass and balls.

I followed Carys to the baby's room, and once again placed Sunny carefully on the mattress. I don't think I'd ever walked slower in my life than I did leaving that room.

Once back in the living room, Carys said, "You really can go home now."

"Ah. I can take a hint."

"Oh, I wasn't trying to get you to leave, if you want to stay. I'm too wired to fall asleep just yet. I'll be up for a while. I'm enjoying the adult company."

It was rare to hang out with a woman without any expectations. I was enjoying her company, too. *A lot.* Carys was real. I didn't have to put on the charm or any kind of a front around her. I could just be myself. That felt good.

When she realized I wasn't rushing out, she looked back toward the kitchen. "Can I get you some..." She hesitated. "Crap, I don't even know what to offer you. I don't have alcohol except for these bottles of champagne I never open. I don't drink too often. And it's late for coffee. I have hot chocolate?"

I chuckled. "That sounds good, actually. I might've chosen that if given the choice between alcohol and hot cocoa."

I followed her as she walked over to the kitchen. She took a couple packets out of the cupboard and filled a tea kettle with water.

I carefully slid one of her kitchen chairs out and sat down. Although this night hadn't turned out the way I'd expected, I was content to be here. I wasn't sure if it was the whole no-expectations thing, but hanging around Carys was very calming. It was nice to just be friends with a woman.

So, you probably shouldn't stare at her ass as she leans over the stove.

The thin material of her nightgown molded to her butt, giving me too good of a view.

Carys looked back at me. "Shit."

"What?" *Does she have eyes in the back of her head?*

"I just realized the tea kettle whistles when it's ready. I wasn't thinking. It could wake her up."

"We can have...*warm* chocolate?"

She laughed. "I'll just listen closely and take it off the heat right when it's about to start." She leaned her back against the counter and crossed her arms as she waited. "It's funny all of the things you forego for the sake of not waking up a baby. Some nights I'll debate for several minutes whether opening a can of seltzer is worth the potential of waking her up."

"So you decide not to bother, only to find that your trusty neighbor has a friend over and wakes her up anyway?"

"No." She laughed. "You only seem to keep *me* awake. Her room is far enough away from *our* wall. But unfortunately, her room *is* right outside the kitchen."

"I did end up moving my bed, just so you know."

"I haven't heard anything since, so it must be working."

The truth was, I'd only had sex in my apartment once since Carys had mentioned being able to hear it. And I'd been extra quiet, to the point that Kendra thought something was wrong. Now that I knew Carys could hear me, it changed things. I couldn't do anything without wondering whether she was listening. The sick thing was, the idea of her listening turned me on a little.

When the water started to boil, she rushed to take it off the heat. She poured two mugs and mixed the cocoa in before handing one to me.

I looked down at the words on the mug she gave me. "I've always wanted to drink out of a mug that says, *Classy, Sassy, and a Bit Bad Assy.*"

She chuckled. "Sorry. I don't have a ton of mugs."

"I love it. And thank you. I haven't had hot chocolate in forever."

"I'd offer you whipped cream, but it makes a lot of noise when it shoots out."

"I think there's a manwhore-next-door joke in there somewhere," I cracked.

"I wouldn't have gone there." She laughed.

There were a few seconds of awkward silence before she said, "Anyway, we should take these out to the living room, so we don't wake her."

"Oh...yeah. Let's do that."

We sat down on opposite ends of the couch and quietly sipped our hot chocolates.

"I hope you don't mind me asking another personal question," I began.

She licked her lips. "Okay…"

"What happened that caused you to not be able to dance professionally anymore? What type of injury was it?"

She shook her head. "You're not going to believe it."

"Why?

"Because it's pathetic."

"Well, now you've got me even more curious."

"I fell down a set of stairs and broke my ankle," she confessed. "Can you imagine that?"

I let out a long breath. "Oh, man."

"That's what makes it so hard. It wasn't like I was injured while dancing, or doing something impressive. It's sad, really."

I felt for her so much. "How long until you realized it would impact your career?"

"I didn't think it would long term—until the company terminated my contract. I always thought they'd give me time to heal, that eventually I'd go back. But apparently they saw my injury as too much of a liability. The doctors seemed to think I'd have recurring trouble with that ankle, even after surgery, so the medical reports only strengthened the company's case."

"You must've been in shock."

She took a sip and nodded. "It's like a death—the death of the future you believed you'd have. I had to reimagine my life. And for a long time there was nothing but a black hole. It wasn't until Sunny came along that I realized I was meant for a new purpose."

Damn. Her words shot straight through my soul. This would have been an opportune time to tell her my story. She'd see just how much we had in common. But ultimately, it wasn't the right time to bring it up. This conversation was about her, not me. Plus, it was late, and I didn't want to open that can of worms.

We talked for a little while longer, and eventually she checked the time on her phone. "I should try to get some sleep in case she wakes up again."

"Yeah. Of course." I stood from the couch.

She reached out to take my mug. "Thank you for everything tonight, Deacon."

"Thanks for the cocoa. This was nice—talking to you, getting to know you better."

"Yeah, feel free to come by again when Sunny isn't wreaking havoc on the building."

"I definitely will," I said, standing in the doorway. "Have a good night."

After I got back to my apartment, I couldn't stop thinking about Carys and imagining what she looked like when she danced. Okay, some of the time I was imagining what she looked like dancing *naked*. But that would remain my dirty little secret.

Most of all, I couldn't rid myself of that old, familiar pang in my chest that had developed when she spoke about her injury. I knew all too well what it was like to have dreams broken.

FOUR

Carys

PROMISE NOT TO LAUGH

The faint noise of traffic from the street below was the only sound in the room as I nervously waited for Cynthia Bordeaux, the director of City Ballet, to begin the interview. Cynthia and I had met years ago when I danced for her competitor.

She finally took a seat across from me and folded her hands.

"So, let's get right to it, Carys. Why do you think you'd be the best choice for the PR position we have open?"

Forcing confidence, I sat up straighter. "Because I know the business inside and out, not only as a performer, but I worked the admin side for a couple of years after my injury. That well-rounded experience, as well as my good writing and speaking skills, makes me a great fit."

She moved her pen between her fingers. "But you don't have any specific public relations experience. So you can understand my hesitation in hiring you for this particular job."

"Well, I never worked in public relations. But months of having to respond to the press regarding my injury

47

while keeping a brave face certainly helped prepare me for anything that might arise. And things like writing a press release are pretty straightforward. In fact, I've already enrolled myself in an online class that teaches the basics in anticipation of this position."

"Well, it's good to know you've been proactive. That shows real interest in the job."

"I am *very* interested, Cynthia."

"I have to say, I'm impressed that you could move on from the traumatic life change of your injury by accepting another position with your company. You chose to keep a foot in the industry, which I like."

"Well, I'd danced all my life and did everything I could to make it professionally. So even when that was suddenly over, I wasn't ready to leave. Being injured didn't take away my love for the ballet."

"What made you finally leave? Was it just your pregnancy, or something else?"

"I stopped working to take care of my daughter, yes."

She tilted her head. "Why are you looking to go back to work now?"

"I've felt a bit antsy lately. I love being home, but I think it's time for me to get back out there. There's also the financial component. But mostly, I feel like having stepped away from the workforce for a while will give me a newfound energy for whatever I embark on next. I'm really excited for the next phase of my life."

She sighed. "I realize you have a lot going on, so I have to be honest in saying that my biggest hesitation in considering you for this position is that you might not be as available as we'd need you to be." She crossed her arms.

"Yes, a good portion of the duties can be performed from home, but there are several events where we'd need you on hand. Sometimes we don't have a lot of advance notice, depending on the situation—say, entertaining a new investor. Do you think you'd be able to manage childcare at the last minute?"

Deep down, I knew that was going to be my greatest challenge. But I wasn't going to let her close the door on me. I was determined to find a way to make it work.

"I'm an expert at winging it, Cynthia. When I was injured, I made the best of it. When I suddenly got pregnant, I knew nothing about raising a child—winged it there, too. I want this position badly enough that I'm willing to do whatever it takes to make it work. Can I promise you that I'd be able to make a hundred percent of the appearances? No. But I can promise you I will make every effort to be where you need me to be. And if I have to miss something, I'll work ten times harder to make it up to you, to make sure you know I'm dedicated to the job." I let out a long breath.

She nodded silently. "There's absolutely no doubt that hiring someone who's been so respected in this industry would be a good public relations move for us. Not to mention, you worked for our competitor, so having you with us would be a *get* of sorts. I've always been looking for a way to stick it to Charles."

I smiled. If that helped justify her offering me the job, I was all for it.

She tapped her pen on the desk. "Tell you what. Let me mull this over. I have a couple other people I'm interviewing, and I want to give them a fair shot. I'll call you when we've made a decision."

The idea of her interviewing people who likely had more experience gave me anxiety. Still, I tried to keep my poker face. "That sounds great." I nodded as I rose from the chair. "And if there's anything else I can answer, please don't hesitate to email or call me. I hope you give me a chance to prove myself."

She reached out her hand. "Carys, it was amazing to see you again. You're just as lovely as I always remembered."

After I left City Ballet, I went to pick up Sunny from Simone's house. Since she lived nearby, she'd graciously offered to watch my daughter. But given her lack of experience, I didn't want to dally in case something had gone wrong.

On the way to Simone's, I checked my email as I walked. To my utter shock, several responses to my inquiry about a part-time childcare worker had come in. I'd figured it wasn't going to be easy finding someone interested in a variable schedule. But it seemed I'd underestimated the number of people who didn't want to be tied to a fixed routine.

Hope filled me. Maybe this was going to work out after all.

Later that afternoon, after Sunny and I had returned home, there was a knock at the door.

Peeking through the hole, I smiled. Deacon stood there with two Starbucks cups in his hands. Lately, he hadn't even been texting me before coffee runs. He'd just proactively get me a latte if he happened to be passing by.

"You're my favorite person right now," I said, reaching for the coffee. "Thank you so much. You have no idea how much I needed this."

His eyes went wide as he looked me up and down. "Look at you. You look great."

I was still wearing my black sheath dress from the interview. My hair was down and styled into loose curls. This was definitely the most dressed up Deacon had ever seen me.

"I do clean up nice when I have to."

"Where did you go?"

I didn't immediately answer, instead walking over to grab my wallet, though I knew he would once again refuse my money.

Deacon held out his palm. "Stop. I won't take it."

"Why are you paying for my coffee again?"

"Because you didn't ask for it. I chose to get it. Now drink it and put away the money."

"You spoil me, Deacon. And given that I have no income, it's most appreciated." I took a sip then smiled. "But that may be changing soon," I added in a sing-songy voice.

He perked up. "You got a job?"

"Not yet. But that's why I'm dressed up. I had an interview today."

"No shit? What's the position?"

"It's a PR gig at a different ballet company than the one I used to work for."

He beamed. "That's fantastic. That'd be perfect for you."

"Well, I can't celebrate until they offer me the job. And I'll have to figure out a situation for Sunny if I get it.

I'd probably be able to work more than half the week from home, but there would be some events I'd need to attend, sometimes with little notice. That's why I have to line a couple people up."

"You got any leads?"

"Actually, yes. There's this company that matches families and childcare workers. A friend of a friend recommended it. They sent me a few people to check out today. I'll have to interview them all, but the company vets them, runs background checks, and makes sure they have appropriate experience. Like, I specifically requested people who have worked with special-needs kids." I took a sip. "I just pray it will work out."

"Well, my gram always says if you think positively, make yourself believe it will all work out, it will. We have no idea how much our outlook affects things."

"I definitely have to work on that."

Deacon took a seat on my couch and picked up a ball of yarn I had sitting there from the night before. "What are you making?"

"Oh. I've been trying to teach myself to crochet, but it's not going well. I wanted to make a hat for Sunny."

"Promise not to laugh, okay?" he said.

"What are you talking about?"

"Don't laugh at what I'm about to tell you."

Before he could say anything further, my phone rang. He waved his hand. "Take it. I'll tell you after."

When I went to pick it up, Deacon walked over to where Sunny was swinging. He knelt down and muttered something to her.

The call was from a number I didn't recognize. "Hello?"

"Carys? It's Cynthia."

I cleared my throat. "Oh...hello, Cynthia."

With wide eyes, I looked over at Deacon. He gave me a fist pump.

"I did a lot of thinking after you left my office today," she said. "I've always been a big believer that you have to go with your gut."

My heart started to pound. "Okay..."

"My gut told me not to waste the time of those other two interviewees. I should just offer you the position. With your history, I doubt anyone could put their heart into it the way you can."

My jaw dropped. "Are you serious?"

"I am. Congratulations. The job is yours if you want it."

"I do. I do—thank you!"

Deacon gave me a thumbs-up and smiled wide.

"Now, I'm assuming you'll need time to line someone up for your daughter, so why don't we select a start date in, say, three weeks? You can let me know if you need a bit longer."

Blinking, I answered, "Sure. That sounds amazing." I had to keep myself from jumping up and down.

"I'll email you an exact date. Plan to work in the office for at least the first three days for training."

"Okay. You got it."

"We'll be in touch."

"Cynthia..." I said before she could hang up.

"Yes?"

"Thank you for giving me a chance."

"I'm certain you won't disappoint."

"I won't."

"Congratulations."

"Thank you."

After I hung up, I waved my hands and screamed, "I can't believe I got it!"

"Hell yeah!" Deacon yelled as he came over and pulled me into a hug.

Whoa.

I hadn't been expecting that, but it sure did feel good to be wrapped in his arms. Now I knew firsthand why my daughter liked it so much.

He pulled back. "I'm so happy for you, Carys."

"This will hopefully be the best of both worlds, if I can make it work."

"Not *if*...but when. You *will* make it work. You have to believe that."

"That's right. I vowed to believe, and I will." I smiled. "Thank you for the reminder."

"Atta girl."

"Would you want to celebrate tonight with me?" I asked, feeling giddy. "My treat. I insist."

His smile faded. "Shit. I would love to. But I told someone I'd go see a show tonight. She already bought the tickets and—"

"Oh my gosh!" I waved my hand. "You don't have to explain."

"No, I do. Because I really would've loved to celebrate with you tonight. This is a big deal."

I felt stupid for having suggested it. Perhaps this job offer had given me a false sense of confidence. "I shouldn't have assumed you had nothing better to do than to celebrate with me on a whim."

"Why? We're friends, right? Friends celebrate with friends."

And there it was. I'd been officially friend-zoned. It wasn't like I didn't already know this. But I suppose a part of me had held a tiny glimmer of hope for something more than platonic. Why did I even want that with—as he'd once dubbed himself—the manwhore next door? That wouldn't be good for me.

"A raincheck, okay?" he insisted.

Since he had to get ready for his date, Deacon left a few minutes later.

When the door closed behind him, I walked over to Sunny, who was still calmly enjoying the baby swing. "Looks like it's just you and me for the celebration tonight. I'm thinking sushi takeout for me, and pureed sweet potatoes for you? What do you say? Sound good?"

She kicked her legs and flashed me a big smile.

Then I remembered Deacon had been going to tell me something before the phone call from Cynthia came in. He'd asked me not to laugh. But I was laughing now just thinking about it—not even knowing what the hell I was laughing about.

———

Later that night, after Sunny went to sleep, I sat down with my takeout maki rolls and popped open a bottle of pink champagne I'd had in my fridge since before my daughter was born.

Turning on the television, I selected On Demand and decided to watch some episodes of *Flip or Flop* on HGTV—

the old seasons from before the stars, Tarek and Christina, got divorced. This was my exciting celebration. But I wouldn't complain. At least I had something to celebrate.

Halfway into my dinner, I got a text. It was a photo of a champagne glass.

Deacon: Cheers to you.

I sent him back a photo of myself sipping my champagne.

Carys: Cheers!

Deacon: Nice!!! Glad to see you're celebrating.

Carys: How was the show?

Deacon: It was okay. I'm kind of looking forward to heading home and going to sleep, though.

Carys: Heading home alone tonight?

Deacon: Yes. Not feeling it.

Carys: Ah. You win some, you lose some. That's too bad. But at least I know I'll get some sleep ;-)

Deacon: That's very true.

Carys: Sorry, couldn't help myself.

Deacon: I can take it.

Carys: This explains why you're texting me from your date. I hope she's not right in front of you?

Deacon: No. The champagne was from earlier (but in your honor). I'm on a bathroom break right now.

Carys: So nice of you to think of me in there.

Deacon: I'm not on the shitter. Don't worry.

Carys: Well, that's good.

Deacon: What did you have to eat with your champagne?

Carys: I got sushi rolls from Miku.

Deacon: That place is good. But have you tried Ichigo?

Carys: No.

Deacon: Ohhh. You need to! I'll pick some up this week and bring it by.

I was already looking forward to that day a little too much. Then I thought of something.

Carys: Hey, what were you going to tell me earlier? When you asked me not to laugh at you? I got that call about the job and you never had a chance to tell me. LOL

Deacon: See? You're already laughing.

Carys: I'm sorry.

Deacon: You really want to know?

Carys: Yes.

The dots moved around while he typed.

Deacon: I used to crochet.

Carys: What? LOL You did?

Deacon: Told you not to laugh.

Carys: I'm not really laughing. I swear. Not out loud. I just wasn't expecting you to say that.

Deacon: It's a fucked-up story how I learned. I was sort of forced into it. I'll tell you the next time we have coffee. I gotta get back to the table or else she'll think I'm whacking off in here.

Well, that provided quite a visual.

Carys: Yeah. I'll let you get back to your date.

Deacon: And I'll let you get back to your bubbly.

Carys: Thanks for checking in.

Deacon: Enjoy the rest of your night.

Carys: My imagination will be running wild, thinking about you being forced to crochet at gunpoint.

Deacon: It's not that bad. But close.

My finger lingered over the keypad. I wanted so badly to tell him he should stop by when he got back. But I thought better of it.

Then he texted again.

Deacon: Okay. I'll tell you real quick. When I was sixteen, I was acting up, getting into trouble. My parents made me live with my grandmother for the summer. All I was allowed to do was go to football practice and come back to her house. At the time, she was crocheting clothes for families in need. Sweaters, scarves, stuff like that for the upcoming winter. She made me learn how to do it. Forced me to sit down with her every night and help.

I couldn't contain the smile on my face.

Carys: Wow. That's sweet.

Deacon: At the time, I was pretty fucking miserable. But when we delivered the items we made, and I got to see the smiles on those kids' faces, it didn't seem so bad anymore.

Carys: That's an awesome story.

Deacon: Take it to the grave, Kincaid. I can't let a rumor about me crocheting with an old lady ruin my game.

Carys: You got it. LOL

Deacon: Okay. Really going now.

Carys: Have a good night.

Deacon: You too.

He closed out our exchange with three little celebration hat emojis, and I wanted to slap myself for being happy that he "wasn't feeling" his date. He'd been thinking of *me* tonight.

FIVE

Deacon

WHAT GOES IN MUST COME OUT

I knew today was Carys's first day of her new job. Over the past few weeks, she'd interviewed a ton of people about watching Sunny. She'd finally found a woman she liked—a retired daycare worker looking for something to keep herself occupied, and who didn't require a set schedule.

I'd gotten up at 5AM and gone to the gym, grabbing Starbucks on the way back so I could drop one off for Carys before she had to leave for work. Even if she'd already had her coffee, an extra might not hurt today.

Holding the cardboard tray, I knocked on her door.

She opened, and it was clear from her face that something was wrong.

"What's going on?"

Her voice was shaky. "Sharon, the woman who was supposed to be watching Sunny today, just called. Her husband is having problems breathing, and she had to take him to the emergency room. She's not going to be able to come." A tear fell down her cheek. "This is my first day, and I'm already flaking out." She blew out a breath. "I'm done, Deacon. So done."

Shit. "The agency couldn't provide you with anyone else?"

"Not on such short notice. I'm supposed to leave in ten minutes." She shook her head. "I'm just gonna have to explain the situation to Cynthia and see if she can extend my start date by a day. But honestly, if I were her, I'd tell me not to bother coming in tomorrow."

This made me angry; it wasn't fair. Carys had all of her ducks in a row. This wasn't her fault. She needed this PR gig, and might not ever find something so perfect again.

She didn't know it, but she and I were kindred spirits. I knew full well what it was like to have to redefine your life. Finding something that gave you a purpose after losing your entire world meant everything.

A voice inside my head urged me to offer help, even though it was way out of my comfort zone. It took several seconds for my fear to step aside.

Although I was probably completely crazy, I refused to let her fail. "You think you can teach me everything I need to know about watching Sunny in ten minutes?"

She looked up as my words registered. Her eyes went wide. "I can't let you do that, Deacon."

"Come on. We're wasting time. We know I have the holding thing down. What else do I need to know?"

She just stood there in shock.

It was up to me to push things forward. "Show me how to change her diaper."

"You're serious?"

"Yes. Let's go. You don't want to be late."

She picked Sunny up out of her playpen and led the way to the baby's room.

Seeming discombobulated, Carys did the best she could to demonstrate the diaper-changing process.

Her words came out rushed. "You roll the dirty one up in a ball like this and put it right in the basket."

"Easy enough," I said calmly, though the diaper thing freaked me out.

"This one was just pee, but if it were poop, you'd lift her legs up sort of like this and use the wipes to clean her. I still use one wipe to clean her after pee, though." She demonstrated the process of wiping Sunny's chubby bottom, front to back.

I swallowed. If it wasn't poop now, the chances of it being poop later were pretty high. I vowed to worry about that when the time came. Couldn't say I was looking forward to it, though.

"You take a new diaper from here and place it under her, then fold the top over and secure the sides with these tabs."

I exhaled. "That seems pretty straightforward."

"Yeah, well, it depends on the situation, but the main thing is, just be careful to make sure she doesn't roll off the table. If you don't change or clean her perfectly, it's not the end of the world."

After that, Carys put Sunny in the baby swing and brought me into the kitchen to show me where the formula was.

She pointed. "These single-serving containers just pour right into the bottle I use right there."

Carys placed the jars of baby food I'd need on the counter along with a plastic spoon.

She began writing down a feeding schedule. "She already had her bottle this morning, so the next meal can be these pureed bananas at eight. She normally has rice cereal for breakfast, but that's a little more complicated to prepare, so I'll just give her that for dinner."

I nodded, trying hard to take it all in.

"Don't worry, it's all down on this pad of paper—what to give her and when."

I scratched my head. "Okay...yup."

"I would change her diaper next around ten. So, approximately every two hours."

I gulped but tried to seem nonchalant.

Carys lifted one of the jars. "Around 11AM, she'll have these sweet potatoes and peas. Then I follow it up with another bottle of formula."

My head started to spin a little. "Got it."

"At noon, you're gonna want to try to put her down for a nap. But change her diaper again first. Text me if you have an issue putting her down. It usually just entails placing her on her back in the crib and turning on her mobile. It's okay to leave her in there awake. She eventually falls asleep if the mobile is on."

Trying to maintain my game face, I nodded. "Sounds good."

"Some babies have two naps, but she only has one. I find she sleeps better at night with just the one."

"And you said in the past, her naps can be anywhere from an hour to three?"

"Yeah. I'm impressed you remembered that." She smiled. "But yes, very unpredictable."

"Alright."

"Depending on when she wakes up, I'd give her another bottle either after her nap or around three. That will tide her over until dinner, and I'll handle that when I get home."

I looked at the time on my phone. It was past ten minutes since I'd arrived. She needed to leave. "You're gonna be late. Don't worry about us. Go."

"You're sure about this?"

"Yes."

"Thank you. Thank you. Thank you. I owe you big time, Deacon. Big time."

She rushed around in search of her stuff.

"Don't forget anything," I warned, taking one of the drinks I'd brought out of the tray. "Take the coffee with you."

She took the cup from me and looked around one last time. "Got my phone, got my purse..." She took a deep breath and ran over to kiss Sunny on the head. "Bye, baby. Be good for Deacon." She looked over at me. "I can't believe I'm saying that—*for Deacon.*"

Me neither. "We'll be fine."

"Text me if you need me. I don't care how often."

"Okay, but I'm only gonna do it if I really need to, like if the apartment is on fire."

"Oh God, don't say that," she said as she rushed down the hall.

After I closed the door, the silence was deafening.

Sunny stared at me from her swing. I was relieved she seemed content. At least one of us was calm.

"Okay...that whole 'we'll be fine' thing? That was just an act so your mom wouldn't worry. I'm freaking out, little girl. You need to help me. No surprises and we'll be good."

She squealed.

"Alright, you cool to just chill there for a few? Looks like, according to your mom's schedule, we don't have anything until eight."

I rubbed my chin. "Actually, I need to go next door to get my laptop so I can use it when you're sleeping. I'm gonna take you with me to go get it. You okay with that?" Unfastening her from the swing, I lifted her out.

We walked over to my apartment, and I grabbed whatever I could fit in my left hand: my laptop, some beef jerky, and chips. I wasn't sure what Carys had to snack on over there.

On the way out, I stopped at the mirror that hung on the wall near my door. I didn't know whether to laugh or cry at the sight of myself juggling all these items along with the baby. When she spotted herself in the mirror, Sunny flashed a huge, toothless grin. Her almond eyes turned to slits at the joy of seeing her own reflection.

Fuck, she's adorable.

"You like mirrors, huh? Well, at least I know one way to entertain you if all else fails." I whispered in her ear, "I'll tell you a secret. I like them, too. I look at myself way too much in this mirror before I go out. But I won't admit that to anyone but you."

She laughed as if she could understand me, but she was probably just still amused by looking at herself.

When we returned to Carys's apartment, it was time for Sunny's breakfast. When I put her down in the highchair, she started to cry.

Shit. I knew this was a bad idea. "What's wrong? What did I do?" I spoke to her like she was going to give me an answer.

After I lifted her out, the crying stopped. She looked up at me with her teary eyes, and I realized this was a repeat of that one night. She wanted to be held.

"Oh. We're back here again?"

She just kept looking up at me until she smiled.

"No, no, no. What's that for? You tryin' to butter me up or something? So I'll hold you? Not gonna work."

She smiled even bigger.

A second time, I put her in the highchair. Once again, she started screaming.

"Shit," I said. Then I cursed myself silently for swearing in front of her. "You didn't hear that."

Picking her up again, I worked to open the jar of bananas while holding her at the same time. I ended up feeding her while standing up. She must have been super hungry because she kept opening her mouth wide before I could even get the next bit of bananas onto the spoon.

"Damn, girl. You're hungry, huh?"

Then it occurred to me: what goes in must come out. I shook that thought from my head, vowing once again to deal with it only when I had to.

The spoon finally hit the bottom of the jar, and there was nothing left.

She licked her lips.

Carys had left another jar of bananas on the counter, so I assumed we'd just keep this going. She devoured that one just as fast as the first.

Still holding her, I grabbed a piece of paper towel and turned on the water to wet it before wiping her mouth clean.

"Alright. Step one finished. You should be good for a while, right? I'm gonna try to put you down in the swing, so I can check my emails."

The second her bottom hit the seat of the swing, she started to fidget uncomfortably and broke out in tears.

Damn it!

I told myself I was going to stick it out. Let her cry. But after five minutes of pacing while she screamed, I caved.

"Okay, okay. You win." I lifted her out.

We walked back over to the couch and sat.

"We have to stop meeting like this, Sunny."

Now, that she was calm, she looked up into my eyes. There was something so amazing about watching a baby stare at you with pure wonder. What was she thinking? Or maybe she was just seeing her reflection.

Then she smiled again.

At least she was happy.

I was already exhausted. It was only two hours into the day, and it had felt like I'd been here for months. If someone had told me yesterday that I'd be stuck inside an apartment today with a baby, I would've dreaded it. But the reality wasn't so bad—just different. Tiring, yes. But I could see, in theory, why people liked children—especially when she was content.

When the clock struck ten, I realized it was time for the dreaded diaper change. I got up and walked with Sunny over to her room. *Please don't be crap.*

After lying her down on the changing table and opening up the diaper at the sides, I was relieved to find only piss.

Score one: Deacon.

Trying to remember the steps Carys had shown me, I changed Sunny into a fresh diaper as fast as possible.

Returning to the main room, I looked at the clock. *Jesus.* Was it only ten thirty?

It felt like eleventy-hundred years at this point.

At eleven, I gave her the sweet potatoes and peas, then followed it up with formula as instructed—all while holding her in my arms so she wouldn't freak out.

The formula went down smoothly. Carys hadn't specified whether to burp her, but it made sense to try. After a moment I was damn glad I had because a belch the size of Gibraltar came out.

A text from Carys came in right around 11:30.

Carys: How is everything going?

I laughed out loud. Could you imagine if I were honest?

Sunny won't let me put her down, so my arm is numb, and I'm trying to figure out how I'm supposed to wipe my own ass later when the time comes. How do you do this every day, Carys? HOW DO YOU DO IT?

I responded using voice-to-text since holding Sunny made it difficult to type.

Deacon: Everything's perfect. Been following your schedule. She just had her lunch and formula.

Carys: Awesome! I owe you huge for this.

Deacon: How's the first day of training?

Carys: It's going great. I'm so glad I was able to make it. I have a lot to learn. But I'm feeling optimistic that I can handle it.

Deacon: Well, keep slaying. I've got everything under control here.

Carys: Thank you again!!!

Deacon: Anytime.

I turned to the baby. "Don't make an even bigger liar out of me, Sunny. Okay? We're gonna turn this around before she gets home."

Returning to the couch, I counted the minutes until naptime at noon, still having no clue how I was supposed to get her to stay in that crib without screaming her head off.

When Sunny smiled up at me this time, I squinted. "What's that for? You enjoyin' watching me sweat? I'm not cut out for this, you know. Between you and me, I have no business playing Mrs. Doubtfire today. No offense, but I don't want kids." I leaned in and spoke in her ear, "But…I guess I can see why some people do. Your mama's lucky to have such a sweet baby."

I made the mistake of placing Sunny on my chest while I lay back and turned on the TV. Within a few minutes, she'd fallen asleep there, and I was now afraid to move.

I wondered if there was any chance in hell that I could transport her to the crib. Movement of any kind was a risk. But I really needed to use the bathroom.

Lifting myself off the couch, I walked as slowly as I could to her bedroom. I'd never moved so carefully in my life as I placed her down on her back. It was like a miracle when she didn't stir. She stayed sleeping, her chest rising and falling with each breath.

I tiptoed out of there, and the first thing I did when I got back to the living room? I danced. *I fucking danced—* fists pumping, hips swaying. And I had to laugh at myself a little. I was a grown man dancing outside a baby's room because it felt like the first time I could breathe since 8AM.

But Carys did this every damn day. Over and over. I'd put in a few hours and thought I deserved some kind of award. I was pathetic for thinking it was some magical feat that I'd managed to get a baby down for a nap. But I didn't care. I silently danced my ass off anyway.

In record time, I did everything I could while Sunny was napping. I used the bathroom. I kicked my feet up on the couch and ate beef jerky. I caught up on my emails. I'd never moved so fast in my life, because I had no clue how much time I had before my freedom ended.

My phone chimed, and I'd never wanted to murder a device so much in my life. I immediately put it on vibrate.

A text had come in.

Katy: You up for a quickie lunch date?

Of course I knew lunch wasn't what she was looking for. Katy was a girl I'd stopped seeing a few months back.

It surprised me that "lunch" was still something she was interested in, considering I hadn't called her.

The thought of a quickie lunch date at this particular moment was comical. *Sure, come on over. But if you make a sound, I'll have to kill you.*

Deacon: Can't. My day's all tied up.

Katy: Maybe next time then.

Deacon: Sorry. Yeah.

Sunny slept for almost three hours that afternoon. I got to decompress, work on a new design concept for my job, and tackle some emails. I considered myself very lucky—until she woke up.

SIX

Carys

MORE IN COMMON THAN YOU KNOW

The sound of running water immediately registered when I walked in the door. Cynthia had sent me home at 2:30 with a bunch of information to review. I was thrilled that I'd be able to relieve Deacon a bit early.

"Deacon?" I yelled.

S"In here!" I heard him holler.

Oh no. This isn't good.

When I got to the bathroom, I said, "I would ask what happened, but I *know* what happened."

Deacon held Sunny stiffly away from his body as the tub filled. She had poop all the way up her back.

"There was no way the wipes were going to clean this," he said, sweat pouring from his forehead.

I rolled up the sleeves of my jacket and took her from him. "I'll take it from here."

Deacon immediately left the room. I thought he ran out to vomit or something, but he returned soon after with a bath towel. "Now I know where you keep them, in that small closet in the hallway."

"Thank you. You don't have to stay. You look traumatized. I'm so sorry this happened." I began cleaning her up.

"It's okay. You saved me in the nick of time anyway." He stood in the doorway for a bit while I bathed Sunny. "I want to hear how your day went and tell you about Sunny's. I'm dying for some fresh air, though. Why don't I go for a Starbucks run and come right back?"

"Okay, that sounds good."

After Deacon left, I looked down at my daughter, who was now laughing and splashing the water with her palms. She'd just started sitting up on her own, so bath time was a lot easier.

"What did you do to Deacon, huh? You couldn't wait till I got home?"

She cooed.

I bent down into the tub to kiss her head. "I missed you so much today."

After I dried Sunny off and got her dressed, I brought her out to the living room and placed her on the playmat.

A few minutes later, Deacon knocked.

When I opened, he handed me my coffee.

"Oh, you're the best," I said, taking the stopper out of the lid.

At the sight of Deacon, Sunny started crying.

He shook his head. "Oh no you don't. Your mommy's home now. You don't need me to carry you."

My mouth dropped. "Don't tell me she cried all day until you picked her up?"

He hesitated. "Not all day—not during her nap."

"Oh my gosh, Deacon! You can't let that happen. You have my full permission to let her cry when she does that. Otherwise, she'll never leave you alone."

"I know. But she does this whole sad-eye, pouty, quivering-bottom-lip thing. And I just...cave."

"She's totally playing you."

Deacon sat down on the couch and rested his head back. "Seriously... I walked outside just now, and it was like I hadn't been out there in *years*. How do you do it every day?"

"It gets easier. The first time you take care of a baby is overwhelming. And in the beginning, it was like that almost every day. But you do get used to it."

"Well, you have my mad respect." He sighed. "Tell me how today went." He gave my leg a smack, and his hand lingered on my thigh for a couple of seconds before he abruptly slid it away, almost as if he'd caught himself doing something he didn't think he should have.

And of course, my body reacted instantly. I felt the effects of that minor contact long after it was over. I cleared my throat. "Today was truly awesome. Cynthia showed me around the office. I have my own cubicle, and it's big. We went through some of the press releases the previous public relations person had put together. She also had me study up on the company—how many dancers, their names, backgrounds, their ranks, stuff like that. The day flew by, and then she randomly told me to go home at two thirty. Sent me home with more reading to do. But I was thrilled to be able to come back here."

"And I was thrilled when you walked in."

"Was that good timing or what?" I laughed. "Seriously, though, you saved my ass today, Deacon. The good news is, the nanny company assures me Sharon is all set to come tomorrow morning, so we won't run in to this problem again. Apparently, it was a false alarm with her husband, and he's home resting."

"It wasn't a problem. As much as she made it challenging by insisting I hold her, it was cool getting to hang out with her."

I knew he was just being nice. I really did owe him.

"Oh..." Deacon snapped his fingers. "I figured out she likes mirrors."

"She does. How did you discover that?"

"I took her next door so I could grab my laptop and a couple of other things, and when I stopped in front of the mirror, she started laughing."

"Yeah. She gets a kick out of herself." Deacon's eyes lingered on mine, prompting me to ask, "What?"

"Nothing. You look really nice. I don't know if I told you that this morning."

His compliment gave me goosebumps. "Thank you."

It would have been easy to take that the wrong way and think maybe he was interested in me—especially with the way his bedroom eyes were fixed on me right now. But I knew better. Even if he were attracted to me, I suspected he wouldn't cross the line—especially after seeing firsthand what my day-to-day life entailed.

Still, I appreciated his company and his friendship. "Can I make you dinner this weekend?" I asked.

He took another sip of his drink and placed it on the coffee table. "You're working all week in between taking care of her, and you want to make *me* dinner?"

"You literally saved my job. I know how you are, that you won't take money from me. It's important that I pay you back in some way for today. I feel like the best way I know how is to make you dinner. I really like to cook. I just don't do it too often, since it's just me."

He nodded for a few seconds, seeming to think it over. "Okay. Yeah, sure."

I smiled, trying not to seem overly excited. "Yeah? You choose the night. Friday or Saturday."

He checked his phone briefly. "I can do Friday."

I smiled wide. "Then it's settled."

"Can I bring anything?"

"No. I insist you don't. But because I know how you are, and you'll likely bring something anyway, a bottle of wine will do."

The rest of that week went off without a hitch. My new sitter, Sharon, showed up on time the following two days, and Sunny seemed to like her almost as much as she liked Deacon. Then I worked from home on Thursday and Friday as planned. Cynthia said she wanted me to come into the office at least two days a week for the first few months, if possible, but she let me choose the days. Sharon seemed amenable to that arrangement, and we decided we'd choose the days based on her availability each week.

Because I worked from home on Friday, I was able to get most of my stuff done early so I could prepare dinner for Deacon. My online grocery order arrived on time, so I got started preparing the food around five. I'd decided to make breaded chicken with a side of risotto, Caesar salad, and roasted Brussels sprouts with cranberries, bacon, and almonds. I ordered a store-bought chocolate cake for dessert. I'd told him to come by at eight thirty, which would hopefully be after Sunny fell asleep.

After slaving away at the stove, I decided to sneak in a shower once I put Sunny down at eight. It was probably the fastest one I'd ever taken because I needed time to get dressed and put some makeup on before Deacon arrived.

As much as I knew this was an innocent, friendly dinner, I couldn't help the butterflies swarming in my stomach. I was incredibly attracted to Deacon, even if nothing would come of spending time with him. My expectations needed to remain low. We were in two different places in life. He had all of the freedom in the world and seemed to be taking full advantage of that, milking the single life. That's likely what I would be doing if I were in his shoes.

And he'd flat-out told me that we were "friends." So the fact that his coming over made me nervous was pretty silly.

I slipped on a gray, fitted sweater dress that landed several inches above my knees and high leather boots. Maybe it was overkill for a night in, but I'd had a really productive week and felt like celebrating in style. I made up my face and had just put the last stroke of mascara on when I heard a knock on the door.

My heart hammered in my chest as I walked to answer it, proof that whatever I tried to tell myself about the platonic nature of our relationship was a crock of shit.

Deacon held a bouquet of flowers and a bottle of wine.

His eyes moved over me. "Wow. Uh...you look fucking amazing."

My cheeks felt hot. "Thank you."

He handed me the flowers. "These are for you."

I took the multicolored tulips. "You didn't have to do that."

"Well, you didn't have to make dinner for me, either."

I smelled the buds. "I keep waiting for you to show me your asshole side, Deacon. But you're sickeningly sweet sometimes. I definitely had the wrong idea about you early on."

"Manwhores can still be sweet. Sometimes we even shop for flowers for our friends." He winked.

Friends. I heard that loud and clear. "Sometimes manwhores even crochet." I winked back.

"Ouch." He smiled through gritted teeth. "Remember your promise, Carys."

My body buzzed with awareness as I took him in. He wore a dark green sweater with jeans and black leather boots. His sleeves were rolled up, and for the first time I got a full look at the tattoo on his left forearm.

"I've never really seen your tattoo before. Does it go all the way up your arm?"

He looked down at it. "It's just the forearm. I got this ink when I first moved to California about eight years ago. It was a work in progress. I kept adding to it."

The design was a mix of roses, crosses, birds, and other ornate imagery. And now I could read the name written in cursive over his wrist. *Kathie.*

"Kathie is my grandmother," he said.

"Ah." I smiled, feeling strangely relieved that I didn't have to be jealous of the fictitious woman I'd created. "I'd noticed the word before but could never make it out. I always assumed it was an ex-girlfriend and didn't want to pry."

"No. Just Gram."

"That's really sweet."

His cologne wafted over me. Deacon looked hotter than I'd ever seen him. Even if we weren't dating, I loved the idea of having him all to myself tonight.

Clearing my throat, I said, "I hope you don't mind, but I think we should eat out in the living room to be as far away from Sunny's room as possible."

"Believe me, if there's one lesson I learned this week, it's the trouble you can get into when a baby wakes up. Sometimes massive explosions, even."

I shut my eyes briefly, remembering the disaster I'd walked in on. "I'm sorry. That was funny, though."

"I'm glad you thought so. I'll send you the bill for therapy." He laughed. "Let's crack open this wine, shall we?" He lifted the bottle of red he'd brought.

"Yes. Be right back." I headed for the kitchen.

My heart pitter-pattered as I grabbed a bottle opener and two glasses before returning to the living room.

My hand brushed against his as he took the opener. Heat zipped through me at the fleeting touch—proof of how desperate I'd been for the slightest contact. It was pretty pathetic that I hadn't been with anyone since Charles.

The cork made a slight popping sound as he opened the bottle and poured the wine. We sat down across from each other on the couch. I was starting to get a good buzz on as he asked me more about my new job.

Then he took a deep sniff. "Whatever you're making smells fucking amazing, by the way."

I was just thinking the same thing about you—how good you smell. I stood up. "Shall we eat?"

"Hell yeah. My stomach is growling."

He followed me into the kitchen, and I sensed every movement of his body as we plated our food.

"Holy crap, Carys. This looks fantastic. I might have to keep creating reasons for you to cook for me."

You've read my mind.

We brought our plates back out to the living room and sat next to each other on the floor, so we could use the coffee table.

Deacon and I were well on our way to polishing off the bottle of wine as we enjoyed the chicken and risotto I'd made.

"How did you learn to cook like this?"

I wiped the corner of my mouth. "Self-taught, mostly. I feel like everyone should be able to follow a recipe, but most people believe they can't for some reason. It's not that hard."

He drank the last of the wine in his glass. "I'm one of those people who assumes I'm gonna burn the place down if I try. I need to get new pans, too. The ones I have are so damn cheap, they burn my hands when I touch the handles. I take that as a sign that I should just stay the fuck out of the kitchen altogether."

I laughed. "Well, it's nice to have someone to cook for."

"I'll be your guinea pig anytime. I haven't had a home-cooked meal like this since the last time I went home to Minnesota."

"None of the women you've met have cooked for you?"

"Not that I can recall. But I don't expect anyone to cook for me."

I smirked. "Yeah...they don't need to know how to cook."

His smile was hesitant. "I know what you're thinking. Despite what you may believe, it's not all about *that*. They have to have half a brain, and they have to be decent human beings. Honestly, there are more duds than not out there."

"It must be expensive to go out all of the time, huh?"

"Yeah, and it costs the same whether it's a bomb or not."

"I never thought about how costly it must be to have a social life."

"If you're gonna date in this city, you expect to pay a fortune in drinks and restaurant bills. Secretly, my favorite thing to do is stay home. But I know I'll regret it if I don't push myself to go out. I feel like that's what I *should* be doing at my age."

"I envy your freedom. I wouldn't change my current situation, but I do miss being able to come and go as I please."

"I really understood that on Monday," he said.

"Yeah." I chuckled. "My life is basically the opposite of yours."

He paused, looking into my eyes for what felt like much longer than normal. "You say that—that our lives are so different—but we have more in common than you know. There's something I've never told you about."

I blinked. "There is?"

He nodded. "I feel very connected to you. And you don't even know why."

I put down my glass and inched a bit closer to him. "Well, now you have me curious."

He emptied the last of the wine into our glasses before turning to me again. "You said once that when you stopped dancing, it felt like the death of the future you'd always imagined. I can relate...because my career was cut short by an accident, too."

My heart sank. "Really?"

"I don't talk about it much. In fact, I don't talk about it at all. I don't think I've told more than one other person since I moved here."

I leaned in a little. "What happened, Deacon?"

He stiffened, as if gearing up for what he was about to divulge. "My father is Jed Mathers, the head college football coach for Minneapolis. And I was the star quarterback for Iowa, one of their biggest rivals in the next state over. We made headlines in those days because of that."

I exhaled the breath I'd been holding. "Okay...wow. You played football?"

"I was on track for a career in the NFL. Our team's record was twenty and six. But...everything ended one day when I crashed my car."

My stomach felt sick. *Oh no.* Instinctively, I reached my hand to his arm.

He looked down at it and continued. "I hit an oncoming vehicle on a foggy night. I was lucky to survive, but my leg was crushed, and my professional football days were over."

I felt his pain intensely. "I'm so sorry. How long ago was this?"

"A little over nine years. I was twenty, a sophomore in college. My whole life had been about the dreams my father had for me, the same dreams I had for myself. From a very young age, everything had revolved around football." He stared off. "After the accident, I didn't know who I was anymore."

Those words resonated so strongly with me. Hearing them come out of Deacon's mouth felt surreal. "I understand that to my core."

He looked into my eyes again. "I know you do. That's why I just awkwardly interrupted our lighthearted dinner to unload my baggage."

"I'm so glad you did. Tell me more about what happened."

He let out a long breath. "My father and I... Our relationship never really recovered. We didn't know how to relate to each other without football. I felt useless for a long time. Eventually, my younger brother replaced me in my father's eyes—became the new hope. While Alex never made it to the NFL, for several years my father chose to focus on him, anything to forget the disappointment I was."

That hurt my heart. "It wasn't your fault."

Deacon frowned. "Well, actually, it was. The night of the accident, I was focused on my navigation app when the car crashed into us. Yes, there was fog, but it was very much my fault for not being more alert."

"Were you alone?"

"No. That's the worst part." He swallowed. "My girlfriend at the time was with me."

I braced myself. "Was she hurt?"

He hesitated. I knew this had to bring back painful memories for him.

"She wasn't severely injured, no. But..." His words trailed off, and he paused. For a moment I thought he might elaborate, but then he simply said, "Things were never the same after that day."

"Were the people in the other car injured?"

He closed his eyes briefly. "No."

I nodded, relieved. "Sorry for all the questions."

"No. It's good for me to talk about it. Normally I just keep that part of my life bottled up."

"So...what did you do to get back on your feet after that?"

"Well, you know how you ended up still working for the ballet after your accident? You kept a foot in the world you loved? It was the opposite for me. I wanted nothing to do with football if I couldn't play. Being around my football buddies, my father and his players, it depressed me. So I transferred to a different college in California, away from everyone, and threw myself into school."

"Did you ever move back to the Midwest after that?"

"No. I've felt very disconnected from my family ever since. I'm closer to my mother and grandmother, but it's been difficult being around my father and brother. I love them, but my relationship with everyone changed after the accident."

"Is it just the one brother you have?"

"Yeah. Alex is two years younger than me. Do you have siblings?"

"I have one brother, too." I took a deep breath, still processing everything he'd told me. "Wow. Here I was thinking I didn't know anyone who could relate to my situation. You've been right next door all this time."

His eyes met mine. "Crazy, isn't it?"

SEVEN

Deacon

THE BLACK SWAN

It felt good to let it all out.

I'd wanted to tell Carys about my background for a while, but the timing was never right. When she invited me over for dinner, part of the reason I accepted was because I figured I'd have an opportunity to finally explain.

"From the moment you told me about your accident," I said, "I've felt very connected to you, like maybe I was meant to meet you, because of our shared experience."

I immediately regretted those words. Too intense. They were the truth, but I didn't want her to take them the wrong way. *Meant to meet you.*

I corrected, "I don't mean to sound—"

"Misery loves company. I get it." She smiled. "I'm really happy you told me."

She placed her delicate hand on my arm. I wished she wouldn't touch me, because my body reacted every time she did. I had no business feeling that way about Carys. My attraction to her made things uncomfortable. She was the first woman since probably high school who I truly considered a friend. And the whole friendship thing would

86

be a heck of a lot less complicated if I didn't constantly imagine what her ballerina body would feel like under mine.

She was like no other woman I'd ever encountered. Carys was elegant as hell. Long, beautiful neck. Soft, porcelain skin. Hair like silk. Didn't need a drop of makeup. But it wasn't only those physical things. Her elegance was more inside than out. It was the way she carried herself. If there was one word to describe her, it was *graceful.*

It was hard not to notice her beauty on an average day. But tonight she was playing up her sexuality with those damn knee-high black boots and slinky gray dress that hugged her body. I couldn't stop staring at her, and I really hoped she didn't sense anything, because that would make things awkward.

Carys was off limits. She didn't need to mess around with someone who hadn't been capable of holding down a relationship in nearly a decade.

You got that, Deacon?

"You know why else I'm glad you told me?" she asked, snapping me out of my thoughts.

"Why?"

"Because now I know I can't put up a front around you. I often try to give the impression that I'm okay with what happened to my career, that being a mother to Sunny more than makes up for everything I might have missed out on. But the truth is, I'm trying to make myself believe it more than anything. Someone who's lost their identity in a similar way knows better than to buy into that so easily."

"Yeah," I whispered. "I definitely know how hard it is."

I was dying to hug her, hold her hand, move the hair off her face—something. But I couldn't. My eyes were glued to hers, and I didn't know how to handle this pull that gnawed at me. I didn't know what to do with my damn hands because all they wanted to do was reach out and touch her, to be as connected physically as we were emotionally at this moment. But I refrained.

Thank God she interrupted the tension. "I forgot," she said suddenly. "There's cake!"

When she stood and started taking the plates to the kitchen, I got up too. "Let me help you."

She held out her hand. "No. Stay. The less people in the kitchen the better. If Sunny wakes up, she'll never leave you alone, and then you won't get to eat your cake."

As I sat down on the couch, I laughed to myself. *You can't have your cake and eat it, too.* That saying was perfect for this situation. Could I continue this friendship with Carys without giving her the wrong impression? I wanted to keep whatever this was going, but given my growing attraction to her, was that realistic? I needed to be careful, maybe take a step back.

Carys returned to the living room carrying two giant mounds of chocolate cake. She handed me mine and sat down. I watched as she took a huge bite of hers and moaned.

"Sorry. I get a little too excited over chocolate." She laughed, covering her mouth.

Well, I get a little too excited watching you eat it. And yet, I continued to stare at her mouth, anticipating each time she'd open it, enjoying every little sound that came out.

The more I looked over at her, the more I wished I could have seen her dance.

"Do you still dance?"

Her eyes narrowed. "How do you mean?"

"I know you don't dance professionally. But do you ever...dance...when you're alone...for yourself? Maybe that's a dumb question. I'm sorry."

"No. It's not dumb at all." She wiped her mouth. "I actually do sometimes. Just to make sure I still have it. It's not the way it would be if I were up on stage, but yeah, sometimes I'll randomly put on my toe shoes and do an arabesque in front of the mirror." She turned a little red. "I can't believe I'm admitting that."

"I think it's awesome. What's an arabesque?"

She pointed to the framed picture on her bookshelf. "Arabesque is what I'm doing in that photo over there. It's one of the hardest positions, even though it might look easy. I should say, it's not easy to do it *correctly*. The perfect turn out...lifted up and forward, relaxed elbow... the right arm placement. No two people do it exactly the same, because everyone's body is different." Shaking her head, she said, "Anyway, I'm going off on a tangent." She rolled her eyes. "Ballet nerd."

She's so damn cute. "Your passion is palpable. Just because you stop doing something every day, doesn't mean you can't have that kind of love for it. That's within you."

She hesitated. "Would you want to..." Then she shook her head. "Never mind."

My heart beat faster. What the heck was she going to ask me? I needed to know. "Say what you were going to say."

89

Her cheeks grew redder. "Would you want to see a video of me dancing?"

A relief came over me. *Jesus.* For a split second, I thought she was going to ask me if I wanted *something else.* Did I really believe she'd ask if I wanted to go back to her bedroom? *Christ, Deacon.* Get your mind out of the fucking gutter.

"I would love that," I said.

"I have one of our old performances on DVD. I haven't watched it in ages."

"Break it out. I'm dying to see it."

She stood up. "Okay, let me get it."

I wiped my sweaty palms on my pants as she took off in search of the DVD.

When she returned, I could've sworn I saw her hand tremble as she popped it into the DVD player.

"Are you nervous to show me?"

Carys smiled shyly. "A little."

"Don't be."

She pressed play. At first, the camera was so far away, it was hard to tell which dancer was her.

"I'm easy to spot. That's me in black," she said, pointing to the screen. "We were performing *Swan Lake.*"

"The Black Swan. I don't know ballet, but I know enough to know you're the Black Swan."

"You must have seen the movie with Natalie Portman." She laughed.

"I did, indeed." I sat transfixed. The orchestral music, the lighting—this was the real deal.

A guy dressed in tights lifted Carys into the air, her legs spreading apart with impressive flexibility. After landing on her feet, she twirled with beautiful precision. The smile on her face exuded confidence and pride as she lifted onto her toes and raised her arms as if reaching for the stars. She *was* a star. And seeing this drove home the loss she'd suffered. This hadn't been a hobby. This was a calling. My heart broke to know it had been taken from her.

Her male partner almost seemed like a tool to showcase Carys's talent. He guided her along, but she was the focal point. She really shined when she danced alone. Without the guy invading her space, Carys spun around free as a bird. Flawless.

"It's like I can feel your emotions," I told her. "Not only by looking at your expressions but in your movements."

"That's pretty much the biggest compliment you could give me."

"Really?"

She nodded. "One of my teachers used to say that was the difference between a good dancer and a great one. She said our purpose in a performance was not to simply move our bodies or entertain, but to express our emotions through dance. Then ideally, those feelings would also be experienced by anyone watching. So I always tried to keep that in mind."

"It's fucking beautiful." My eyes met hers. "Truly." I didn't merely mean *it*. I meant *her*.

Her eyes glistened. "Thank you."

For the first time in a long time, I felt like tearing up, too, and it had nothing to do with my own shit. What a tremendous loss she'd suffered—the world had suffered the day this woman stopped being able to perform. The emotions pummeling me were too much. It was time to go before I did or said something I'd regret. I didn't want to be rude and leave before she turned off the video. But I vowed to make my exit at the first opportunity.

"I'm blown away by your talent," I told her when the video ended. "Thank you again for showing it to me."

"You're welcome."

Carys put the DVD back in the case and stared at it a moment before snapping it closed.

"I think I should probably head back," I said.

She seemed surprised. "Oh...okay. Yeah. It's getting late, I suppose."

"Yeah."

We stood and faced each other. A few tense seconds passed—tense seconds where the right thing to do felt like kissing her, even though I knew that would be very wrong.

Carys rubbed her arms. "Thank you for coming."

"Are you kidding? Thank you for having me, for preparing that amazing food, for listening to my sob story, and most of all, for sharing that video with me. It really means a lot that you did."

"After what you told me tonight, I definitely felt more comfortable."

"Yeah." I smiled, and after a few seconds of awkward silence, I said, "Well...have a good night."

I wasn't prepared for her to reach out and hug me. I stiffened. But once the initial shock passed, I relaxed into her embrace. Feeling my heartbeat accelerate, I moved back before it became too obvious that her touch had wreaked havoc on me.

I nodded and didn't say anything else, heading to my apartment in a brain fog.

EIGHT

Carys

DID YOU LOOK IN MY BOX?

A few days went by before I heard from Deacon again. I'd had this funny feeling he was keeping his distance because things had teetered on crossing the line during our dinner—not necessarily on a physical level, but certainly on an emotional one. Sharing that video of my *Swan Lake* performance was like taking the Band-Aid off a wound that hadn't quite healed yet. But somehow, after letting it air out, I didn't feel like I needed the Band-Aid anymore. Reliving my past, even for that brief moment, had been therapeutic. And my confidence in doing so had everything to do with Deacon first opening up to me.

The story he'd told me about his past made me feel less alone. I'd never imagined my happy-go-lucky neighbor was hiding something so painful.

I got a text from him on Monday afternoon while Sunny was napping.

Deacon: Hey... I got a package that was meant for you. Delivery guy got the apartments mixed up. I ripped it open before I realized it didn't

93

have my name on it. Want me to leave it outside your door?

It seemed strange that he wanted to leave it outside rather than just come over with it—further evidence that he was avoiding me. That bummed me out.

Carys: Yeah. Sure. Thanks.

I couldn't remember what the hell I'd ordered. Lately, I'd been up late at night one-clicking all kinds of crap I didn't need. I bought pretty much everything online, because it was easier for me, so this could have been anything from baby food to shampoo and tampons.

A few minutes passed before I opened my door to find a medium-sized box on the ground. The top had been ripped open. I brought it into the apartment and looked inside.

A package of pacifiers.

Banana chips.

Black licorice bites.

Diaper cream.

A Woman's Guide to Self-Pleasure.

I paused.

A Woman's Guide to Self-Pleasure.

My stomach sank.

Oh. No.

Now I knew exactly why he'd chosen not to knock on the door.

I spent the rest of the day stewing over what Deacon might have been thinking about me ordering that book. I didn't know why it bothered me so much. Did it make me seem lonely or desperate? Or was it just the sheer embarrassment of needing a how-to guide on touching myself in the first place. The book had seemed like a good idea the other night at 2AM. Now? Not so much.

I wished I could just not mention it. But I knew myself. The next time I saw Deacon, my preoccupation would be written all over my face. I'd act all awkward. Eventually, I'd stammer my feelings out in a less-than-articulate attempt to explain myself.

It was better to acknowledge it calmly and get the awkwardness over with now. Grabbing my phone on the nightstand, I scrolled down to Deacon's name and typed.

Carys: Hey.

He responded almost immediately.

Deacon: Hey. Everything okay? You don't normally text at this hour.

Carys: Everything's fine. Are you out?

Deacon: I'm in bed, actually.

Carys: Did I wake you?

Deacon: No. I was watching some documentary. What's up?

My fingers lingered over the keys before I mustered the courage to type.

Carys: Did you look in my box?

Ew. That didn't come out right. Or maybe that was the perfect lead-in to this awkward-as-fuck conversation.

Of course, he picked up on it.

Deacon: Huh? LOL

Thanks for letting it slide, Deacon. I rephrased.

Carys: I assume you saw what was in the box you dropped off earlier?

My pulse raced as the little dots floated around.

Deacon: Yeah, and I have to say, I'm pretty surprised.

My heart hammered against my chest. But before I could reply, he sent another text.

Deacon: I didn't take you for a black licorice person. Worst candy ever.

Oh my God.

Carys: Nice try pretending you didn't see the book.

I shut my eyes tightly and cringed.

Deacon: What book? ;-)

Carys: The winky face gave you away. You know what book.

Deacon: I had no plans to mention it. It's none of my business.

Carys: I wanted to acknowledge it before you did. I'm a bit embarrassed.

Deacon: I wouldn't have acknowledged it. And if I did, I certainly would never shame you for reading about something that's natural. Not only would that be wrong, it would be hypocritical.

Carys: Hypocritical...because you have a similar book? LOL

Deacon: No. Because self-pleasure is one of my pastimes. I'm pretty damn good at it.

Carys: I take it you don't need a book then.

Deacon: I could WRITE the fucking book.

Well, then...

Carys: I know I don't have anything to be embarrassed about, but I still feel weird that you saw it.

Deacon: Why?

Carys: Because it makes it seem like I don't know my way around my own vagina! I'm not totally clueless. I just figured, you know, since it's just me...I need ways to be motivated. Thought I'd check it out. See what it has to say. It sounded like a good idea at 2AM.

Deacon: Have you read any of it yet?

Carys: No.

Deacon: I thumbed through it.

Shit. This is worse than I thought.

Carys: You did?

Deacon: Yeah. And I don't think it's what you need.

Carys: Meaning?

Deacon: You really want to talk about this?

Carys: Aren't we already?

Deacon: Okay. Just wanted to make sure, because you seemed embarrassed a minute ago.

Carys: I'm over it now. What did you read?

Deacon: That shit's too clinical. The steps she goes through...there's too much choreography. Honestly, I was bored when I should have been turned on. Worrying about where the fuck you put your hand is not going to help you get off.

Carys: Yeah. That doesn't sound like something I have time for.

Deacon: Pretty sure what you need is to relax with a good fucking glass of wine and some hot porn. The book you bought will have you thinking too much. What you need is to NOT think. Getting off is not so much about technique. It's about losing yourself until you can't help but touch yourself. When that happens, you don't give a fuck how you're doing it.

It suddenly got really hot in my room. My nipples hardened as I reread that last message a few times.

Deacon: That's just my two cents.

Carys: Is that what you do when you're alone? Have a glass of wine and watch porn?

Deacon: Occasionally.

Carys: Do you always need porn to get off?

Deacon: No. It's a mood thing. Sometimes I don't need it at all.

Carys: Like when?

Deacon: When I'm turned on by someone or something that happened. Or sometimes, I'm just turned on for no reason. If I'm stressed, I might need more assistance.

Carys: I see.

If he only knew how aroused this conversation had made me. Until this very moment, I don't think I'd realized just how hard up I'd been. The muscles between my legs ached. That was ironic, because it proved his argument. If you were turned on enough, the mechanics didn't matter. I knew if I touched myself right now, I could make myself come—all because of this conversation and the fact that I was now imagining what Deacon looked like when he pleasured himself.

There was so much more I wanted to know: what exactly turned him on, who had turned him on last, what he thought about in those moments when he made himself come all alone. I didn't need a freaking book. I needed more of *this*—but I wouldn't dare ask for it.

Instead, I chickened out before I made a total fool of myself.

Carys: Headed to bed. Thanks for the chat.

The three dots moved around for a lot longer than usual.

Deacon: Sweet dreams.

———————

A couple days later, a box arrived at my apartment. Given my penchant for online spending lately, I once again had no clue what it might contain.

When I opened it and reached inside, I wasn't even sure what I was holding. It looked to be a pair of men's leather pants with the ass part cut out.

What the hell?

Then I noticed the name on the billing receipt. Deacon's. Although the address was mine.

Even more confused, I took out my phone. I couldn't even type the question without laughing.

Carys: Did you order assless chaps and have them sent to my apartment?

Deacon: Wow. They came fast.

Carys: So this isn't a mistake? Do I want to know what you'll be doing with these?

Deacon: They're a gag gift for my buddy, Adrian. He and I are always sending each other weird shit as practical jokes. He was complaining that he had nothing to wear for this costume party he's going to. So, voila.

Carys: And you thought to send them to ME because???

Deacon: Just wanted to see your reaction. Plus, I figured this would make us even. You accidentally sent a masturbation book my way. And now I sent you assless chaps.

Carys: That was so thoughtful of you.

Deacon: Thank you. Just trying to be a good friend. ;-)

Then came the worst thing that could have possibly happened. I meant to send the laughter emoji. Instead, my finger hit...the tongue.

Ugh! It was at the top of my choices, since I responded to Simone earlier after she sent me a photo of her dessert. *I just sent the tongue in response to assless chaps.*

Deacon: Okay???

Carys: Sorry! Wrong emoji! My finger slipped. It was supposed to be a laughing face.

Deacon: So you're not an ass licker then.

My jaw dropped.

Deacon: Not that there's anything wrong with that.

I was mortified.

Deacon: Too much?

Carys: YES. Just a tad, TMI King.

Deacon sent a zipper-mouth emoji.

I threw the phone across the couch, still embarrassed—but laughing.

NINE

Carys

WE'RE JUST FRIENDS

Fall flew by, and before I knew it, winter was upon us in New York. I couldn't believe I now had a nine-month-old. Over the past couple of months, my friendship with Deacon had grown stronger, but it was still just that—a friendship and nothing more.

He'd chosen not to go home to Minnesota for Christmas, instead going to Vail on a ski trip with friends from New York. While he was away, my mother came for a two-day visit from Florida. And that was enough. By the end of her stay, I'd had enough of her criticisms about my parenting and ignorant questions about Sunny. I loved my mother but could only take so much of her.

Now it was January, and I looked forward to what the new year would bring. My job was going well, and Cynthia had given me more responsibilities.

Since I was working in the office today, Simone and I met for a quick lunch. We hadn't gotten together in a long time, so we had a lot to catch up on. I'd only now told her about the day Deacon had to watch Sunny—the day he'd saved my ass.

Simone dabbed her pizza with a napkin to soak up the grease. "I can't believe he watched her for the whole day. What a trouper."

"Yeah. It was pretty amazing."

She squinted and examined my face. "You like him..."

"No." I shook my head and lied, "Not that way."

Says the girl who still masturbates to the transcript of our text chain about masturbation two months later.

"Why not?"

"Because he's a friend. It's not like that with us." I took a bite of my pizza.

"Are you just telling yourself that?"

Speaking with my mouth full, I said, "Unfortunately, no. Deacon has had plenty of opportunities to make a move. He's not interested in me romantically."

"But you like him, and you'd want him to be your boyfriend if you thought he was interested, right?"

Feeling hot all of a sudden, I snorted, "Boyfriend? Deacon? Deacon is the *anti*-boyfriend."

"What does that mean?"

"It means he's the opposite of someone who would be settling down any time soon—if ever. He loves the single life too much."

Simone glared at me, seeming to see through my defensive attempt to hide my feelings. Still, I wouldn't admit that my hopes had been dashed too many times already.

Taking a long sip of my water, I decided to be partially honest. "I have a crush on him, okay? I'll admit that. A pretty big one. And maybe sometimes things border on flirtatious, but that doesn't mean I expect it to go anywhere.

He and I are in two different places in life. What does a single man living in New York City want with a girl who has a baby?"

"Don't be so hard on yourself. You're a very beautiful woman. And it doesn't sound like he minds having Sunny around." She tilted her head. "How old is he?"

"Twenty-nine."

"Hmm. So, pushing thirty, then. How do you know he wouldn't change or grow to want a family? He seems good with kids."

"Okay. Now you're taking this too far." I laughed. "Being a helpful next-door neighbor and all-around nice guy doesn't mean he wants the real responsibility being with me would bring. He has enough women without baggage lining up at his door."

Her face turned serious. "You don't know he wouldn't want Sunny."

Her words made my heart clench. Just the thought of any man not wanting my daughter, or worse, someone leading her on and leaving, made me so sad.

"I pretty much *do* know, Simone. He's made it clear in subtle ways that he wants nothing to do with me—with us—that way. He leaves abruptly anytime things get a little tense between us. The answer is in his body language and behavior. He doesn't need to say anything for me to know where he stands. And that's perfectly fine. We're just friends. To be honest? It's kind of nice to have someone I can turn to right next door without having to worry about complications."

"Well, that's too bad. I think you guys would make a cute couple."

Feeling flushed, I looked down at my phone. "Shit. I have to go. I'm gonna be late getting back to the office."

"Way to escape the uncomfortable convo."

I laughed as I got up from the table and dropped a twenty in front of her. "That should more than cover me. I'll call you. Let's do this again soon."

When I returned, Cynthia asked if I could accompany one of our potential investors, Neil Spectra, around the city for the remainder of the afternoon. She was supposed to do it, but apparently had gotten called home for a family emergency.

Neil was the son of Albert Spectra, a multimillionaire who'd contributed generously to the arts over the years. Word was that Albert's wife, Ginny, had recently passed and had requested that a portion of her money go to one of the two major ballet companies in New York. But it was apparently up to her son, Neil, to decide which company would receive the funds.

We visited a new exhibit at the Met. Then he expressed interest in going for coffee after so he could ask me some questions about our company. I suggested the Starbucks near my apartment so I wouldn't be late getting home. Neil had a driver, so I wasn't really putting him out.

Once we got to Starbucks, though, it seemed Neil was more interested in learning about *me* than City Ballet.

"Carys, I hope it's okay that Cynthia told me a bit about your history with City's competitor, The Manhattan Ballet. I was intrigued to learn about your background."

"Yes, I have fond memories of my time there both as a dancer and behind the scenes."

"I was kind of hoping since you have experience with both companies that I could pick your brain."

Feeling unsure about where this was going, I nodded as I sipped my latte. "Sure."

He clasped his hands together. "This decision is very important to me. It meant a lot to my mother. She grew up in this city with very humble beginnings, and one of the rare luxuries was going to the ballet with her grandmother. Ballet got her through some rough times when her mother—my grandmother—was sick. So, as you know, in her will, she asked that a major donation be made to the company of our choosing."

"If you don't mind my asking, why do you think she would be opposed to splitting it between the two ballet companies?"

"I'm not entirely sure. I guess, perhaps, she figured a higher amount given to one company could make a bigger difference. She asked that it go to the company we felt deserved it the most. I have to follow her wishes."

"I see."

"I'm not as well-versed in the arts as my mother was. But my father tasked me with overseeing this decision. I've learned a lot by visiting the two companies, and this experience has given me a greater appreciation for something my mother loved so dearly."

"Well, we're extremely grateful for your consideration. I think it's safe to say there's no wrong decision."

He took a sip of his espresso. "I have to tell you, you're a lot more gracious than your competitor."

"Why do you say that?"

"The gentleman I spoke with over there seemed to point out all the reasons I shouldn't give my money to City, rather than trying to sell me on why his company was the best fit. Turned me off a little, to be honest."

Charles. I knew it had to be him, but I didn't dare mention his name so as not to have to get personal with Neil.

"Anyway, today has been a...refreshing change," he said. "And that's due mostly to you."

He was definitely giving me a vibe that he might be interested in more than just my expertise on the ballet.

A couple of minutes later, I was surprised to see Deacon walk in. Well, it shouldn't have been a surprise. He hit this Starbucks daily, but it was rare for me to be in here.

When Deacon spotted me, his eyes went wide. "Carys...hey." He turned to Neil and extended his hand. "I'm Deacon, Carys's neighbor."

"Neil Spectra."

Deacon nodded a few times before he turned to me. "I didn't expect to see you here at this time of day. Thought you were across town at work."

"I am...at work, actually. Neil is a potential investor. So this is a business meeting. We just had it here so I could get home in time."

"It *is* a work meeting," Neil interjected. "But Carys has done a tremendous job of making me forget this is still business. She's a joy to be around."

Deacon stared at Neil for a few seconds. "I'd have to agree with you." He looked at me and nodded. "Well,

109

I'll let you get back to your meeting. Just gonna grab a cappuccino and head back."

"Okay…" I smiled. "See you later."

Deacon proceeded to the line. Was it my imagination, or was this run-in a little awkward? My eyes wandered to where Deacon stood at the register. He seemed fidgety as he waited for his drink. I wondered if it bothered him to see me with Neil. Maybe that was wishful thinking.

A few minutes later, Neil was talking when Deacon walked past us with his coffee. Rather than interrupt to say goodbye, he winked at me before heading out the door. My eyes lingered on the exit. I wondered if Deacon thought there was something going on between Neil and me.

It was as if Neil could read my mind. "So, I hope this doesn't come across as inappropriate, Carys, but I've really enjoyed your company and was wondering if perhaps before I return to Palm Beach next week you might let me take you to dinner?"

Oh boy. Neil was decently attractive, smart, and successful. It was tempting to take him up on his offer. But there was no point, especially since he didn't even live here. And mixing business with pleasure was never a good idea, as I'd learned the hard way.

"That's really nice of you to offer, and I'm flattered, but I don't think I have the availability. Not sure if Cynthia mentioned it, but I have an infant daughter. I'm a single mother. So, it's not easy for me to get childcare on a whim."

His eyes widened, and for the first time today, Neil seemed speechless. "Cynthia hadn't mentioned that, no," he finally said. "You're so young. I never imagined…"

"Yeah. She was a surprise."

I could've used this opportunity to tell him the man he'd met with over at our competitor was also the deadbeat father of my daughter, but I didn't. And Neil didn't try to convince me to go out with him after my revelation. Apparently having a child was enough of a deterrent.

We stayed at Starbucks for the better part of the next hour as the conversation moved back to business. He grilled me about my history as a dancer and asked for my honest opinion about how the money might be put to use at both companies.

When five o'clock finally rolled around, I was relieved to have to walk only a block down the street to get home.

Once I got to my door, I was surprised to hear music playing inside my apartment.

And not just any music. The song was an old one: "How Deep is Your Love" by the Bee Gees.

The Bee Gees?

I only knew them because my mother had loved disco when I was growing up.

I assumed maybe Sharon had a thing for the seventies until I opened the door and saw Deacon standing there. The music came from his phone.

What the hell?

TEN

Deacon

THE BIRTHDAY GIFT

After I'd returned to my apartment, I couldn't stop thinking about Carys and that guy in Starbucks. *Fuck.* Why had it bothered me so damn much? Seeing her with a dude who looked like he wanted to eat her up definitely got under my skin. I'd always told myself nothing could come of my attraction to Carys, yet I seemed unable to turn off the jealousy. That was messed up, because it couldn't work both ways. That old saying came to mind again. *You can't have your cake and eat it, too, Deacon.*

It may have been a business thing, but there was no way Carys was walking away from that meeting without an invitation for something more. And why wouldn't she take it? He looked like he had his shit together.

It was only a matter of time before she started dating, anyway. As her friend, I'd have to suck up my feelings on that. She had needs—as her masturbation book had proven. What I'd neglected to tell her back then was that she needed a good fuck more than any self-service, whether she realized it or not. I just couldn't be the one to give it to her. But I wasn't going to encourage her to go out and get it from some asshole who didn't deserve her, either.

My coffee was cold, and I'd tried to force myself to get some work done, but I couldn't concentrate. Although it wasn't because I was thinking about Carys anymore. It was Sunny. She wouldn't stop crying. Sharon was next door with her, so I knew she was in good hands. But when the crying hadn't stopped after a full thirty minutes, I'd decided to head over there to make sure everything was okay.

Sharon had opened the door looking completely frazzled. We'd met once before, so she knew who I was, and Carys had always told her to call me in the event of an emergency.

She'd thrown her free hand up, carrying Sunny with her other arm. "I can't get her to stop crying. I've changed her diaper. Fed her. I don't understand. She hasn't done this before."

I pressed the back of my hand to Sunny's forehead. "What's up, Sunny?" She didn't feel hot or anything. I took her from Sharon.

Her crying slowed before it eventually stopped.

"Oh no you don't. We can't go down this road. There needs to be another way to get you to stop."

Sharon seemed amused. "Does she always stop crying when you hold her?"

"Most of the time, yeah."

"That's so cute."

"It is until you can't put her down."

When I placed her in the swing, the crying started again. I was determined to help Sharon find a solution that didn't involve me picking Sunny up.

I took out my phone and scrolled over to my music-streaming app.

Kneeling down next to Sunny, I said, "We're gonna find something you like."

Song after song, nothing seemed to stop the crying—until I got to the seventies station. "Stayin' Alive" by the Bee Gees was on.

Little Sunny's eyes went wide as she listened. I started bopping my head to the music and watched as she fell silent and remained content.

"Did we find a winner?" Sharon asked.

When the song ended, a Donna Summer tune started, and Sunny wasn't having it. She started wailing. So I tried a little experiment. I pulled up the same Bee Gees' song on YouTube, and sure enough, Sunny stopped crying again. When it ended, the next video was another song by a different artist. Again, she started crying.

The Bee Gees definitely had a unique sound. I wondered if it was the song she liked or the pitch of their voices. So I pulled up "How Deep is Your Love," a slower ballad. Sunny again quieted and listened intently.

No shit? This is gold.

At that point, I downloaded the whole freaking *Best of the Bee Gees* album onto my phone.

Then Carys walked in. I couldn't imagine what she was thinking.

She looked concerned. "What's going on? Why are you here, Deacon?"

"Deacon is a genius," Sharon said. "He figured out that Sunny likes the Bee Gees. Listening to their music keeps her from crying. He heard her from next door and came over to help."

"Well, she stopped crying when I picked her up, but I didn't want to encourage that habit," I explained. "Decided to try something new. But the only thing she likes is the Bee Gees, apparently."

Carys's mouth hung open. "The Bee Gees? They're ancient! What made you think of that?"

"It was luck," I said. "They just happened to come on. That's when she calmed down."

"That's so bizarre. But...thank you for figuring it out."

"I downloaded their whole best-of album. I'll get it for you, too, so you have it."

After Sharon left, we kept the album playing. Carys walked over to the swing to kiss Sunny's head. She then kicked off her heels and plopped down on the couch, putting her feet up on the coffee table. I had the urge to grab her feet and massage them, but I refrained.

"What a day." She sighed.

"As in bad?"

"That guy you saw me with is a huge potential investor. Cynthia sprung him on me because she had a family emergency. It's been nerve-wracking trying to make a good impression."

"It seemed to me he felt you made an *excellent* impression."

"Yeah, so much so that he asked me out."

I swallowed. "Really?"

She nodded. "But that interest got squelched as soon as I mentioned I had a baby."

Despite my jealousy, I was actually offended for her, which seemed hypocritical coming from me—a guy who didn't want kids.

115

My fist tightened. "He said something negative?"

"No, no. Nothing like that. But his tone changed. It went from flirtatious to a bit more guarded." She waved her hand dismissively. "It doesn't matter. I wouldn't have gone out with him anyway."

I shouldn't have been thrilled to hear that. I should've wanted her to find someone who could make her happy. Instead, my selfish ass was relieved that she wanted nothing to do with that rich prick.

"I need a drink the size of my head tonight," she said. "And I don't even drink much."

"After Sunny goes to bed, you should have it. You deserve it."

She turned to me. "Hey...thank you for coming over to help today. That's not your responsibility."

"Well, now that I know Sunny, it's hard to ignore her when she's crying. I'm just glad we discovered something that can pacify her."

Our eyes locked for a few moments before she asked, "Big plans tonight?"

I hesitated to answer. I did have plans—with a woman I'd met online. Couldn't say I was too excited about it, though.

"Uh...just dinner."

Her brow lifted. "Anyone interesting?"

"Not sure yet. The verdict is still out. Haven't met her in person."

"Gotcha." She played with some lint on the couch. "Well...if it doesn't work out...you know...if she doesn't make the cut to come back and...play *Parcheesi*, maybe you can stop by and have a late drink with me."

Play Parcheesi. I remembered I'd once used that as a metaphor for sex.

"Yeah. Maybe," I answered, sweating a little and feeling oddly anxious. *This* felt different. Was it just in my head?

Carys had no idea how badly I wished I could play Parcheesi with *her* tonight.

———————

Her name was Allie, she worked for the city's water board, and she liked karaoke bars. That was about all that registered. Everything else was in one ear and out the other.

I would've loved to believe I just wasn't that into her, but I knew it was more than that; I couldn't stop thinking about Carys—her invite and whether I was going to take her up on it. Aside from that one dinner, our get-togethers were always during the day—innocent. Her inviting me over for a drink in the late evening felt different.

Allie was attractive enough. If this were a different time, I might have taken her back to my place for a nightcap. But I had no interest in that tonight. Believe me, I *wished* I did.

Finally, we came to the point in the evening where we needed to leave the restaurant and figure out the next step. Allie asked the question that forced me to make a decision.

Out on the sidewalk, she flicked her curly blond hair to the side. "Would you be interested in seeing my apartment? It's small but cozy. We could have drinks there instead of going somewhere else."

Code for: would you like to come back to my place and fuck?

I could practically hear the ticking in my head as my brain formulated a response. "You know, I actually have an early appointment tomorrow. So I'd better head home."

"Oh." Disappointment was written all over her face. "That's too bad. I would've liked to hang out some more."

"Next time, maybe." I forced a smile.

"Yeah." Her tone proved she knew there wouldn't be a next time.

Once I separated from Allie, I grabbed a cab back home.

My palms were sweaty as I texted Carys from outside her door. I'd gone to her apartment many times, but somehow the vibe from earlier had stuck; it felt different this time.

Deacon: Still up for that drink?

A response came in almost immediately.

Carys: Yes.

Deacon: I'm outside your door. Didn't want to knock and wake Sunny up.

A few seconds later, she opened. "Hey."

"Hey." I swallowed at the sight of her.

Carys wore black leggings, showcasing her toned legs, and a vintage Bon Jovi T-shirt. Her hair was damp. She must have just come from the shower. My eyes wandered down to her bare feet. Her toes were painted a light pink, like the color of a ballerina slipper. *Fitting*. She wasn't even trying to look good, and I couldn't remember her ever looking as beautiful as she did right now.

Fuck me.

She blinked a few times as she looked up at me. "I didn't think you'd come by."

Following her inside, I said, "Why not?"

"Just a feeling, I guess."

Conflicting emotions rushed through me as I towered over her, continuing to take her in. She was right in that I hadn't been *planning* to come over. But she was wrong in probably assuming it was because I was more interested in hanging out with someone else. Just the opposite. Not only was I physically attracted to this woman, I connected with her in a way I'd never felt before. It scared me.

"Did she get to bed okay?" I asked.

"Hmm?" Carys seemed as much in a daze as I was.

"Sunny. Did Sunny go down okay?"

"Oh. You mean after several full rounds of *The Best of the Bee Gees*? Yes."

"You're welcome?" I joked.

Carys yawned as she laughed.

"You said you'd be up for a drink, but I have a feeling I'm late to the party."

She shook her head. "I think my body is tired, even though my brain isn't. This day is just catching up with me. But I have no desire to sleep. Not sure I feel like a drink this late, though." She rolled her eyes. "God, I'm twenty-five, and I sound like such an old lady."

"Twenty-five? Am I missing something? When did you turn twenty-five?"

She looked down at her feet. "Today."

What? My eyes widened. "Carys...today is your birthday?"

"Yes."

"Why didn't you tell me?"

She shrugged. "Because I didn't want you to feel obligated to hang out with me. I wanted you to choose to come over because you wanted to have a drink with me, not because you felt sorry for me on my birthday."

Wow. If I'd known, I would've *definitely* canceled my plans.

"Confession..." I said.

"Yeah?"

"I didn't come for a drink," I admitted. "I came because I wanted to hang out with you. But if I'd known it was your birthday, I definitely would've been here earlier. We could've ordered Ichigo. I wish you would've told me."

That was the most honest I'd been about my feelings since we'd met. Maybe it was dangerous to admit I would've dropped everything for her tonight, but it was the damn truth.

Carys blushed. "I'm sorry."

"Goddamnit, girl, you only turn a quarter of a century once." Wracking my brain, I scratched my head before turning back toward the door.

She followed. "Where are you going?"

"Don't worry about it. I'll be back in a few."

I'd done the best I could on short notice. Hitting the two grocery stores within walking distance, I managed to find Carys a cake and a present.

It still floored me that she was going to let this day pass without doing anything special.

Carys looked down at the cake I'd found. It had probably been baked a few days ago. It had orange and blue frosting, which reminded me of the Florida Gators. If I'd had more time, I might have found a way to write *Happy Birthday, Carys*, but this would have to do.

"So just imagine it says, 'Happy birthday, Carys-Like-Paris', okay?"

She smiled. "It's the thought that counts, and it was an amazing gesture. Thank you."

We sat on the floor, eating directly off the cake with our forks.

"This ain't bad," I said with my mouth full.

"Not sure I want to know where you even got a cake this late, but I have to say, it's pretty damn good." She had blue frosting stuck on her teeth, and I had the urge to take her mouth in mine and lick it off.

Whoa.

Distraction needed. Stat.

I reached into my pocket and took out the gift card I'd purchased from the kiosk at the store. "There weren't a lot of options. So I hope you can use this."

She took the gift card from me. "I love Macy's. Maybe someday I'll get a sitter for Sunny and spend the whole day shopping. That sounds divine." She placed the gift card aside and stuck her fork in the cake. "You spent too much. You didn't have to do that. You've made me feel incredibly special."

I stopped chewing. "You *are* special. You've become a really good friend."

There I was again, attempting to define our relationship, mainly as a means of reminding *myself* that I couldn't cross the line, though I wanted to so desperately right now.

She seemed to remember something. "Oh! I forgot! I actually have something for you, too." Carys disappeared into her bedroom.

She returned, holding something she'd apparently crocheted, but I couldn't identify it.

Carys smiled proudly. "Your little crochet story inspired me to give it another go." She handed it to me. "I made this for you. Can you guess what it is?"

I didn't want to insult her. But it didn't look like... anything. A tiny umbrella slipcover? What the hell was it? Actually, to be honest, it looked like a...cock sock.

"Is it a crocheted condom?" I finally asked.

She covered her mouth. "Oh my God." Looking over at it, she said, "Actually, you're right. That's exactly what it looks like. Shit. But no."

"So, it's not a cock sock?" I teased.

"It's a cover for your pan handles! You said you burn your hands on your cheap frying pans. I made you a little cover for them. I thought I was being clever. It was also easy to make compared to the hat I'd been failing at. I actually found someone who made these online, and she listed instructions. But apparently, I made you something else."

She was so fucking sweet. I couldn't believe she remembered I'd even said that about my damn pans.

"Actually, that's really cool. Who knew there was such a thing? Thank you for thinking of me. And I promise not to try it on for size."

Carys turned red and hopped off the couch. "Maybe we should have that drink, yeah? I feel like I'm getting a second wind."

Licking the frosting off my lips, I agreed. "Okay. Yup."

She retreated to the kitchen and brought out a large bottle of pink champagne.

"This is my last one. I've had two bottles chilling in there for months—since before Sunny was born. The first one I opened the night I found out I got the job. Just not sure how to open this without waking Sunny."

I took the bottle from her. "Let me take it next door and open it over there."

"Good thinking." She smiled.

After I returned with the open bottle, we settled into the couch with our respective flutes.

"So..." She took a long sip and swallowed. "If you're here...then obviously your date didn't go as well as you might have hoped."

It upset me that she thought she was someone I only turned to when things went wrong. Of course, I'd given her that impression.

"Actually..." The words were at the tip of my tongue— that I'd specifically canceled the date early because I wanted to come here instead. I thought better of admitting that, though.

"Yeah. The date was just...meh."

Feeling more comfortable with each sip, I lay back into the couch and put my feet up. She did the same from her spot at the other end of the sofa, her bare toes taunting me. Toes were not normally something that attracted me. But *this girl's* toes? I wanted to take each and every one into my mouth and devour them. *Fuck.* I needed help.

Carys downed the last of her bubbly before setting the glass down on the corner of the coffee table. Then she stared up at the ceiling and said, "You know...I used to imagine where I'd be at twenty-five. My life looks nothing like that. But I'm okay with it."

I turned to her. "You should be. You're doing everything right. You're an amazing mother, and your career is thriving. You've accomplished more than most people your age."

She smiled over at me, then stared into space for several seconds.

"What are you thinking about?" I asked.

"Neil—the guy you saw me with today—he mentioned that when he went to our competitor, The Manhattan Ballet, the man he spoke with over there was basically badmouthing us."

It hit me. "Sunny's father..."

She nodded. "Yeah."

"What an asshole."

She sighed. "I talk a lot about how he abandoned his daughter, but I don't often deal with my feelings about what he did to *me*. And hearing that today opened up so many old wounds."

Anger filled me at the thought of how he'd hurt her. I wanted to beat the shit out of him.

"You want to talk about it?"

"Not really. I wish I wasn't focusing on him tonight, but the more I think about what he might have said to Neil, the more it enrages me. I'm sure he knows I work for City Ballet now. You'd think, at the very least, he wouldn't try to jeopardize a company that's basically the hand that feeds his child."

My fists tightened. "It's one thing to be competitive and want to win. It's another to knock someone else down."

"Exactly." She exhaled and shook her head. "Anyway, I'm sorry. I shouldn't have brought him up."

"It's okay. You need to get it out. You can vent to me anytime."

She closed her eyes a moment. "I hadn't had a lot of experience when I got involved with him. I had one boyfriend in high school back in Jersey, but my focus was always on dancing. After I moved to New York, I dated a little, but never anyone exclusively. Charles was my first serious relationship, the first man I gave my heart to. It's going to be a very long time before I trust someone again because of my experience with him. The problem is, I..." She shook her head. "Never mind."

"Don't stop. What were you gonna say?"

"It's a little bit TMI."

Now she really had me curious. "TMI? Are you forgetting the circumstances under which we first got to know each other? I'm the TMI king, remember? Nothing is off the table, Carys."

Her face turned red before my eyes. Then she finally said, "Okay...what I was going to say is...I really miss having sex. Unfortunately, I can't have it without a man. And I'm in no place to trust one right now, so I'm not likely to let a man into my life long enough to have sex. It's a conundrum."

My dick hardened, and my heart began to race. "How long has it been exactly?"

"Well, do the math. Sunny is nine months. I was pregnant with her for nine. So, eighteen months?"

Jesus. I'd always assumed she hadn't been with anyone since Sunny was born, but I really *hadn't* done the math. I couldn't imagine going more than a few months without sex. But a year and a half? That would kill me.

I swallowed hard. "That's a long fucking time, yeah."

"And the worst part is, something happened with my hormones after I had Sunny. They went crazy, and I've been hornier than ever. As you now know from my unfortunate book order, I struggle with getting myself off. Because there's nothing like human touch. So I'm in this constant state of frustration."

Fuck. Me.

Hearing her say that made me practically cream my pants. I'd never been more turned on by a conversation in my life. It felt like my hormones were raging worse than a teenage boy on Viagra. There was nothing in the world I wanted more than to make her come. Right here and now.

"Have I stunned you into silence?" she asked.

God knows how many seconds went by. But I knew the reason I kept my mouth shut: the words begging to be said were dangerous. If I spoke, they were going to come out.

As the seconds wore on, the need to say them became unbearable.

My voice was barely audible. "I could give you an orgasm...if you want."

She turned to me suddenly. "What?"

Clearing my throat, I said, "I could make you come. We wouldn't have sex, but I can give you a damn good orgasm."

It was like I'd lost my damn mind.

She moved back a little. "I'm not some charity case, Deacon."

Shit. She'd taken it the wrong way.

"No. I didn't mean to imply that this was about charity. It's not. Let me rephrase." I took a deep breath and exhaled. "I would *love* to give you an orgasm."

Carys stared at me in disbelief. "That's not why I told you about my issue—so you would offer to get me off. I was just venting. I—"

"I know. I know you weren't expecting me to say what I just did. Honestly, I can hardly believe it myself. But all I could think when you told me you wanted an orgasm is that I...*really* want to give it to you."

You could cut the tension with a knife as she just continued to stare at me. My heart pounded, hoping I hadn't made a huge mistake, one that would cost us our friendship.

She blinked several times. "I appreciate the offer. But I would feel weird saying yes. Because it would be one-sided if you gave me an orgasm, and we weren't having sex."

So, let's fuck then, a voice inside my head suggested. Actually, that voice was likely coming from below the belt. As much as I wanted that, going there would be too dangerous. "You underestimate the enjoyment a man gets from pleasuring a woman."

It was like someone had removed every shred of sense from me tonight. My words were completely bypassing my brain.

"I can't let you do it." Her face was beet red.

I didn't want to make her uncomfortable, and it seemed I had. Now was the time to drop it.

"Okay. Fair enough. I'm sorry if I crossed a line."

She let out a long, shaky breath and closed her eyes. "No. You didn't. It's okay."

I watched her as she stayed in that meditative state. I wondered what she was thinking, but I was too afraid to ask. It was better if I said nothing at this point. My mouth had already gotten me into enough trouble.

After a while, she turned to me. "Are we supposed to just go back to normal conversation right now?"

"We can try." I forced a smile. "I'll go first." Clearing my throat, I asked, "So how was Sunny tonight when you put her to bed?"

"You asked me that earlier."

"That's true." I scratched my chin. "Fuck. Okay. Did you see they're raising the rent?"

"Yeah. That sucks."

"This isn't working, is it?"

"No." She laughed nervously. "Not in the least."

ELEVEN

Carys

USE ME

Deacon and I ended up putting on a movie—some old Jason Bateman comedy on HBO—but I hadn't heard a word of it. The vibe was completely awkward. He'd shocked me with his proposition.

His expression was stoic as he watched the movie alongside me. I couldn't tell what he was thinking, whether he was unaffected or disappointed by my refusal of his offer.

I, on the other hand, couldn't stop thinking about it, and I wasn't sure if that would ever change. Would I be able to think about anything else around him ever again?

But the bigger question was: why did I not entertain his suggestion? It wasn't like I had any other gorgeous men knocking down my door. I trusted Deacon, and I knew he meant well in wanting to "help" me. His intention wasn't to hurt me. He cared about me and wanted to offer me a safe way to get off without involving a stranger.

I spent the next several minutes making a case to change my mind as the movie played in the background.

My brain went in circles. *How exactly did he plan to get me off? Was he going to use his mouth? Stop thinking about it. It would ruin your friendship. But oh my God. What would it be like?* As uncomfortable as I was, I could feel myself getting wet at the thought of what might've been.

It was past midnight now. The movie was nearing the end. When I looked over at Deacon this time, I realized he hadn't been staring at the screen. He was looking at me.

When he realized I'd caught him staring, he started to apologize. "I'm sorry if I fucked up, Carys. I—"

"I want it," I blurted.

His jaw fell. "You want...what?"

My breathing was erratic. "You're gonna make me say it?"

He straightened in his seat. "Yeah. I need to hear you say it."

My words came out in a whisper. "I want you to make me come."

His breath hitched. "You sure?"

I looked into his eyes so he knew I was serious. "Yes."

His breathing grew heavier. Now I had no doubt he was turned on. It wasn't just me.

"You have to promise me something," he said, turning his whole body toward me.

"Okay," I said shakily, my palms sweating, so nervous but wanting him more by the second.

"Don't overthink it. Just lie back and relax. Don't think about anything but enjoying it. And after you come, I'm gonna leave. No awkward talk. I'm gonna pleasure you, and that's all there is to it. And when we see each other again, we don't need to talk about it or analyze it. Promise me that first."

Beyond the point of no return, I would have agreed to just about any terms now. "I promise."

"Good. Because turning something that's supposed to make you feel good into something that makes you anxious or worried is counterproductive."

"I get what you're saying." Trying hard to reassure him, I nodded. "I'm good."

Looking deeply into my eyes, he confirmed it one last time. "You sure?"

"Yes."

After a long pause he finally said, "Let's go to your room."

He stood, reaching out his hand. With my heart pounding in my chest, I took hold of him as he led me into my dark bedroom. He didn't turn on the lights, but there was enough light coming in through the window to see him.

Is this really happening?

My knees shook as I sat down on the bed, feeling a mix of nervousness and excitement, the muscles between my legs giving new meaning to the term *eager beaver*. I had no idea what Deacon was going to do to me; I just knew I was going to let him do it and that my body was incredibly excited, as nervous as I was.

Apparently my nerves were obvious.

He placed his hand on my legs to still them. "You okay?"

"Yes, I promise. I am."

His voice was low and gravelly. "Is there anything that's off limits? Anywhere you don't want me to touch you or anything you don't want me to do?"

His words alone were unraveling me, never mind anything he might do.

"No. Do anything you want."

He closed his eyes briefly, as if to compose himself. Standing at the side of my bed, he whispered, "Lie back."

Deacon's eyes were glassy as he looked down at me. He placed his large, warm hand on my stomach and moved it lower to pull down my leggings. After he slid them off, goosebumps peppered the skin on my thighs.

He sat at the edge of the bed as he rubbed my legs. "You're cold. Let's warm you up."

As he ran his calloused palm along my legs, I practically melted into my mattress. His touch felt so damn good—not to mention surreal. It had been so long since I'd been touched by a man. But being touched like this by *Deacon*? It was my ultimate fantasy come true.

After a few minutes, I felt his fingers grip the elastic band of my panties. Then he slowly worked to move them down. My clit was already throbbing, and he hadn't even touched it yet.

"Take your shirt off."

The demanding tone in his voice made me quiver. I lifted my T-shirt over my head but kept my bra on, mainly because it was the only article of clothing I had left.

Deacon lowered his head and gently kissed down the length of my stomach. If I'd thought his hands felt good, that was nothing compared to his mouth. The stubble on his chin was rough against my skin.

Then I felt his fingers at my opening. It was almost embarrassing how wet I was.

"Jesus Christ, Carys."

"What?" I asked stupidly.

"You're so wet. It's beautiful."

As soon as I felt his fingers pushing inside, my body clenched. It had been so long. My muscles were tight, and it actually burned a little. But within seconds, he was fingering me with ease. Then he added his thumb to the mix, circling and pressing on my clit, and I knew it wouldn't be long before my body gave in to this.

I could hear the sound of my own wetness as he moved his fingers in and out, landing so deep each time he pushed in. He'd barely done it for a minute, and I could've come if I let myself.

Deacon's eyes were on my face the entire time. He seemed fixated on watching me come undone.

He reached for my chest. I felt a nudge on my bra before his fingers fumbled around the material. "Front or back?"

After a brief thought that maybe he was asking how I wanted to take him, I realized he wanted to know where the opening of my bra was.

My nipples hardening, I unhooked it from the front and tossed it to the floor.

He pulled his fingers out of me suddenly, and my clit throbbed harder than before, longing for his return.

Deacon moved to hover over me, one leg on each side of my body. He was so much bigger than me, and I loved the feeling of being locked in under him. He lowered his mouth to my nipple. The sexiest groan escaped him when he took it into his mouth. His teeth nipped at my tender bud, and I grabbed the back of his head, pushing him into my breast as he sucked my nipple harder. My fingers raked through his silky, thick hair. I writhed beneath him as my body longed for more.

And then he gave it to me. He lowered his hand and pushed his fingers back inside of me, moving them in and out in a rhythm that complemented the way he sucked my breasts.

It nearly did me in when he mumbled over my skin, "Fuck me. You're even wetter than before. Amazing." Pausing, he looked up at me. "*You're* amazing."

Even in my lust-induced haze, I warned myself to take those words with a grain of salt, given the circumstances.

And now he was doing that circling thing with his thumb again, rubbing my arousal over my clit, which felt ready to explode. But if I thought that was the pinnacle, I was wrong. Because when he pulled his fingers out and stopped sucking my breasts, Deacon slid his head lower and lower until it was right between my legs. I hadn't been sure he was going to go there. I'd REALLY hoped he would. And it seemed he was.

Oh God.

He spread my knees apart, and at the first touch of his tongue to my clit, I let out an unidentifiable sound— certainly not one I remembered making before. He groaned in response against my tender flesh.

"You taste so good, Carys. I've always wanted to fucking taste you." His words vibrated through my core. Then he lapped at me faster, pressing his tongue harder against my clit.

It felt like my body was here, but my mind had been transported to some other realm. There was no more concern about how I looked, how wet I might have been. I was too far gone now, gripping Deacon's head and guiding his movements as his tongue pushed all the way inside of me and he massaged my clit with the top of his jaw.

"That's it. Grab my head. Show me what you like. Use me," he muttered.

Use me.

I nearly came. Instead, I clenched hard and pulled his hair in an effort to prolong this, because I never wanted it to end.

His breathing and the sounds emanating from him continued to prove this wasn't merely an act of kindness. He was losing it right along with me, and I wanted nothing more than to give him the same satisfaction he was giving me.

I gasped. *Holy shit.*

After a few minutes of hanging on for dear life, I panted, "I want to feel you inside of me, Deacon."

I could hardly believe those words had escaped me. But I guess when you need something badly enough, you have no choice but to ask for it.

Despite the fact that I'd just begged him to fuck me, he didn't budge. If anything, he buried his face deeper between my legs.

Had he not heard me? Or was he pretending he hadn't? I didn't want to presume anything, so I chose not to repeat my request, as desperate as I was to be fucked by him.

He slid his mouth down farther and began to fuck me again with his tongue. I gripped the sheets for dear life, because I knew this was going to be the end of me.

His beard scratched against my ass as he continued moving his tongue in and out of me, stopping only long enough to say, "Fucking hell. I can't get enough of this."

The muscles between my legs contracted. I was losing it. And he knew.

"Come. Come all over my mouth. Give it all to me."

Those final words were enough to push me over the edge.

I bucked my hips, circling my clit against the pressure of his tongue as a rush of adrenaline hit. It was painful to keep quiet as my orgasm coursed through me—more like barreled through me. Waves and waves of pleasure rocketed throughout my body. When I fully released it all, Deacon was still lapping his tongue slowly over my flesh, as if to eat up every last drop of the evidence.

My body was blissfully limp as I recovered from the single most erotic experience of my life—one I knew I wouldn't get over anytime soon.

Eventually, Deacon kissed up to my stomach. He hadn't kissed me on the mouth once. I assumed it was some sort of boundary he'd set, an attempt at not pushing what had happened into intimate territory. I longed for at least one kiss, though, my lips practically trembling from the starvation.

But I was too high to let that disappoint me right now. Because I'd just had the best damn orgasm of my life.

When Deacon moved off the bed, even in the darkness, I could see the bulge in his jeans. I knew he had to be hard, but actually seeing it, the proof that he was aroused, pleased me. My body could have immediately gone for round two. I longed to lie naked with him, to do so much more.

But that wasn't happening.

When he leaned down toward me, he placed a gentle peck on my forehead and said, "Get some sleep."

How does one even respond after the kind of orgasm he'd just given me? There was really only one thing to say.

"Thank you."

"Happy birthday, beautiful," he said. Then he walked away and slowly shut the door behind him.

Happy birthday, indeed.

The next morning, the faint smell of Deacon's cologne lingered on my sheets. Desire pooled in me all over again. As I forced myself out of bed, I could still feel his mouth on me.

Once my feet found the cold bedroom floor, though, everything hit me like a ton of bricks.

Holy shit.

Deacon went down on me last night.

He gave me an orgasm—on my birthday—then left like a bat out of hell.

How would I ever look at him again? How would I ever have a casual conversation, stare at his lips and not remember what they felt like between my legs while his tongue was inside of me? How could I ever forget the way he groaned when he was pleasuring me, as if he'd been starving for it? Or the fact that he told me I was amazing while he sucked on my breasts and fingered me? God, his words. His freaking words.

Use me.

Use me.

Use me.

I walked across the apartment to Sunny's room in a daze. She was awake but quiet, which was rare.

"Thank you for sleeping in this morning, baby girl. Because Mommy really needed it."

My brain felt foggy.

After I changed Sunny, I brought her out to the kitchen and placed her in the highchair.

A few minutes later, my phone chimed.

Deacon: Morning.

What the heck do I say?

Carys: Good morning.

The little dots danced as he typed.

Deacon: You okay?

I wasn't sure whether he was being polite or really wanted to know what I was thinking this morning. I wanted to type a diatribe about my feelings, how I was scared things would never be the same, how I couldn't stop thinking about him, how I craved the return of his mouth, yet I opted for a simpler response.

Carys: Yeah. I'm great.

Deacon: Good. Just making sure.

What else could I say? Thanks again for last night?
Instead of making a fool of myself, I didn't text back.
And neither did he.

TWELVE

Deacon

THE ELEPHANT IN THE ROOM

My friend Adrian waved a hand in front of my face. "Hey, man. What's up? You seem distracted."

Adrian was one of the few close friends I had here in New York. When I first got to town three years ago, he and I had randomly met in Bryant Park and struck up a conversation. At the time, I'd been staying at a hotel while I apartment hunted. He ended up giving me a room until I could find a permanent place. He was probably my best friend now. But I'd never mentioned Carys to him, mainly because he was so good at seeing through me.

It had been two days since Carys's birthday "surprise," and I decided to take Adrian up on his offer to meet for lunch just to get out of the damn apartment.

I looked down at the menu in front of me and brushed off his concern. "It's nothing."

"If you say so. But if you wanna talk about it, I'm here."

I let out a long breath. If I couldn't talk about it with Adrian, who could I open up to?

"I fucked up," I finally said, closing the menu and sliding it away.

"Okay. Be more specific."

"I crossed the line with someone I shouldn't have."

"*Someone* meaning a woman, I take it."

"Yeah, one who's supposed to be a good friend. That's the fucked-up part."

"So you crossed the line with a friend? That's a tale as old as time, man. Nothing wrong with going out of the friend zone if it feels right. You're an adult."

"There's more to it than that. This girl...she's different. She's been through a lot. And she deserves someone who has his shit together, someone who'll be there for her and Sunny long term. I'm not that person."

"Wait..." He narrowed his eyes. "Sunny? Who's Sunny?"

"Her daughter."

"Ah. She's got a kid." He now seemed to understand why this was complicated. "How old?"

"Nine months."

His eyes went wide. "A baby?"

I chuckled at his reaction. "Yeah."

"Where's the father?"

"He's not in the picture. He left when he found out she was pregnant. Sounds like a real gem. Went back to his ex-wife."

"What's this chick's name?"

"Carys—with a C." I smiled. "Carys like Paris."

"That's different."

"Yeah, so is she—in a good way."

He squinted. "You really like her. I can tell. I haven't heard you talk about a woman like this since I met you."

I pondered his words. "She and I have a strong connection. We also have a lot in common. She was a ballet dancer before an injury took her out."

"Oh, shit, like you." He laughed. "Well, not the ballet part. But same idea."

"Yeah, so we can relate to each other. But also, we just jibe, you know? Our conversations are comfortable and easy. She's beautiful on the inside and out. And the way she handles everything life's thrown at her? It's like the personification of grace under fire."

A look of amusement crossed his face. "Yeah, you don't like this chick *at all*."

Though my feelings were apparently transparent, I shook my head and laughed in an attempt to brush off his statement. "And her daughter is a sweet little thing. Even in the short time I've known them, Sunny's gotten used to me. She knows me. That's dangerous. I don't want her to wonder where I am when I inevitably stop coming around." I sighed. "It's just hard because they're right next door."

"Shit, okay. This is your neighbor. The one you mentioned having coffee with."

"Yup."

"I hadn't put two and two together." Adrian looked perplexed. "So, we never really talked about this, but why is the kid thing a problem? You don't want to be a dad someday? Or is it just that you don't want to be a dad to *someone else's* kid?"

The thought of rejecting Sunny because she wasn't my blood hurt my heart a little. It wasn't about that. This was about me, not her. She deserved better.

"I made a decision a long time ago not to have kids." I had my reasons; I just preferred not getting into them right now—maybe ever.

"Why?"

"Just a personal decision. If I know I don't want kids, it's not fair to get involved with a woman whose entire life is her daughter."

"So if you feel that way, what happened? You just slipped?" He leaned in and whispered, "You fucked her?"

"Actually, no. Things didn't go that far. But they shouldn't have gone as far as they did."

"What kind of stuff did you do?"

For some reason, I didn't feel comfortable telling him. It felt like I was exploiting what had happened somehow, which was weird because I never hesitated to talk about sex. But I felt protective of Carys. I wasn't going to kiss and tell.

I held my palm up. "It doesn't matter what we did. I just don't think I can look at her the same way now. That really sucks, because I don't want to lose her friendship."

He scratched his chin. "If you didn't live right next door, it would be easier to avoid her."

"That's the problem. I don't *want* to fucking avoid her. I just don't want to mess things up any more than I already have."

"You think she has feelings for you?"

Deep down, I believed she did. "Possibly."

For a long time, I hadn't been sure. But lately, even before her birthday night, there was something about the way she looked at me—probably the same way I looked at her. And what happened between us had confirmed that she was attracted to me, at the very least. For as long as I lived, I would never forget her begging me to fuck her. Pretending not to have heard that in the moment was nearly impossible, and I'd thought about little else since. My mind kept wandering back to her words, to the need in her voice. I'd spent that entire night hard, even after I jacked off. I'd stayed up until morning, unable to forget how she tasted, still savoring her on my tongue and smelling her on my body. And right now, I was nearly hard again just thinking about it.

Adrian snapped me out of my thoughts. "Well, if you think she has feelings for you, and if you're a hundred-percent sure you don't want anything more than a friendship, continuing to be around her is a recipe for disaster. You can't have it both ways, you know? Sounds like you've reached the point of no return. You can't go back to being friends once you've crossed the line with a woman. Speaking from experience, it just doesn't work. You can't have your cake and eat it, too."

There was that fucking saying again. It kept haunting me. Except now, the word *eating* conjured up images of her sweet pussy. My jeans tightened.

I shook my head. "I don't want to lose her as a friend, but I also don't think I can forget what happened between us."

"I don't think you have a choice. You already *did* ruin the friendship. Honestly, was it ever really 'just a friendship' if you were attracted to her from the beginning?"

He had a point. From almost the first day I'd hung out with Carys, I'd had to fight my attraction to her.

"So how do I handle it?"

"You stop trying to be her friend. I hate to say it, but this is a 'shit or get off the pot' situation. If you continue to stick around, you *will* cross the line again. Someone's gonna get hurt."

Adrian was a straight shooter; he was seldom wrong. And I hated that I knew he was right in this case. It wasn't fair to toy with Carys's emotions. I wanted to be there for her if she needed me, but I needed to stop trying to get closer if I couldn't trust myself.

Despite Adrian's warning, when I passed Starbucks on the way home, I walked in and picked up a latte for Carys. My plan was to go over to her apartment and see if things seemed different between us. If they did, I'd know I'd fucked everything up beyond the point of no return. If by chance she acted normal, maybe that would mean I hadn't totally ruined our friendship.

Once I got to her apartment, I texted her from outside her door in case the baby was napping.

A few seconds later, she opened. "Hey." Her face seemed flushed.

"Hey," I said.

And there it was. Immediately. An unspoken energy that was different than what I normally felt.

I handed her the coffee.

She took it. "Thanks for this."

"You're welcome." After I entered, I looked down at my shoes for a moment. "After the other night, I, uh, wanted to come by and...see you...feel you up." I shut my eyes and corrected, "Fuck. *Out!* Feel you *out*."

Jesus Christ. Not even a minute here, and I was already acting crazy. It was one thing to tell myself to act normal, but now that she was right in front of me, I was incapable of that. Her scent immediately fucked with my head, brought me back to my face buried in her pussy. I didn't think I'd ever be able to smell her and not lose my mind again. I was a lost cause and an idiot for thinking things could go back to the way they were before.

"I'm glad you came," she said, turning red. She shook her head. "I guess I'm speaking in ambiguous sexual phrases, too."

"What the fuck is wrong with us?" I asked.

When I noticed Sunny kicking her legs in the air on her playmat, I put my coffee down on the table and walked over.

Kneeling down, I said, "Hey, Sunny Side Up. How ya doin'?"

I'd never been more grateful for Sunny's presence, because it was just the buffer I needed right now. She cooed but didn't cry to be held.

I turned to Carys. "How's Bee Gees therapy going?"

"It's amazing. I had the album on a little while ago, and it put her in a really good mood. It's a miracle. You see how she's not even crying for you to hold her? I guess we weaned her off that habit."

"Who knew the answer was some high-pitched disco dudes all along?" I stood up. "Glad to help."

About fifteen seconds of silence passed, but I swear it felt like fifteen minutes.

Then we both started to speak over each other.

"You first..." I told her.

Then she said the dreaded words. "About the other night..."

Here it comes.

My heart started to pound. "Yeah..."

"I don't want things to be weird between us."

I let out a long breath, happy she'd articulated what I'd been struggling to. "Neither do I, Carys."

"There's no reason why they should be, right?" She shrugged. "I mean, we're both adults."

I forced honesty out of myself. "What happened...felt right at the time. In retrospect, I probably took things too far. I care about you and would never want to do anything to ruin our friendship."

She blinked several times and whispered, "It's not ruined."

Relief washed over me, though I didn't exactly believe her. I *wanted* to believe her. "I'm glad you said that. You have no idea how much."

Then my chest felt heavy again, because while the elephant in the room was no longer present, that unspoken tension remained. No matter what we told each other right now, something had changed. Our words weren't coming as easily, and I could hardly look at her without remembering how she tasted. In fact, I could hardly look at her at all. Meanwhile, her eyes were on my lips. If coming over here was a test to see if things could feel "back to normal," we'd failed miserably.

I had to give her credit for trying to convince herself our friendship could pick up where it left off. But it wasn't working because I could see in her eyes that she felt the change in our dynamic, too.

Adrian was right. He was damn right, and I didn't know what to do about it.

I ended up taking the cowardly way out.

"Alright, well, I have a phone meeting with my supervisor. I just wanted to bring you your coffee and see how you're doing."

"Thanks." She smiled, but it seemed fake.

Fuck.

I walked over to Sunny. "Be good for your mama." She took the toy she was biting on out of her mouth and flashed me a wide grin. Not sure why, but that smile kind of hurt this time. Maybe because deep down, I knew I'd be seeing it a lot less. That is, if I could stick to doing what I needed to.

THIRTEEN

Carys

HE WASN'T ALONE

I couldn't believe I was thinking this, but I wished Deacon had never gone down on me. I wished I had never heard him groaning against me. I wished he'd never given me the most amazing orgasm of my life. I wished I could erase that night altogether, because nothing had been the same since.

I wasn't stupid. I knew he'd been keeping his distance since my birthday. It had been a week now, and it was clearer by the day that we'd ruined a perfectly good friendship. What bothered me the most was the sense of false hope I'd had after that night—that somehow Deacon would decide he wanted to be more than friends. Instead, I hadn't seen or heard from him in days. Normally he would've stopped by with another coffee by now, but he had chosen to distance himself. Not sure I could blame him. The last time he was here, things were awkward. And I hated that. Things had never been that way before—sexually tense, maybe, but never awkward.

Poor Sunny.

As I sat ruminating about Deacon, I'd been feeding her mindlessly, causing some of the rice cereal to dribble down her chin.

"I'm sorry, baby girl. Mommy's mind is somewhere else today."

Thankfully, Sunny simply opened her mouth wider for the next bite. Didn't take much to please her.

After Sunny's early-intervention therapist came for her visit that morning, I decided we needed to get out of the house. I found a "Mommy and Me" class with drop-in availability in the afternoon, so I packed up a diaper bag and took my daughter out for a change of scenery.

For an hour, I did yoga poses while holding Sunny, and she seemed to love it. I also got to talk to other moms, one of whom was single like me. It felt damn good to get out, and I vowed to do it more often. The only times I usually left the house were to go to the office or for some quick food shopping. That needed to change.

After the session, I took Sunny to the neighborhood Starbucks. After wiping down the highchair, I fed her bananas while I sipped my latte. It had started to rain, so I was thankful we'd made it close to home before the weather got bad.

It had been such a relaxing day. But that all ended when Deacon walked into the café. Raindrops covered the front window, so I'd had not even a few seconds' warning before he entered. My heart beat faster as I watched him. The worst part? He wasn't alone.

I recognized the girl with him—Kendra, the redhead he'd taken back to his apartment at least once before.

Why did this have to happen? Both times I'd come here recently I'd run into him. Maybe a part of me *hoped* to run into him. But certainly no part of me had hoped to run into him with *her*.

When our eyes locked, I swallowed the tension in my throat.

He had no choice but to come up to us, but I wished we could've bypassed this uncomfortable run-in altogether. I wished we were invisible.

"Hey, Carys," he said stiffly.

"Hi." I could barely look at him. Instead, I looked at her. "Nice to see you again," I lied. It was pretty sad that looking at her was easier than looking at him.

"You, too," she said.

He placed his hand on Sunny's head. "Hey, Sunny Side Up."

It broke my heart a little to see her face light up. That's how I used to feel when I saw him, too. Sunny flailed her arms and legs in her highchair.

"How long have you guys been here?" he asked.

"Not long."

My answer was curt, and I still didn't look him in the eyes. I couldn't help it. Seeing him with Kendra hurt, and I wasn't in the mood for small talk.

He likely sensed my disdain. "Well, I'll let you two be," he said. "Enjoy."

"Yep," I said, still not making eye contact.

I knew he hadn't brought her around to hurt me, but it stung. He was spending time with her instead of me.

I tortured myself by sneaking glances in their direction as they waited in line. When he took out his wallet to pay, my eyes zoned in on his big, strong hands. Hands that had touched me so intimately, hands that had made me feel things I'd never felt before. Hands that would be touching *her* later.

The milk turned in my stomach as jealousy burned through me.

———

That evening, just when I'd thought my day couldn't get any worse, the phone rang. I looked at the caller ID and realized it was Charles—Sunny's father.

Why is he calling? "Hello?"

"Carys..."

"What do you want?"

"I wanted to congratulate you on City Ballet winning the donation from Neil Spectra."

"Thank you. You didn't need to do that."

"I also wanted to see how you're doing, in general."

Is he serious? "Why? You never normally care."

He sighed. "I know things have been rough between us for some time. That's something I deeply regret."

I looked over at Sunny, who was peacefully swinging and oblivious to the fact that her "father" was pulling some shit right now.

I got a little choked up. "You should regret not acknowledging your daughter, aside from throwing money our way from time to time. That's what you should regret."

"I know. And I do regret that. I really do."

"Well, it's too late. You had your chance."

He paused. "I messed up royally."

"What's the real reason for this call, Charles?"

After a short delay, he finally said, "I want to see her."

"Why? Why now?"

"Because she's my daughter."

"Wait...you're only now realizing this? I thought you didn't want anything to do with her. You're not even on the birth certificate, per your request."

"I know. I was scared, Carys. At the time, Violet had threatened to take everything if I acknowledged Sunny. She didn't want Talia and Xavier to know. Still doesn't. I handled everything wrong. I shouldn't have given in to her."

"Why are you realizing this now?"

"Things have been bad at home. It's become clear to me that I threw away everything with you for nothing. Not only did I make a mistake abandoning Sunny, but you, too. I really did love you, Carys. I don't know what I was thinking going back to that woman when I had you. I was trying to save my family."

The nerve of him. "Oh, I see. You save one family by throwing the other one away. That makes perfect sense." *Is he seriously expecting me to be receptive to this bullshit?* He was more than a little too late.

"Please hear me out, Carys. I—"

"I'm not sure what you expect me to say, Charles, but—"

"Say you'll speak to me." His voice grew louder in my ear. "Say you won't shut me out. Say you'll consider letting me see my daughter."

Looking over at her, I felt conflicted. "I don't know. I still have a lot of negative feelings toward you, and she's very intuitive. She'll be able to sense things. I don't want negative energy around her. And I certainly don't want you coming into her life only to leave again. I don't trust you and never will."

"I have to accept that as my own fault. But please say you'll consider talking to me again. Maybe that can eventually lead to my being able to see Sunny—on your terms."

"Are you going to tell your children about her? Because you shouldn't be allowed to see her if you're not willing to acknowledge her like you acknowledge them."

"You know it's not my choice. Violet doesn't want them to know. And I can see her point. They're still very young. When they're older, I may be able to tell them. I *do* plan to tell them eventually."

That was the only one of his arguments I sort of understood. It would be devastating for them to find out their dad had fathered a child with another woman. Xavier was thirteen and Talia was ten. His daughter, in particular, wasn't even old enough to understand sex.

After I didn't say anything for several seconds, he said, "Talk to me, Carys."

"I honestly have nothing to say. I'm confused by what you're throwing at me. I don't think you deserve to see her, but at the same time, Sunny deserves to know who her father is, even if you've been a disappointment. So I guess I'll think about the pros and cons of letting you be around her."

"That's a start." He let out a breath into the phone. "Thank you. That's all I needed to hear."

FOURTEEN

Deacon

CALL ME DICK

A few days after I'd seen Carys at the coffee shop, Kendra was over again. She bent down to pick up something off the floor.

"What's this?" she asked.

It was a pacifier. I couldn't believe I hadn't noticed it before.

"Where was that?"

"Underneath this table. I went to slide my shoes under there and found it."

I had a small table where I dropped my keys near the door of my apartment. It was right next to the wall mirror—the one Sunny had loved to look at herself in. I had no idea she'd dropped the binky, which had been clipped to her shirt that day.

Taking it from Kendra, I looked down at the dusty rubber tip. My chest felt heavy. It hadn't even been two weeks since I'd vowed to stay away from them, but I missed Sunny. I missed Carys. I missed them.

"Why do you have a pacifier here?"

Still gazing down at it, I said, "It belongs to the baby next door—Sunny. I had to watch her in an emergency one day. She must have dropped it."

"Oh." She cocked her head to the side. "What's their deal anyway?"

"What do you mean?"

"Why is there no father in the picture?"

The first time Kendra met Carys, I'd mentioned my neighbor was a single mother. Carys' story really wasn't any of Kendra's business. So, I shrugged. "It didn't work out."

"That's too bad. The baby is so young to not have a father around. Especially given her condition. It's such a shame."

My body stiffened. Then a rush of adrenaline ran through my veins. "Why a shame?"

"You know…"

My tone was harsh. "No, I don't. Why is it a shame?"

"The fact that the baby has something wrong with her."

My blood started to boil. "There's nothing wrong with her." I gritted my teeth. "Nothing. Do you understand?"

"Jesus. I didn't mean any harm."

"She might look a little different, but there's nothing wrong with Sunny. It's time people like you started realizing that. She's just like any other baby. And happier than most people. There's no reason she can't grow up to be just like any other adult. She has an extra chromosome. That's it."

"Okay." She held out her palms. "I'm sorry if I upset you."

"You didn't. I just felt I should educate you on that."

Her voice softened. "Understood."

Things went quiet for several minutes before Kendra escaped to the bathroom.

I felt a little bad for snapping at her, but I understood Carys's frustration now. Down's didn't have any impact on who Sunny was, only how people saw her.

Kendra and I watched a movie in silence, and it was early evening by the time we even spoke to each other again.

After we shut off the TV, she took me by the hand and led me to my bedroom. We hadn't had sex in a while, and she'd given me every indication earlier today that her expectations were set on getting some. But I didn't know if I could go through with it. Not only was I not feeling it tonight, but how would I deal with Kendra making noises Carys could hear? No freaking way was I going to put Carys in that position. But if I was serious about moving on, I couldn't stay celibate forever.

When Kendra and I started kissing, it felt...off.

Then the sound of crying next door killed any last shred of hope. Even though my bed was now on the opposite end of the room, away from Carys's wall, I was still able to hear Sunny pretty clearly.

After I pushed back, Kendra rolled her eyes. "Well, this is déjà vu."

I sighed. "Yeah. I suppose it is."

"What...does that baby have a radar that detects whenever we're about to have sex?"

"I know. It's pretty funny," I said.

She crossed her arms in a huff. "I don't think it's funny at all. Glad you do."

Kendra was probably more pissed that I found the timing amusing than the interruption itself.

"You know what?" She hopped off the bed. "I need to leave."

"You're gonna leave because the baby's crying?"

"No, Deacon. I'm leaving because you find this funny—that our privacy doesn't really matter to you. I'm *also* leaving because you reamed me a new asshole earlier for feeling sorry for that poor little baby."

Remaining silent, I didn't try to convince her to stay as I followed her out of the room. I watched as she slipped on her shoes.

She threw her coat over her shoulders dramatically. "Call me when you're ready to stop laughing at me or reprimanding me." She slammed the door behind her.

I was a dick, because as upset as she was, it didn't really faze me. In fact, her leaving was a relief. Continuing to see Kendra had been more about trying to move on from Carys than anything else. Kendra was merely a distraction, and she deserved more than that. So let her be mad, and let her find someone else to spend her time with.

I had bigger fish to fry tonight. I really wanted to go next door to see if Carys needed anything. Sunny was still crying, and when I heard the Bee Gees playing and realized that hadn't calmed her down, I decided that was my cue.

My heart raced as I went next door. I'd use returning the binky as my official excuse.

When she opened, I couldn't believe what I saw. I had expected Carys to look flustered or disheveled after

Sunny's meltdown. Instead, she wore a black sequin dress and looked like a million bucks.

She's going out?

Carys was out of breath as she stood there, holding a crying Sunny. "What's up?" she asked.

"Are you heading out?"

Instead of answering my question, she blew air up toward her forehead. "What do you want, Deacon?"

Nice to see you, too.

I held up the pacifier and wiggled it between my fingers. "I wanted to return this. Found it on my floor. I probably should've washed it but figured you'd throw it in the dishwasher. Not sure of the proper way to sanitize these things."

She nodded once. The fact that she was still cold toward me wasn't a surprise. I knew seeing me with Kendra the other day must have sucked. But the fact of the matter? That was exactly what I was aiming for. I was trying to get over Carys and hoping she'd see things were "back to normal," back to the way they were before I'd royally fucked up.

Sunny kicked her legs, seeming to want out of Carys's arms.

I reached out. "May I?"

Carys looked down at Sunny, then back at me, as if accepting my offer wasn't an easy decision. But eventually, she handed Sunny over.

After a couple of minutes in my arms, Sunny's wailing had reduced to quiet sniffles.

Bopping her up and down, I asked, "What happened to the Bee Gees? I heard the music earlier. They didn't help much this time, huh?"

"No. I guess they've run their course...like a lot of things."

Ouch. I pretended that went over my head. "That sucks. We'll have to find something else."

A few seconds of awkward silence passed. "Why did you really come over here?" she asked. "I doubt it was to return this dusty binky."

I looked down at Sunny to gather my thoughts. "I wanted to check in on you, see how you're doing. It's been a while."

"Well, at the moment, not good, Deacon. Because I'm supposed to be attending an important event for work tonight, and Sharon had to cancel."

Shit. "Why didn't you call me?" I asked without thinking.

"Do you really not know the answer to that?"

Of course, that was a dumb question. "What time are you supposed to be there?"

"I was supposed to be there fifteen minutes ago."

I waved my hand. "Go. I'll watch her."

She shook her head. "I can't let you do that."

"Carys...I know I fucked up our friendship. And I'm sorry. But I still care about you. And I don't want you to miss this thing if it's important. So maybe just take me up on my offer so you don't have to piss off your boss. Then you can process it later. We'll talk when you get back." When she didn't say anything, I pushed. "You need that job. Now's not the time for pride."

She sighed. "I don't know..."

"Look how calm Sunny is right now. It'll be fine. We'll be fine."

We'll be fine.

Sunny and me? Yes.

You and me? Not so sure.

Blinking several times, she finally conceded. "Okay."

"Good," I said. "Now go, so you don't miss too much."

Carys rushed around in search of her things, grabbing her purse and a quick glass of water. She wore high, red-bottomed heels. Fuck, her legs looked good in those shoes. My mouth watered as I admired the curve of her little, round ass in that dress. Then jealousy set in at the thought of men ogling her tonight.

Kissing Sunny on the head, she said, "Be a good girl."

I took a deep breath of her scent for the few seconds she was close.

She finally looked up at me. "I won't be back too late."

"Take as long as you need."

Another whiff of her perfume hit me as she blew out the door.

After she was gone, I looked down at Sunny.

"We got this, right? No surprises tonight." I put my forehead against hers. "And you know what that means."

When she smiled, it reminded me how much I'd missed her pure, non-judgmental sweetness. No one ever looked at me like Sunny Kincaid did. And I didn't deserve a shred of it. I wished I could warn her not to get too attached to the man next door. I'd only end up disappointing her, like I had so many other people who'd trusted me.

Wandering the room with her in my arms, I spoke in a low voice. "Do you ever wonder who the hell I am? I'm not even sure I formally introduced myself, Sunny. You probably just look at me as the weird, big guy who comes over sometimes and holds you." I smiled. "Anyway...I'm Deacon. Can you say Deacon?" I pointed to my chest. "Deacon."

She cooed.

Sunny actually let me put her down on the playmat, which surprised me.

I spent the better part of the next hour sitting on the couch while I watched her play on the floor. "Deacon," I kept repeating, to see if by some chance she'd try to say my name. I'd pretty much given up when I heard her say what sounded like...*dick.*

Then she repeated, "Deek."

I cracked up. "That's right!"

She'd babbled many different sounds tonight, and it could have been a coincidence, but I had myself convinced she was trying to say Deacon. Or maybe *Dick* was a more accurate description of me lately. Either way, it worked for me. Deacon or Dick. Tomato, Tomahto. I'd take any D sound she wanted to give me.

A knock at the door interrupted my little celebration. I assumed it might have been Carys returning early, though that didn't make sense.

After I opened, I regretted not checking the peephole first, because it was a man I didn't recognize. He wore a black tuxedo and looked to be in his late thirties.

"Who are you?" he asked.

My body went rigid. "Shouldn't I be asking you that question?"

"I'm Charles, Sunny's father."

What the fuck? Gritting my teeth, I clenched my fists. "Does Carys know you're here?"

When he didn't immediately respond, I knew the answer was no.

This guy wasn't exactly what I'd pictured. He was average-looking, with blond hair and shorter than I'd imagined. Basically, Carys could have done a lot better.

"Let me guess... You expected to find some vulnerable, old woman watching the baby so you could weasel your way in here while Carys was out?"

When he took a few steps forward, I held out my hand. "No. Stay back. I'm not letting you in."

He let out a frustrated breath. "Look, man to man, I just want to see my daughter for a few minutes."

"Man to man?" I scoffed. "A real man wouldn't have to sneak over to see his daughter, because he'd be in her life already."

"Look, I'm going to the same gala Carys is at. My colleague told me she was there, so I wondered if I could just stop by to see Sunny without having to upset her. I don't mean any harm."

He tried to look beyond my shoulders, but I adjusted my body so he couldn't see past me.

I crossed my arms. "Well, it's not gonna happen—not without Carys's permission."

He grimaced. "Who did you say you were?"

"The name's Dick. And I suggest you leave before I show you exactly why they call me that."

He let out a frustrated breath, huffed, and made his way back down the hall.

After he was out of sight, I shut the door, locked it, and went over to where Sunny was still playing on the floor.

I lifted her up and held her for a while, feeling protective. It angered me that Carys's ex tried to pull that shit, and now I'd have to tell her.

Sunny stared up at me, this time not smiling as she normally did. Maybe she sensed I was pissed.

"You deserve better than that dude. I'm sorry you have a crappy dad. But your mom makes up for it."

I walked over to the window with her, and we looked out at the traffic below. "Can I tell you a secret, Sunny?" After pausing for her response, I said, "Okay. I'm gonna tell you anyway." I looked at her. "I really screwed up with your mother. You got any tips for how I can make it right?"

A few seconds later, I felt a vibration from her bottom.

Well, I guess that's my answer.

FIFTEEN

Carys

SUCK IT UP

I ended up leaving the gala early. I couldn't relax knowing Deacon was stuck taking care of Sunny. Maybe if things had been different between us, I would've been more comfortable with the situation.

And when Charles showed up, I knew that was my signal to leave. I wasn't surprised to see him—it was an industry event—but that didn't make having to deal with him any easier. I managed to avoid him while doing the remainder of my obligatory schmoozing. Then I told Cynthia I needed to leave. She seemed fine with it, since I had shown my face for a while.

It was eleven when I walked into my apartment. I was surprised to see Sunny not in her crib, but lying on her stomach atop Deacon's chest. Both of them were asleep on the couch. I stopped for a moment to take in the sight, which tugged at my heart in a bittersweet way.

Why do you have to be so sweet and such an asshole at the same time, Deacon?

I tiptoed over to them and slowly worked to remove her from his grasp.

Deacon's eyes blinked open. "Hey. Did you just get in?" he whispered groggily.

"Yes. Gonna put her to bed. Be right back."

I placed Sunny in the crib and waited to make sure she didn't wake up. After confirming she was asleep, I returned to the living room. Deacon was now standing, his thick, copper hair a tousled mess. He slid his hands into his pockets, seeming tense.

"There's something I have to tell you," he said.

My heart sank. "Did something happen?"

"Your ex came by tonight. He knew you were out. He tried to take advantage and see Sunny."

"Oh my God. What?" My heart began to race. "He knew I was at the arts gala. He showed up late. Now it makes sense why. I can't believe he'd do that."

"I wanted to punch him, but instead I scared him away. He definitely wasn't expecting to find me here."

"No. I'm sure he wasn't." I clutched my chest.

"I don't mean to upset you, but obviously I had to tell you."

"Thank you for handling that."

"Sunny was on her playmat when he came by. I don't think she sensed the drama. Has he ever pulled anything like this before?"

I shook my head. "No, but he called me the other night, out of the blue, asking if he could visit her. I told him I had to think about it. Apparently, that answer wasn't good enough."

"Why does he want to see her all of a sudden?"

"I haven't figured out if his intentions are genuine, or if there's something more to it. He mentioned that he's having problems with his wife."

Deacon pursed his lips. "You think he's trying to use Sunny to get back together with you?"

"I don't think so. I just think his ex was the driving force in his staying away from Sunny all this time. And now that they're having trouble, he probably sees it as an opportunity to do something he should've done a long time ago. Maybe he has a heart in there somewhere and feels guilty."

Deacon's eyes narrowed. "You won't ever trust him again, will you? After all the shit he's put you through? Tell me you won't let him into your life again."

"Not romantically." I exhaled. "While I don't like what he tried to pull tonight, I've been torn ever since he called. Sunny deserves to know who her father is and see him, even if he's not worthy of her love. I hadn't decided what to do, but him showing up like that certainly doesn't help his case." I sighed. "Thank you again for protecting Sunny."

"There was no way I would've let him near her."

Closing my eyes, I let out a breath and fell back onto the couch. "Charles was the second man I ever trusted. And both of them let me down."

"Your father was the first." He guessed correctly.

I nodded.

As Deacon took a seat across the sofa, it hit me how much I'd missed talking to him. I needed to repair our friendship, so I opened up a little. "You wanna know the weird part? My mother had gotten involved with an older guy, too, when she was around my age. That was my dad. He also left Mom to go back to his wife. How freaky is that?"

"No shit?"

"Yup. Talk about history repeating itself. Except unlike my situation with Charles, my father was still *with* his wife when he started dating my mother. He had three kids. It's a very similar scenario, though Charles has two kids and not three."

"Have you ever met your father's other kids?"

"No."

He'd touched upon a sore subject. My dad had come around a tiny bit when I was little, but by the time I was old enough to remember anything, he was gone. He lived in Delaware, and his children were in the same area. No one ever reached out to me, though I did find out through a mutual friend that my father ended up telling his kids about me. It is what it is. But I wanted better for Sunny. I just didn't know what that was as it related to Charles.

"You said you have a brother," Deacon said. "Different fathers?"

I nodded. "My mother married my stepfather a few years after I was born. He's my brother Aaron's biological dad. Then they got divorced, and I never saw him much after, either. Nice family life, huh?"

"Everybody's got their shit, Carys." He placed his arm over the top of the couch and settled into his seat. "My parents have a pretty good relationship on the surface, but my father's focus was always his football-coaching career and not their marriage. I know he and my mom have had their share of troubles over the years. Pretty sure there was some infidelity on his part that he never owned up to. No family is perfect. But I do realize how lucky I was to grow up with two parents when so many people don't."

"Yeah, and neither will Sunny."

His eyes softened. "Sunny has an amazing mom. I know you'll make sure she doesn't want for anything, least of all love and security." He looked down at his shoes for a moment. Then his eyes met mine. "I'm sorry I've acted like an ass."

Shaking my head, I said, "It's okay, Deacon."

"No, it's not. I took the cowardly way out when I stopped coming around instead of addressing things with you. Sunny called me a dick tonight, and she's right."

I couldn't help but chuckle. "What?"

He shrugged. "I was trying to teach her to say Deacon. It came out 'Deek'. Sounded like 'Dick'." He sighed. "Anyway...she's right. I *have* been an absolute dick, Carys, and I'm so fucking sorry."

"Maybe a little," I agreed. "But deep down, I understand, Deacon. I take responsibility for what happened between us that night, too. I was...horny. We'd both had a little too much to drink and got carried away. And now you don't know how to handle the tension. Because you don't think we can be anything more than friends. You can't ever...*go there* with me. I get it."

He looked torn. "I feel like you think I've shied away because I don't want you enough to accept your situation. That's not it. I've been struggling with my feelings when it comes to you for a while—long before that night. This has nothing to do with not wanting you. It has everything to do with not being good for you long term, certainly not good enough for Sunny. I haven't held onto a normal relationship since God knows when, and I've hurt people I cared about in the past. I don't want to end up hurting you or Sunny down the line—especially Sunny."

As much as I admired his honesty, it still hurt to hear him confirm what I already knew. There was no chance for us.

"I get it." I sighed. Who was I to convince him to trust himself? I didn't trust anyone.

Then he continued. "I pretended to make what happened on your birthday night mostly about you, but I wanted it more than you could ever know. And I wanted more than that, too. I just wouldn't let myself take it. I don't want to hurt you, Carys. You're one of the best people I know and a good friend, and I crossed the line. But it's too late. I can't take it back. I know I ruined our friendship in the process, regardless of what you say."

"You're right," I agreed. "You did kind of ruin our friendship as we knew it. Not because I'm mad at you or respect you less, but because I can't stop thinking about what that night felt like or how jealous I was when I saw you with Kendra. I can't control my feelings. As much as I don't want things to be awkward between us, they are now."

"Yeah. Don't I know it." He exhaled. "I don't want to lose you as a friend. And I don't want to hurt you. So tell me what I should do."

There was only one way to handle it, short of one of us moving.

"I think we have to be adults about it. We need to accept that things might be a little awkward between us and let them be awkward. It's either that or never see each other again. I'd personally rather know that I can go to you if I need you. If that means dealing with a bit of uncomfortable sexual tension, so be it. I want to have coffee with you and be able to talk about my day. I don't want to lose you, Deacon. So I think that means we only have one choice. And that's to suck it up."

He stared into my eyes for a while. "I don't want it to be the end of us, either. I really don't. I value your friendship so much."

"It's settled, then. We just deal."

His mouth curved into a smile. "You may be younger than me, but you're a fuck of a lot more mature, you know that?"

"Well, I guess I've had to grow up fast."

"Yeah. You have."

I stood, prompting him to do the same. "Thank you again for tonight," I said.

"Anytime, Carys."

I closed the door behind him and knew it would be a long time before I fell asleep.

SIXTEEN

Carys

BLINDSIDED

Six Months Later

A lot had changed over the past several months, and it was more than the weather transforming from frigid to hot in the city.

It was now July, and I had a fifteen-month-old who was attempting to walk, albeit unsuccessfully thus far. The months were flying by. It seemed like yesterday that she'd turned one. When Sunny had marked that milestone in April, I'd had a small party for her at the apartment with a few friends from our Mommy and Me class. Simone had been there, too, and, of course, Deacon. Charles, on the other hand, hadn't been invited. He continued to call occasionally, and had apologized multiple times for coming by without permission earlier this year, but I still hadn't warmed to the idea of having him around Sunny. However, I suspected one day I would.

My feelings for Deacon had been put to the test more than ever. Kendra was a thing of the past, but he'd begun dating someone new in May—Rachel. She had long, dark hair and big green eyes and worked behind the scenes for a modeling agency. She was gorgeous, and I hated her. He'd been open about her from the beginning, never tried to hide it, but it still sucked. The whole thing sucked. I wasn't sure how serious they were, but his meeting her had been the final nail in the coffin of my heart.

If Deacon and I were going to be friends, I had to accept everything—as did he when I'd decided to put myself out there in the dating world last month. I'd informed Deacon that Sharon was coming over in the evening to watch Sunny while I went on my first official date in ages. That'd been an awkward conversation. I could've sworn Deacon seemed jealous. He'd wanted to know the guy's name so he could do a background check.

Sean Colmes was the man I'd met online, and Deacon had dubbed him "P-Diddy" because he had the same name as the singer, only spelled differently. Anyway, the date didn't amount to anything—he didn't knock my socks off. I hadn't been on a date since then, but it had felt good to return to the dating scene. Lord knows I needed the practice.

Deacon still brought me coffee almost daily. He didn't talk much about Rachel, which I appreciated. On the outside, it seemed our friendship had survived the blip of my birthday night last January. So it was important that I not let on that my feelings for him had only grown. I wanted Deacon more than ever. Whenever Rachel was over at his apartment, I was a mess.

A mess.

I'd thought my complicated feelings were my biggest problem when it came to him. That is, until one afternoon when he stopped by with his usual coffees. The unusually somber look on his face told me something was up.

"What's wrong?" I asked.

"You could tell, huh?"

"Yeah. I know your face pretty well. The smile's not here today. Did something happen? Is everything okay with your family?"

"It's nothing like that. Everyone is okay." He handed me my coffee. "Let me say hi to Sunny Side Up first. Then we'll talk."

Deacon walked over to Sunny's swing and seemed to take a much longer time than usual rubbing her head and whispering gibberish.

An ominous feeling came over me. "What's going on, Deacon?"

He stood up. "I have some news."

My heartbeat accelerated. "Okay..."

"I got a promotion."

My first reaction was...confusion. "That's great. That's good, right?"

"Yeah. It pays almost double. Which is nuts."

"Oh my gosh, wow."

"The only problem is...the new position requires me to work out of the Tokyo office. I'd have to move there."

"Oh." My heart sank.

He swallowed. "It's a different role, a managerial position with less design work. So it's not remote. I'd have to report to the office every day because I'd be training people on our software. And I'd still be designing my old series on top of that. So it's more work, but a big opportunity."

It took what felt like forever to form a response. Despite all the complex emotions I'd felt toward this man—jealousy, longing, frustration—*nothing* felt as horrible as the thought of him disappearing from my life.

"Wow...I don't know what to say, Deacon."

He let out a long sigh. "I'm having my doubts about whether to take it. It sucks, right? That something good happens and there's such a price to pay. I love my life here, and I don't want to leave."

Fighting off tears, I said, "I don't want you to leave, either. You're like...family."

"I know. I feel like that about you guys, too. You have no idea how much I want to stay. But...at the same time, I'm torn. This opportunity could lead to better things, even if I just stick it out for a year and come back."

The words *come back* gave me some hope. But who was I kidding? If Deacon left for a year, things would never be the same again.

But I steeled myself to be the best friend I could be. "This sounds like a once-in-a-lifetime opportunity, right? I mean...you can't turn it down?"

He seemed to think long and hard before he answered. "Probably not." He nodded. "I probably should take it."

"Well, then, you have your answer."

He stared down at the floor and muttered, "Fuck."

My emotions soon transformed from shock to heartbreak. Not only had he been offered a position across the world, he was taking it.

Deacon's leaving.

There would be no more daily conversations. No more coffees. No more security of knowing he was just next door if I needed him. No more hope that one day he'd come to his senses and lose control again with me—and choose to never let me go this time. All hope was gone now.

"How long have you known this would be a possibility?"

"About a month. I threw my hat into the ring, but I didn't think I'd get it. That's why I didn't mention it."

I stared into space and nodded in an attempt to let it sink in.

"You okay?" he asked.

I shook my head. "Not really. But I'll have to be." I continued to fight like hell against the tears forming in my eyes. "I'm gonna miss you."

"I'm gonna miss you, too." He frowned. "I actually found out I got the job yesterday, but I didn't know how to tell you. I slept like shit last night. There was just no good way to break this news."

I knew he meant it when he said he was going to miss me. The way he was looking at me, deep into my eyes, gave me chills.

"When will you move?"

"They told me I'd have to start in about a month. I have to see if the landlord will let me out of my lease."

Despite feeling hopeless, I tried to feign optimism. "So we still have a little time, yeah?"

"Yeah," he muttered.

Unexpectedly, Deacon leaned in and pulled me into a hug. Many seconds passed where he just held me. I let out a long breath of frustration into his chest. I could feel his heart beating in my ear, and I wondered if he could feel *my* heart breaking.

The two-and-a-half weeks that followed Deacon's announcement went by way too fast.

He managed to get out of his lease and began packing up his things, a little each day. The landlord told him he could leave his furniture for the next tenant, so Deacon didn't have to worry about cleaning the place out. He was glad not to have to figure out how to get his stuff out of there.

Each day he'd bring by coffee, and we'd pretend things were normal, even though it was the opposite. Each day felt more somber than the last.

On his second-to-last weekend in New York, we decided to do something we'd never done together: take a little trip out of the city. Since Sunny hadn't been to the beach before, and the weather was supposed to be hot, we rented a car and planned a drive out to the Hamptons. Getting out of the usual environment would be one way to distract from what was happening. Or one way to say goodbye, however you looked at it.

Deacon's friend Adrian's family owned a small house in Easthampton and offered it to him free of charge. The plan was to head out on Saturday morning and spend the night there before returning on Sunday. It would be bittersweet to spend time with Deacon like this, knowing soon I might never see him again. At the same time, that was exactly why I'd taken him up on the offer of this trip.

I'd tasked him with going to the store to buy some beach supplies.

A text came in while he was out.

Deacon: What's the difference between a swim diaper and a regular diaper?

Oh boy. Here we go.

Carys: Regular diapers become too heavy, super saggy, and fall off when they're wet.

Deacon: Man, that sucks.

Carys: Yep. So the swim diapers don't do that.

Deacon: What do they do, then?

Carys: I've never really thought about it, but basically they don't absorb.

Deacon: So what good are they? Sounds like a false sense of security.

Carys: I guess the pee just goes in the water. LOL

Deacon: What a waste. Why not have her free-ball it?

Carys: Well, for one, she doesn't have balls.

Deacon: Let her go commando.

Carys: The diaper will protect her bathing suit.

Deacon: Okay. There are three types of swim "diapers."

I was cracking up.

Carys: Any kind is okay.

Deacon: How do you reuse a swim diaper? This one here says reusable. Why would someone want to do that?

Carys: You could take it home and wash it.

Deacon: Three hours after it bakes in the sun at the beach? Seems like a lot of trouble. And what if she had a big explosion?

Carys: Then you'd probably throw it away.

Deacon: So it's really disposable.

Carys: Right. LOL. Get the disposable.

Deacon: The only swim diapers in her size are blue ones with boy stuff on them.

Carys: She'll live.

Deacon: Wait! Score! Got one in the back with flowers.

Carys: They're all going to the same place ultimately. But that's cool.

Deacon: I'm getting a bunch of buckets and shovels.

Carys: We don't need more than one of each. It's just her.

Deacon: And me. And you. We need buckets, Carys. And shovels.

Carys: Ok. LOL

Deacon: What about this hat?

He sent a photo of something that looked like a pink bonnet.

Carys: For who? My grandmother?

Deacon: For Sunny.

Carys: That's for a woman, isn't it?

Deacon: I don't know. Maybe?

Carys: Pretty sure that would eat up her whole head. Anyway, I've got a hat for her.

Then he sent a photo of himself wearing the bonnet. It swallowed his head.

Deacon: You're right. Okay...moving on. Sunscreen.

Carys: Just get the highest SPF. One of the baby kinds with gentler ingredients.

He sent a photo of a tube of sunblock.

Deacon: This one is the best.

Carys: How do you know?

Deacon: Consumer Reports.

Carys: You're checking Consumer Reports?

Deacon: Yeah.

That was adorable.

Carys: Thank you. Get that one.

Deacon: Does she have shades? You didn't put them on the list.

Carys: No. But that might be a good idea.

Deacon: Got some little ones! Heading back now.

Carys: Okay :)

My smile faded. *I'm going to miss this.*

My heart felt like it was being choked. I kept staring at the phone as a tear fell down my cheek.

SEVENTEEN

Deacon

PSEUDO-FAMILY

After double parking the rental car outside our apartment building, I put my hazards on and ran upstairs to help Carys bring down our stuff.

"You ready to go?"

"Yeah," she said, carrying Sunny, who already had on her sunhat.

I nudged on the hat. "She looks so cute in that."

"Yeah, well, though her name might imply she likes the sun, her fair skin certainly doesn't."

"Well, Sunny, don't you worry because Deek bought you sunscreen."

When my eyes moved to Carys, I saw a huge smile on her face.

"What?" I asked.

"Nothing. Just happy to be spending this time with you."

Her words hit me in the gut. She had no idea how down I'd felt all morning, though I was trying to put on a happy face. Every moment I doubted my decision to move. I hoped our trip would mean a break from the second-guessing.

The ride out to the Hamptons was long and congested—no surprise that everyone had the same idea with the weather being so nice. It had taken me a minute to figure out how to install Sunny's car seat in the rental. It was rear-facing, but we could see her little face through a mirror Carys attached to the back of the seat. We played *The Best of The Bee Gees* for most of the way, which kept Sunny relatively calm. She even fell asleep at one point.

It was hard to believe I'd be leaving in little over a week. Even though I'd tied up most loose ends, mentally I was nowhere near ready to leave New York. I'd ended things with Rachel, the girl I'd been seeing—not that there was much to end. We hadn't been dating for very long. We'd had fun together, but I knew there wasn't a long-term future there, even if I hadn't been leaving. Ending that hadn't affected me in the least. Leaving Carys and Sunny, on the other hand? That wasn't something I'd yet come to terms with. Leaving was going to have to be like ripping a Band-Aid off, because there wasn't an easy way to say goodbye.

After the long drive, we finally pulled up to Adrian's family's house. It was a small cottage with two bedrooms—perfect for what we needed. Main Street was a walkable distance, and the beach only a short drive away.

Carys beamed as we walked into the bright space. "This is so amazing, Deacon. Look at all the sunlight coming in. Thank you again for inviting us."

I carried Sunny inside. "Are you kidding? There's no one else I would've rather brought with me."

When Carys smiled, it literally hurt. I'd spent a lot of time burying my feelings for her. But doing that today felt impossible.

We set up the Pack 'N Play in the room Carys would be sleeping in with Sunny. It wasn't worth trying to find a crib for one night. Carys said Sunny sometimes slept in the playpen with no issues, so I hoped it worked out. Otherwise, I'd probably be the one up holding her all night. And secretly, I wouldn't even mind, because the days of holding Sunny, being able to calm her down and make her smile, were about to be over. Soon, I'd be out of her life, and she likely wouldn't remember me. I felt a pain in my gut, but Sunny forgetting me would be for the best, wouldn't it? Isn't that what I wanted?

I clapped my hands together to snap myself out of it. "You feel like hitting the beach first, or should we go grab some groceries so we don't have to later?"

"We still have a few more good hours of sunlight. I'd prefer to go to the beach when the sun isn't as strong anyway. So maybe we hit the market first?"

"You wanna stay while I go, or do we bring her with us?"

"I'd like to go," she said. "I want to pick out stuff to make a nice dinner."

We got back in the car and drove to the nearest market, which happened to be an organic grocery store about two miles from the house. Carys was like a kid in a candy store, taking her time perusing the aisles. Sunny got a little antsy, so I carried her around and tried to keep her entertained while her mom shopped. I knew it was rare that Carys got to browse the aisles alone, so I wanted her to take her time and enjoy herself.

At one point, I took a seat with Sunny at a table in the eating area of the market. Since they sold prepared foods, it was basically a restaurant.

This woman seated at the table next to us smiled over at me. But when Sunny turned toward her, the expression on the woman's face changed. My heart sank. It was exactly that look Carys had described getting from people. It felt awful. I suspected Carys never said anything when it happened. But I couldn't help myself.

"Excuse me."

She turned to me and smiled again. "Yes?"

"I couldn't help but notice the way your expression changed when my little friend here turned toward you. I know you didn't mean any harm, but you should know there's no reason to feel differently about her. She's the happiest baby I know. And the most beautiful. She can't understand what your change in expression means right now, but someday when she's older, she'll be able to sense what people might be thinking when they look at her a certain way. So please save your sympathy for someone who needs it."

The woman frowned, taken aback. "I-I'm sorry. I didn't mean any harm. I didn't realize I had done that."

Rather than respond, I stood up and walked outside with Sunny to get some air. She leaned her head on my shoulder, and I kissed the top of it.

My reaction in there was probably a bit overboard; my emotions were out of whack with my impending departure. I guess I felt like I needed to stick up for Sunny now because I wouldn't be able to do it later.

After I'd grabbed my bearings and walked back inside, the sight of a smiling Carys brought me back to the present. She approached us with her cart full of food.

"This place is great. Sorry I'm taking so long. I just never get to do this."

"I know. That's why I gave you space. Take your time."

"Oh, no. I'm done. Let's go check out so we don't miss the sunlight."

After we got back to the house and put away the food, Carys took Sunny into their room to change.

Carys emerged wearing a sundress that covered the swimsuit underneath. The tie of her swimsuit was knotted around the back of her neck. Sunny wore a little polka dot bathing suit with a hat to match.

I pulled on the edge of Sunny's hat. "Are you ready for the beach?"

She wriggled her legs and squealed.

While they were getting ready, I'd packed snacks and drinks into a cooler. We loaded the car and headed out. The beach was only a few minutes down the road.

After we parked, we found the perfect spot on the sand, a ways away from the nearest group of people.

We laid down a blanket, and Carys pulled out the beach toys I'd bought.

My attention briefly wandered to a Jack Russell terrier playing in the sand.

When I turned back around to look at Carys, she'd removed her sundress. My heart raced as I took in her bikini-clad body. I'd been looking forward to and dreading this moment at the same time. Immediately, the sight of her pert breasts straining through the fabric of her top reminded me of the way they'd tasted the night I sucked them into my mouth, reminded me how perfectly they'd fit into my palms. My hands tingled with the need to touch the taut, peachy skin of her stomach. Her body couldn't have been more perfect. I hadn't ever seen her so undressed in broad daylight. I couldn't stop staring. When my eyes met hers and she blushed, I realized she knew exactly what I'd been thinking.

"I was gonna put on sunscreen," she said. "But I don't think there's a need, since the sun isn't that strong right now. I put plenty on Sunny back at the house, though."

I knew it would kill me to touch her, but the opportunistic side of me couldn't contain itself.

"Better safe than sorry." I grabbed the bottle. "Let me."

Carys slid over, and I began massaging the lotion onto her back. She had the smoothest skin I'd ever touched. My dick immediately stood at attention in my swim shorts. This was not good. After I finished, I turned away to focus on the Jack Russell again, hoping my erection would subside before she noticed.

"Can I put some on you?" she asked.

"Yeah. Thanks."

Now there was no chance of my dick downsizing. The feel of her soft hands rubbing over my back was fucking heaven.

I let out a frustrated breath as she continued.

"Thank you," I said when she stopped. I didn't turn around, though, not wanting her to see that I was hard.

Focusing on some seagulls, I worked to distract myself. When it was finally safe to turn around, I noticed Sunny slapping her hands in the sand. She was having a freaking ball.

Over the next several minutes, Carys ran back and forth to the shore to grab water in the buckets.

I couldn't contain my smile. "I can't believe this is Sunny's first time at the beach. I'm so glad she likes it."

"Yeah. I'm gonna have to find a way to take her more often—not exactly easy when you live in the city."

After grabbing my bucket, I built a sandcastle that Sunny soon mashed down into nothing. We were having the best time. People looked at us and smiled, probably assuming we were a family. *In a way, we are.* A pseudo-family. From almost the very beginning, Carys and Sunny had felt like family to me, though I'd tried hard to resist that feeling.

Sunny enjoyed playing in the sand until we decided to take her for a dip before the sun went down and it got too cool. We took turns holding her as she splashed and laughed. I spun her around, her feet grazing the water, and lifted her over the small waves that came in. I couldn't remember the last time I'd had this much fun. Something about being around Sunny made you forget about all the unnecessary bullshit in the world. Her smile and laughter were contagious.

When we got back to our blanket, Carys wrapped Sunny in a towel and sat for a while, cradling her and looking out at the water. An ocean breeze blew her damp hair around. Carys' strawberry blond hair looked more reddish brown when wet.

While they were chilling, I opened the cooler and cracked open a beer. I continued to watch them as they faced the water. I would never forget this peaceful snapshot in time. *I will never forget them.*

Droplets of water dripped down Carys' smooth skin, and I wished more than anything I could lick them off. My dick twitched, and I scolded myself for turning what was supposed to be an innocent moment into something else.

When Sunny resumed playing in the sand, Carys turned toward me, her lean body now facing mine, providing a clear view down her top. My eyes were glued, my ogling obvious. I couldn't help it. She was so fucking beautiful.

The next thing I knew, a pile of wet sand hit me in the face. I'd been so wrapped up in eye-fucking Carys, I hadn't noticed Sunny getting ready to propel it toward me. That woke me up for damn sure. Carys and I broke into laughter, and Sunny squealed.

I should've been completely content, but there was a tightness in my chest that wouldn't subside. Pretty sure it was my brain battling with my heart.

Later that evening, Carys took a shower while I watched Sunny out in the living room. Lately, Sunny had been holding on to furniture and trying to walk. But I never expected to see her take a few steps toward me on her own. She fell on her butt soon after, but it was a valiant effort.

Carys had told me that while many babies walk by the time they're a year old, there could be a delay with Sunny. Kids with Down's typically walked later on average, closer to two. At fifteen months, Sunny was apparently ahead of the curve, because she was definitely attempting it.

I turned on the TV and kicked my feet up, never expecting to see her moving toward me again from the corner of my eye. I soon realized she wasn't holding on to anything. One foot in front of the other, Sunny was walking toward me.

"Whoa, whoa, whoa," I said, moving my feet off the ottoman.

Struggling to balance, with a wide stance and wobbly legs, Sunny had a huge smile on her face. My heart raced as I reached my hands out to receive her. Her smile grew bigger until she landed in my arms.

Oh my God. Sunny had officially walked. *She walked. She was walking.* Holy shit. I'd just witnessed her first steps, and Carys was in the damn shower! She'd missed the whole thing.

Lifting Sunny up, I rushed over to the bathroom door and knocked. "Carys!"

"Yeah?"

"Sunny just walked! She walked several steps toward me."

Her voice echoed. "Are you kidding?"

"No! I wish I'd gotten it on camera, but it happened too fast."

I heard the shower turn off.

A few minutes later, Carys emerged, wrapped in a towel, her hair drenched.

"I can't believe I missed it. I've been trying to get her to walk to me for weeks with no luck. She's come close, but it never happened."

"I know. That's why I feel so damn guilty. I didn't even do anything. She just...did."

Carys' skin was flushed, probably from the hot water. She shook her head. "She loves you, Deacon. You just have to exist, and that's enough to motivate her."

I swallowed, unsure how to respond. I didn't want Sunny to love me. I sometimes wished she'd forget me the second I left, so she wouldn't wonder where I was.

I looked at Sunny as she babbled, then turned to Carys. "Why do you think she loves me?"

"I guess she has an innate sense that there may be some good in you—something the rest of us might not see." She winked. "Kidding." Then she disappeared into the bedroom to get dressed.

After Carys came back out, we tried to get Sunny to walk again. But despite lots of encouragement, she wouldn't repeat it. She made me seem like a damn liar.

Later, I leaned over the kitchen counter, watching Carys as she cooked dinner while Sunny played with her toys in the playpen. She'd prepared scrod with lemon and herbs, which was baking in the oven, and she was now chopping a salad.

Once again, I couldn't take my eyes off her, unable to stop thinking about how some lucky bastard would come along in the not-so-distant future. This would be his life; he would be just as content as I was right now. The difference was, he wouldn't hurt them like I inevitably would. I knew I wasn't right for Carys, but that didn't take away how I was feeling right now. The thought of leaving made me sick to my stomach.

I'm fucking crazy about her.

I was about to ditch someone I cared about very much. I'd been pretending, when the truth was I ate, slept, and breathed Carys, probably from the first day we'd had coffee together. She just didn't know it. And I was too much of a damn coward to admit my feelings. The past had proven that I couldn't trust myself to keep them safe. They would eventually get hurt. And I'd be damned if I was going to let that happen.

EIGHTEEN

Carys

TELL ME TO STAY

The weekend after our getaway, I forced myself to get dressed up, despite feeling like the world was about to end. It was the night I'd been dreading. Deacon's friend Adrian was throwing him a going-away party at a restaurant downtown. Sharon, who loved Deacon ever since he'd come to her rescue with the Bee Gees, had no problem coming to watch Sunny on a Saturday night so I could attend.

It wasn't often that I got dolled up and left the house these days, so I went all out, putting on a sexy, hot pink dress and sparkly heels I knew my feet would regret later. I used my new hair iron—another late-night impulse buy—to create large waves. It seemed kind of silly trying to impress Deacon's friends when he was leaving in two days, but in all honesty, I knew it was Deacon I wanted to impress. Which was ridiculous. Did I think he would take one look at me and magically decide not to move, turning down a position that paid double? Yeah, that made a lot of sense.

Before I left, Sharon said, "Carys, if for any reason you want to spend the whole night out, I can crash on the couch. My husband won't mind parting with me for one night, and I won't mind a break from his snoring."

I narrowed my eyes. "I don't have any plans to be out all night. I have to come back at some point to sleep."

A slight look of amusement crossed her face. "Well, I was thinking maybe you and Deacon might want to be... alone."

I felt the need to clarify. "You know he and I aren't *together*, right?"

"Oh, I know... I just...can tell there's something there and can imagine how hard his leaving must be. Thought maybe you'd want to say a *proper* goodbye. You know..." She winked.

Is she serious? My cheeks heated. "That's not going to be happening."

She nodded. "Okay. I just wanted to put it out there that I can stay the night. Didn't want you to be uncomfortable asking me."

"Thank you, but that won't be necessary." When she kept looking at me, I felt the need to continue. "I mean, it's not that I wouldn't have wanted that with him. Deep down, I have...wanted that. It just didn't work out, and now of course he's leaving." *And that's a little too much to be divulging to my babysitter.*

"Well, something tells me he's going to take one look at you in that dress tonight and lose his mind."

I smiled. She was giving me a false hope I didn't need right now. On that note, I kissed Sunny goodbye and made my way out.

Mrs. Winsbanger opened her door just as I headed down the hall. That was a rarity. She never opened the door, only spied. She wore a floral house dress and fur hat. I don't know if she constantly had a head cold or what, but the fur cap was apparently part of her standard attire. It certainly didn't make sense for the middle of summer. She was probably in her mid-seventies and couldn't have been more than four-foot-five.

I looked down at her. "Oh hey, Mrs. Winsbanger."

She lifted her chin. "I hear Fuckboy is moving."

"Yeah. I'm actually going to his goodbye party."

"Haven't heard a peep from him in a long time. Not since the day you yelled at him."

Come to think of it, she was right. No vocal action had come from Deacon's bedroom since that day I'd announced I could hear him through the wall. I knew he'd had sex since then, but he must have chosen to do it away from home. Either that, or he'd taped someone's mouth shut. I cringed.

"He's actually become a very good friend since then, Mrs. Winsbanger. And I'm sad to see him go."

"Watching him go is my favorite—nice ass." She winked and abruptly shut her door.

Hornball. She's worse than me!

Deacon's friends and co-workers had gathered in a private room Adrian rented out at the back of a restaurant downtown. It was a mix of well-dressed late-twenty-somethings, laughing and drinking. There were a fair number of attractive women, and I wondered how many of them had been with Deacon in ways I hadn't.

I spotted Deacon in the corner, talking to a couple of guys. He looked so painstakingly handsome, wearing a Polo shirt that clung to his contoured chest. His thick hair was parted a bit more than usual off his face. He was taller than most of the men in the room and stood out in the crowd. I was sure most of the women here wanted to climb him like a tree—myself included.

He hadn't noticed me yet. I waited in one spot for a bit, observing his interactions with his friends. He sipped some amber-colored liquor and seemed a little off—his smile forced as he made conversation. I wondered if the impending departure had him on edge. He looked around mid-conversation, as if searching for something. Or someone. *Is it me?* When his eyes found mine, he smiled wide and immediately excused himself to walk over. Maybe it *was* me he'd been looking for.

To my surprise, he leaned in and pulled me into a tight hug, whispering in my ear, "Thank you so much for coming."

His hot breath sent chills down my spine. "I wouldn't have missed it for the world."

When he let me go, he took me in from top to bottom. "Carys...you..." His words trailed off. "You look absolutely stunning."

Feeling my cheeks heat, I looked down at myself. "Thank you. I tried. I wanted to look good for your party."

"You don't have to try. You're so beautiful. Always. Even when you're in a fucking T-shirt with coffee stains or food stuck in your teeth. But right now, you're taking my breath away."

I didn't know what to make of this, except to say that for several seconds, it felt like we were in our own world. Everyone faded away.

Then he took my hand. "Come on. I want you to meet my friends."

I relished the warmth of his hand as we made our way across the room.

Deacon brought me over to a group in the corner and introduced me to several friends and a few people who also worked for the same company he did.

A handsome man with dark, curly hair and broad shoulders joined us. "You must be Carys."

Surprised that anyone knew my name without being introduced, I smiled. "Yes."

"I've heard a lot about you." He held out his hand. "I'm Adrian."

"It's really great to meet you. Deacon talks about you all the time, too."

"I don't know if I like that." He winked. "Anyway, really happy to put a face to the name."

"You, too. And thanks so much for letting us use your family's cottage. We had the best time." The reminder of our overnight trip to the Hamptons made me momentarily sad.

Deacon spoke in my ear, "What can I get you to drink?"

Again, feeling his breath against me put my body on alert. This "celebration" definitely called for something stronger than my norm.

"A dirty martini?"

"You got it."

Deacon left the private area to head over to the bar in the next room. Things felt colder in his absence, a taste of what was to come in just a couple of days.

When he returned with our drinks, he must have noticed my somber look. "Everything okay?" he asked as he handed me my martini, which had several Spanish olives floating in it.

"Yeah...I guess it just hits me in waves that you're actually leaving."

He nodded slowly. "It's strange that we've never been out like this together in all the time we've known each other."

Forcing a smile, I replied, "Better late than never?"

"I guess. Yeah. Just wish we had more time." Deacon took a long sip of his drink.

I stuck a toothpick into one of my olives and popped it into my mouth. "How are you holding up?"

He sighed and stared blankly into his glass. "Honestly?"

"Yeah...honestly."

"Not good. This party is great." He looked around. "But it feels surreal. These last hours are moving too fast."

"I know. I don't think it's really going to sink in until after you're gone."

He stared at me, and his eyes wandered down the length of my body. "You look so beautiful it hurts, Carys."

My nipples hardened, and my heartbeat accelerated, but before I could respond, one of his friends interrupted.

"There's the man of the hour," the guy said, patting Deacon on the back. "Come on, we need your input on a bet we're placing."

"I'm sorry," Deacon said as he got dragged away. "Be right back," he mouthed.

"It's okay." I laughed it off and tried to do something other than ruminate over what he'd just said to me.

While Deacon was talking to his friends, a guy approached and held out his hand. "Hey. I'm Scott."

"Hi," I responded uncomfortably, not in the mood to make small talk. "I'm Carys."

"Karen?"

"Carys...like Paris."

"Ah. Pretty name. Are you with Deacon Mathers?"

"I'm a friend of his. We live next door to each other."

"I see. Well, I couldn't help admiring how lovely you look tonight. That pink is definitely your color. I was kind of hoping the D-Man hadn't claimed you for himself."

When Deacon noticed him talking to me, his eyes darkened and he moved away from his friends to rejoin me. His eyes shot daggers. "What's up, Scott?"

"Nothing much. Just chatting with Carys here."

Deacon grabbed my hand. "Can you excuse us?"

The next thing I knew, he was ushering me to the bar area in the next room.

"Want another drink?" he asked.

"What was that all about?" I responded.

"I don't like that guy."

"Then why is he at your party?"

"I didn't invite him. He's a friend of a friend who tagged along. I know that was rude of me, but I don't give a fuck right now. I don't want him anywhere near you. He's an asshole to women."

A sheen of sweat covered Deacon's forehead. He seemed very on edge. I decided to drop it.

He went up to the bar and got us two more drinks, an amber-colored liquid for him and another martini for me. He took a long gulp of his as I watched.

"Are you okay?" I asked.

He made a face that looked like the alcohol burned his throat going down, then wiped his mouth with the back of his hand. He finally said, "Am I making a mistake?"

"About leaving?"

"Yeah. I mean…I'm happy here. There's no part of me that *wants* to move. I feel obligated to take the job because it's a great opportunity. But I can't help wondering if I'll regret leaving." When I didn't respond, he shook his head. "What am I even saying, right? My apartment is mostly cleared out, and I'm supposed to be reporting to the new office on Wednesday. I guess it's too late to change my mind."

It was the first time I realized he might be having serious doubts. I'd assumed it was a no-brainer based on the money. My true opinion on the matter wouldn't have been helpful—I was too biased—so I tried not to make him feel badly about the decision he'd already made. My heart, however, screamed, *"Don't go! Please don't go."*

If Deacon never wanted to take a chance on us, maybe it was better if he did leave. Maybe he *had* to leave in order for me to get over him. Whether he left or stayed, I was destined to get hurt, considering I couldn't seem to shut off my feelings for him.

"What time is your flight again?" I asked.

"Eight thirty Monday morning."

Tears formed in my eyes, but I wouldn't let them fall.

"I need to say goodbye to Sunny," he said. "I wasn't sure how best to do that. I feel like she'll notice me gone and wonder what happened. I don't want to make her sad. But I feel like I owe her an explanation, even if she can't fully understand."

The thought of him saying goodbye to my daughter, who I knew cared so much for him, hurt my heart. I could no longer control my emotions. I needed to escape to the bathroom to cry.

I placed my hand on his arm. "I'll be back, okay? I have to use the restroom."

Without waiting for his response, I weaved my way through people to get to the single, unisex bathroom in the back of the place. After knocking to make sure it was empty, I entered and wiped the tears that were now falling down my face as I looked in the mirror.

Shit. Shit. Shit. Why didn't you tell him not to leave when he expressed doubt? Maybe he would have listened. Maybe he would stay.

I knew that was crazy talk. It would have been selfish to convince Deacon to stay for my own self-serving purposes. But he seemed sad tonight, didn't he? Almost like he wished someone would give him a good reason to stay. Despite my internal argument, I knew it was a losing battle. The sadness Deacon felt tonight was normal— fleeting. He'd go to Tokyo, settle into his new and amazing job, and never look back.

Visions of Deacon wandering amidst the bright lights and vibrancy of that foreign city ran through my head. He'd have his pick of any beautiful Japanese woman he wanted. And they'd all flock to the gorgeous, larger-than-life American man.

Someone knocked on the bathroom door. *Crap.* I'd spent way too long in here. Deacon was going to wonder what happened to me.

"Be right out!"

My eyes were still red. Deacon would know I'd been crying if I returned now. With someone waiting, though, I felt pressured to leave. I'd have to sneak outside for a few minutes before going back.

When I opened the door, a woman stood there. She looked pissed.

I walked past her and made my way to the exit. The cool outside air hit my face as I leaned against the brick building, planning to take out my compact and make myself look presentable before returning to the party. Hiding my tears with more makeup was going to be a challenge, but I would manage. Masking my emotions on the other hand? That had never been my forte, especially when they hit me as hard as they had tonight.

Before I had a chance to dig my mirror out of my purse, I heard his voice.

"Carys—Jesus. Adrian told me he saw you walk out the door, and I didn't know what to think. I—" He stopped talking. "Are you crying?"

Am I supposed to deny it? A sniffle escaped me. "I'm sorry. I didn't want you to see me like this. I came out here to get some air." Looking down at the sidewalk, I said, "I feel so stupid that you caught me. It's just...when you were saying all that stuff, how you were sad to leave, saying goodbye to Sunny, it brought out everything I've been feeling since the day you told me you were moving away." I looked up. "Deacon, what if after Monday I never see you again? This sucks. And I'm sorry I'm not handling it better. I didn't want to show it."

I shut my eyes, regretting having let my vulnerability escape. Then I felt his hands wrap around my face. My eyes flew open, only to close again at the feel of his hot mouth on my lips. I might have stopped breathing for a second. My legs felt weak as I melted into him. When it hit me that this was really happening, I opened wider, letting his tongue inside and remembering all too well what it felt like on other parts of my body. But despite the intimacy of that night, this moment was different—more passionate than sexual. I tasted him for the first time, breathing him in like oxygen. And I couldn't get enough.

He flicked his tongue to nudge my mouth open wider. His chest pressed into mine, my back still against the brick of the building. Deacon's heart beat rampantly as our tongues circled in frantic competition. I lifted my hands and placed them around his head, pulling him deeper into me and inhaling his heady scent. The vague sense of people passing us registered, as did the muffled sound of talking around us.

His groan vibrated down my throat as he fisted my hair. "Fuck, Carys."

I could feel his erection through his pants as it rubbed against me. My clit was throbbing with need. If he'd wanted to take me on this damn sidewalk, pretty sure I would have let him.

An indeterminate amount of time passed, our kiss lasting what felt like several minutes, neither of us willing to stop. I was certain this was going to make his leaving even worse for me, but that wasn't enough to pull me away. Nothing could have torn me from the delicious taste of his hot lips or his intoxicating scent.

Deacon finally broke our kiss, but not before returning his mouth to mine to bite my bottom lip before letting it go.

He panted as he placed an arm on either side of me, locking me in against the wall. "Your fucking lips. I've dreamed about doing that for so long. And it was even better than I imagined. I could kiss you forever."

"I wish you hadn't stopped," I said, my hands still wrapped around the back of his neck.

The streetlights reflected in his eyes. "I'm gonna go back in there and apologize to my friends, let them know I have to leave early. Half of them are so sloshed they won't even care. Then I want you to come back to my apartment so we can talk. Okay?"

I had no clue what was left to talk about, but I nodded in agreement, still dazed as he walked away. I rubbed my bare arms as I waited.

A few minutes later, Deacon reappeared and grabbed my hand as I followed him to the curb. As luck would have it, an empty cab approached almost immediately. Deacon lifted his arm to flag it down. We both got in, and he gave our address to the driver.

I couldn't believe he'd left his own party. Deacon gripped my hand as we sat close together in the backseat. His leg against mine was enough to keep my entire body on alert. I wanted to straddle him right here. But the vibe he gave off right now was not exactly a sexual one. I wished he would kiss me again, but he faced away. He seemed tense as he looked out the window, his knee bopping up and down. Whatever he wanted to say was clearly weighing on his mind, and he stayed that way—distant—the entire ride home.

After paying the cab fare, we exited the vehicle and made our way inside the building and upstairs. It felt strange passing my apartment without stopping in to check on things. Deacon fumbled with his keys before he finally managed to open his front door.

My heart pounded as I entered his place. It was the first time I'd ever been inside it alone, without Sunny. I got a look at myself in the mirror just inside his door, the one I knew my daughter loved. My lips were swollen, my lipstick smudged, my hair a mess. *What is happening tonight?*

Deacon still seemed tense as he threw his keys on the table. He hadn't said a word to me since we left the restaurant. I looked around at his barren apartment. A box of stuff he'd apparently planned to ship to Japan sat on the floor. There was a large suitcase in the corner—no photos or artwork hanging. It made me incredibly sad.

"Can I get you a drink?" he asked.

"Maybe some water."

I followed him into the small kitchen, noticing for the first time how similar the layout was to mine.

Deacon took a glass out of his cabinet before opening the fridge and pouring filtered water out of a jug. He handed it to me and watched as I drank it down in one long gulp. The water felt like rainfall over a desert.

He held out his hand to take the empty glass. "More?"

"No. Thank you," I said, handing it back.

He slammed the glass down on the counter, harder than he'd probably intended to. His chest heaved as he stood across from me.

"Tell me to stay," he finally said.

My eyes went wide. "What?"

"I haven't been honest with you, Carys."

"Okay..." My heart thundered against my chest.

"I've given you the impression that there are things more important to me than you—like the job I accepted or the money. But all I've wanted is to be with you. I've told you before that I struggle with my feelings for you, but I made it sound like something I could control or dismiss. But I want you, Carys. Not just as a friend, but in every way—and not telling you that has been a lie of omission."

Even though I should've said something, nothing would come out. I was in shock.

"After I officially accepted the position, I got this sinking feeling that I'd just made a huge mistake. It's gotten worse every day. But here's the thing: I'm a risk, Carys. A huge risk. I don't know that I'm right for you. And I sure as hell can't assure you I won't fuck everything up eventually." He moved closer. His lips were almost on mine when he said, "But I want to stay. I just need to know that's what you want. It might be the biggest mistake you'll ever make, but if you tell me to stay, I will."

My heart pounded. "I've wanted to tell you to stay from the second you told me you were leaving. But I never thought it was an option. I thought this job opportunity meant a lot to you."

"Fuck the job." Deacon leaned his forehead on mine, his breathing intensifying. "Fuck the job. Tell me to stay."

A tear rolled down my cheek as I whispered, "Stay."

The moment the word escaped me, his lips were on mine, even more intensely than they had been back at the restaurant.

"I need you, Carys. Right fucking now," he growled.

Deacon lifted me off the ground. It felt like I was floating on air as he wrapped my legs around his waist and carried me to his room, our lips never separating.

On all fours, he pinned me beneath him on the bed. "Tell me to stop if you don't want this."

"No," I panted. "Please don't stop."

I flipped over, knowing he would have to unzip me from behind. He lowered my zipper before turning me back around to face him. He slid my dress off and removed my bra, unsnapping it effortlessly. The cold air hit my breasts, and my nipples hardened. Goosebumps covered my skin.

"I've missed these beautiful tits," he groaned as he sucked my nipple into his mouth. "Dreamed about them every night since your birthday."

My clit throbbed as if readying to come. I was already so incredibly wet, the muscles between my legs pulsating with the need to feel him inside of me.

Deacon showered my chest with kisses as he traveled down to my belly button. "You're so freaking gorgeous, Carys. I love your body so damn much." He kissed his way up again, and his mouth returned to mine.

I couldn't get enough of his taste and the smell of his cologne. I tugged on his shirt and pulled it over his head. Throwing it aside, I kissed him harder as I relished the feel of his hard chest pressed against my bare breasts. His body felt heavy over mine. I'd always wanted to feel him on top of me like this. Being skin to skin with Deacon was heaven. The muscles between my legs clenched, so eager to receive him.

He stopped kissing me long enough to say, "You're the most beautiful girl I've ever touched. I never thought I'd get to have you like this. It's literally a dream come true."

I didn't care if he was saying all those things in a sex-induced fog. My desperate and horny self loved every word.

He pulled away from me to slide my panties down my legs. I shimmied to speed the process. Deacon returned his mouth to my breasts, sucking even harder. No one had ever worked my body like this, so unapologetically.

Threading my fingers through his hair, I thought I might explode if he didn't enter me soon. Lowering my hands to his waist, I unbuckled his belt and threw it across the room with a clank. I unbuttoned his pants, slipping my hand inside to touch him.

"Easy now," he muttered over my mouth. "You have no idea how close I am to losing it, beautiful. If you touch me, I might come in your hand."

Deacon reached over to his side table and fished in the drawer. He took out a strip of condoms and ripped one off the top.

"You sure about this?" he asked.

"Believe me, I'm sure."

His mouth curved into a smile as he lowered himself to devour my lips. When he moved back, he opened the condom wrapper with his teeth. He slid his boxer briefs down and lowered his body over me again. I felt his hot, thick cock against my abdomen. I wanted so badly to reach between us and touch the length of it. As he kissed me, his shaft slid against my clit. I pressed myself harder against it, my wetness covering him.

He pulled back and rushed to slide the condom on. I followed every step of the process, marveling at the girth of his veiny cock. I'd imagined what Deacon might look like naked, but nothing prepared me for the sheer magnificence. He was beautifully hung—gorgeous and manly in every way.

Before he could enter me, I wrapped my hand around his length and stroked slowly.

"Be careful," he warned. "When you're ready, put me inside of you."

As hard as it was to resist pushing him inside, I rubbed the head of his cock against me. I had only been with a few guys, but I certainly didn't remember being so incredibly ready for a man.

Unable to hold back any longer, I placed him at my opening.

Within seconds, he pushed himself inside of me. "Fuuuck," he breathed over my neck. "I'm sorry. I couldn't wait."

His thick cock entering burned a little. When he was balls deep, I wrapped my legs around his back.

He pumped into me slowly, quickly moving on to fast and hard thrusts.

"Fuck. You feel so good, Carys. So fucking good, beautiful girl. Holy shit."

Not sure if it was because it had been so long for me, or because he was so thick, but I felt a mixture of pleasure and pain—everything I'd ever imagined. I didn't care if it hurt. I *wanted* it to hurt.

"Nothing—and I mean *nothing*—has ever felt better than your wet pussy around my dick. It feels better than anything."

I writhed under him. "Fuck me harder, Deacon."

"If you don't stop moving like that, I'm gonna lose it. You're so tight. Incredible."

With that, I contracted my muscles, tightening even more around him.

His body shuddered as he groaned, "Shit."

I gripped his ass as his hips moved in a circular motion. He couldn't have been deeper inside of me. Again, I tightened my muscles around him.

"Stop that. I almost lost it." He laughed over my lips.

So naturally, I squeezed tighter.

"You're so bad. Just for that, I need to fuck you harder."

Spreading my legs wider, Deacon pumped in and out of me so hard I was sure I was going to come any second. I held my breath, hoping I could prolong this a bit more. He took my nipple between his teeth, and I nearly lost it.

Then he brought his mouth to mine, kissing me forcefully. This was so different from the first time we'd "experimented." To be able to have *all* of him, to taste him, smell him, feel him inside of me, and most of all, to know I was causing him so much pleasure amplified my own arousal tenfold.

Deacon abruptly slowed down, his chest heaving over me as his kisses slowed. I continued to throb, craving more as he tried to prolong the inevitable. His hair was a tousled mess. I loved him so out of control, knowing I was the cause of it.

Slowly but surely, his movements quickened again, and his balls slapped hard against my ass. I moved my hips to match the intensity, and my muscles contracted as I suddenly orgasmed.

"I'm coming," I breathed, surrendering to the loss of control. "Oh my God, Deacon."

"Thank fuck." Deacon trembled as he finally allowed himself to let go, rocking into me deeply as he climaxed. I could feel the warmth of his cum through the condom as he let out a loud groan that echoed through the bedroom.

Our movements finally slowed, and I wished he could have stayed inside of me forever. After we came down from the high, he slowly pulled out, leaving a chill in his wake.

He kissed me on the nose. "Be right back."

Still in a hazy delirium, I admired his sculpted, naked body as he got up to discard the condom.

What is this life?

Deacon just fucked me—hard.

And he *wasn't* leaving?

It felt like the best dream ever. I never wanted to wake up.

He returned to the bed and nuzzled his nose in my neck. "I don't want to spend the night away from you. Can I come over?"

"I have a better idea." Grabbing my phone, I searched for Sharon's name and texted her.

Carys: Is the offer to have you stay the night still open?

A few seconds later, she responded.

Sharon: Yes. No need to explain. Your walls are thin. ;-)

Oops. I couldn't even be mortified right now because the euphoria made it impossible to feel anything but over the moon.

The following morning, the sun streamed into Deacon's bedroom window. I woke to the sight of him staring at me from a few inches away. How long had he been watching me sleep?

"Did last night really happen?" I asked.

He leaned in to kiss my nose. "It did."

"And you're not leaving?"

"How could I leave you after what we did last night?" He pulled me closer, his rigid dick against my leg. "I'm gonna need more of it, Carys, so much more of you. Every damn day."

Now that I'd come out of my sex-induced fog a little, I managed to pose a legitimate question. "As amazing as last night was, I guess I'm a little wary of how fast you changed your mind about leaving. Like, could it change again when sanity hits?"

He closed his eyes and nodded, seeming to understand my concern. "The thing is, it wasn't as sudden a decision as you think. Like I told you last night, from the moment I accepted the offer, I wondered if I was making a mistake. I've told you before that I wrestle with my feelings for you. I've wanted to be with you, but worried I wasn't right for you and Sunny. I've made mistakes I don't want to repeat..."

He paused and rubbed his hand over his face. "This isn't coming out the right way. Seeing you cry outside the party—that was my tipping point. That's what I needed to take a chance on what my heart has been telling me all along. I don't want to hurt you. I want us to be happy. That's what I've always wanted."

That sounded great, but my disbelief remained. "What are you gonna say to your job?"

He sighed. "I'm gonna tell them the truth—that I made a mistake, that I mistakenly thought I could leave the people I care about behind. They deserve someone who can give them his all, not someone who's pining over a woman and regretting every second he's away from her. There are plenty of people lining up for that position, don't worry. The company will be okay." A slight look of doubt crossed his face. "And if they give me shit, I'll find another job. I'm banking on not having to do that, though."

"What about this apartment? Did the landlord already give it to someone else?"

"I have no idea. Should that matter?"

"Hell no. I was just wondering."

"Hopefully, I can get it back. If not, I think I might know someone who'll let me crash until I can find a place?"

The idea of Deacon moving in gave me a momentary thrill, though it was way too soon for that. I didn't want to get my hopes up about any of this.

I shook my head. "I'm sorry. I'm still wrapping my head around this. I can't believe you're staying."

He placed his hand on my chin. "Promise me something."

"What?"

"We're gonna spend time getting to know each other even better. Once a week, I want us to get a sitter—I'll pay for it. I want us to go out and spend time alone, just the two of us, even if it's only an hour or two."

"I would love that."

He placed his hand behind my head and brought me in for a kiss, our naked bodies pressed together. He was so hard.

I could faintly hear Sunny next door. Even though I was just beyond the wall, being holed up in Deacon's apartment made me feel a world away.

Deacon lowered his hand, placing it behind my ass, his erection still hot against my leg. "I probably need to give Sunny back her mom soon, but I don't want to let you leave this bed."

"I do have to get going. Sharon has to head home." I brushed my thumb across his gorgeous lips. "Will you come over today?"

"How about I go get us breakfast and bring it to your place?"

"I would love that. That's nice of you."

"Not really. I have an ulterior motive."

"Yeah?"

"Feed my girl so she has energy when I have my way with her again later while Sunny's napping."

My girl. He had no clue what hearing that did to me. "Don't worry. I'm nowhere near worn out."

"Good, because I'm nowhere near done with you."

NINETEEN

Deacon

SAY MY NAME

Three weeks since I'd decided to stay in New York, and there wasn't a single moment I'd regretted my decision. I felt like the luckiest guy on Earth. I'd managed to keep my old job, despite fucking management over with my last-minute one-eighty. I got to keep my apartment because my landlord hadn't given it to anyone else yet. But most of all, I'd managed to snag the girl of my dreams, somehow pushing aside my fears enough to allow myself to be with her.

Carys found a new sitter who watched Sunny for a few hours every weekend so the two of us could have a date. My alone time with her was precious.

Today was a day date, and it had been epic. We went to a diner for breakfast and talked in the window seat over waffles and endless cups of coffee. It was a rainy morning in New York City, so we were spending the last hour of our alone time at my apartment before she had to go back next door.

And I'd just returned from the bathroom to a sight better than anything my imagination could have conjured up.

Carys was stark naked in front of the full-length mirror in my bedroom. And she was *dancing*. Dancing so gracefully, like the ballerina she was. With her heels together, she lifted her arms above her head. Then she raised herself up on her toes as if they easily carried the weight of her body. She landed on her heels briefly before her right leg flew into the air. Then she spun. Naked fucking ballet starring Carys Kincaid was the best damn thing I'd seen all year—maybe in my entire life.

She jumped when she noticed me watching her in the mirror, placing her hand over her chest. "Oh my God. You scared me."

"That was fucking amazing," I said, entering the room.

"You came back faster than I thought you would. Otherwise I wouldn't have—"

"I know. That's what's so amazing about it, getting to see you in your natural element." I slid my hand down the smooth skin of her back. "You're beautiful and brave. I wish I could've seen you dance on stage, but seeing you dance like this? Naked in my room? That's the stuff dreams are made of."

She got up on her tippy toes to kiss me. I loved that she wasn't rushing to put clothes on, that she was comfortable baring herself in front of me.

"I would've loved to see you play football," she said. "I know how painful it is for you to even think about those days, but I bet you were incredible in action."

I sighed. "I wish I could go back to playing casually. Just because something stops your professional career doesn't mean you can't ever do it again—I get that. But every time I've considered returning to it for fun, I chicken out. I haven't touched a football in years. On some level, though, I know figuring out a way to play would be good for me. It'd be therapeutic." I brought her lips to mine. "Maybe someday I'll get there. You motivate me."

Carys grabbed my ass. "I can imagine how sexy you looked all suited up in that gear, too."

I still had my old jersey tucked away in a box at the back of my closet. It was the one memento I'd kept and taken with me everywhere I moved. I walked over to my closet and located the box. When I took out the royal blue jersey, my heart raced. I hadn't so much as touched the fabric since the day I'd put it away nearly a decade ago. Seeing my number and *Mathers* written across the back gave me chills.

Carys's jaw dropped. "Oh my God. Is that—"

Still looking down at it, I nodded. "My jersey."

"Number eight."

I sighed. "Yep."

Slipping it over my head, I quickly realized it was a little tight. I'd bulked up a bit in muscle since college. I looked at myself in the mirror for a while. Carys stood next to me, still gloriously naked. I was almost a foot taller than her.

She moved behind me, wrapping her arms around my waist. "I know it wasn't easy for you to put that on."

"Well, you've inspired me. You always do." I turned around to face her.

She flashed an impish grin. "Seeing you in this shirt is turning me on a little."

My brow lifted. "Yeah?" I pressed my chest into her naked body. "You want to fuck the quarterback, you dirty girl?"

"Actually, yeah. I do. Only if he's you."

I lowered my hands to her pussy and circled her opening with my fingers. "Holy fuck. You're wet."

Her cheeks flushed. "It doesn't take much with you."

My dick felt ready to explode, and I wasn't even inside her yet. I'd never been as insatiable in my life as I'd been the past few weeks with her. This moment might have been the pinnacle.

She slipped her hands up through my shirt as I continued to finger her, devouring her lips. With every moan, I got harder until I couldn't take it anymore. We collapsed onto the bed. We'd had sex a half-hour ago, but I needed her again.

I fished a condom out of the drawer as fast as I could and sheathed my engorged shaft, so eager to slip inside of her.

I nearly came the second I felt her hot, tight pussy wrap around my cock.

Even though I was conscious of the sitter next door, I couldn't help myself as I thrust in and out of Carys, causing the bed to creak and the headboard to bang against the wall. It would be a while before I got to do this again—at least until tonight—and that wouldn't be soon enough. What can I say? We were making up for lost time.

"Deacon," she panted as I rammed into her.

I fucking loved when she said my name while I was inside of her. I loved when she said anything at all during sex. She wasn't always vocal, but when she was, it put me over the edge.

"Say my name again."

"Deacon."

"Again." I thrust into her harder. "Say my fucking name."

"Deacon...Deacon...Deacon."

"Fuck, Carys. What am I gonna do with you? I want you all freaking day."

She grabbed my ass and pushed me deeper. "Take me whenever you want me."

At that, I lost it. I shot my load prematurely, something that hadn't happened since high school. But lately it had been happening quite a bit.

"Shit. I'm sorry. I just can't control it with you sometimes."

"It's okay. I love it when you lose control."

When my breathing finally calmed, I turned to her. "I might need a shot to calm myself down, like the opposite of Viagra."

"Do you hear me complaining?" She flashed me the most adorable smile.

Since I'd come before Carys had a chance to finish, I pulled out and buried my head between her legs, bringing her to orgasm with my mouth a few minutes later.

After, we lay across from each other, savoring the final moments of alone time.

Holding her close, I confessed, "I can't remember the last time I was this happy. Thank you for making it impossible to resist you, so I didn't make a huge mistake by going to Tokyo."

"You make me happy. But you scare me, too," she admitted.

I nodded, feeling my heart squeeze. I'd given her every reason to be scared, because I'd told her I was destined to fuck up. I vowed to do everything in my power to not let that happen, though.

"I know I scare you. And that's mostly my fault. I haven't been in a relationship since I was in college. I hadn't wanted to be in one until I found you. You've changed me. You make me want to be a better man. I still don't trust myself. It comes from years of self-doubt, but those are *my* issues and have no bearing on how I feel about you."

Carys looked deep in thought. "We're all fucked-up in different ways, Deacon. I never planned on being in another relationship. I had all but written it off. So in a sense, we're both learning as we go here."

I smiled, her words warming me, making me feel like I didn't need to have all the answers right now. "I've spent way too much time sabotaging myself by worrying about the future. Let's just take one day at a time. I promise you I'll do everything in my power not to hurt you."

"It's not me I'm worried about. You know that, right?"

Sunny. I nodded. "I know."

She grabbed my hand and locked my fingers with hers. "But you're right... Let's take it one day at a time."

Carys returned to her apartment around two in the afternoon, and I went to the gym to burn off some energy.

Then I met Adrian at the Starbucks near my apartment. We hadn't seen each other since the goodbye party he'd thrown me almost a month ago—a wasted effort.

He smiled from ear to ear as he watched me approach the table with my cappuccino.

"What's that look?" I asked, sliding my chair out.

"Nothing. Just happy to see you and curious to hear what you've been up to." He snickered.

"You mean you're curious about me falling off the deep end for a woman."

"I never thought I'd see the day, man."

"Yeah, well...it happened." I took a sip, smiling behind my cup.

"I knew the second I met her that you weren't gonna let her go."

I squinted. "You did?"

"When I saw what she looked like, I knew you were in trouble. But the way you ran over there when that dude was talking to her at the party? That sealed the deal. I was like, how is this man gonna move halfway around the world when he's clearly in love with this girl?" He chuckled. "Then you left your own damn party to chase after her."

In love, huh? He'd just put a label on my feelings for Carys. I knew that was the official name for what I'd been feeling, but I hadn't acknowledged it—not to myself or anyone else, least of all Carys. Maybe it was time I did.

"I'm glad I saw things clearly before I moved to Japan."

"So, what does this mean—you guys shacking up yet?"

"No. I was able to keep my apartment. And we're taking things slow, trying to get to know each other on a deeper level."

He wriggled his brows. "I bet."

"Yeah, that too. *Lots* of that. But we have time set aside to go out and be alone together. It's not easy, so we make the best of whatever time we get."

"So...if you don't mind my asking, what the hell changed?"

"What do you mean?"

"You said before that you never wanted to get involved with someone who had a kid, that you didn't want to be a father. Your feelings for Carys changed that? Like she has a magical pussy that makes you want to have kids?"

That made me cringe. And he'd just touched on my sore spot, the one thing eating away at me, the thing that made it impossible to fully exhale when it came to my relationship with Carys. I'd learned to appreciate Sunny in my life, but the fear of being responsible for her, of somehow letting her down, still paralyzed me. But the selfish part of me didn't want to face my doubts right now—because I enjoyed being with Carys too much.

"I'm still working through that part," I answered.

I wasn't about to delve into all this with Adrian right now—or ever, really. This day had been perfect, and I wanted to keep it that way.

"I care about Sunny a lot," I said. "And I want what's best for her. Time will tell if what's best for her...is me."

"Okay, fair enough. I'll stop prying. I just don't want to see you getting in over your head."

"I get it. Thank you for your concern," I said. "I'm just going to try to be honest with her every step of the way."

He changed the subject to Formula One racing, and I blew out a sigh of relief.

After Adrian left, I waited in line for a latte to take back to Carys. It had only been a couple of hours since we were together, but I missed her. I realized just how strong my feelings for her had become.

When the barista grabbed a venti cup off the stack for Carys's drink, I asked if I could borrow a Sharpie to write something on it.

My heart raced as I waited. When the barista finished steaming the milk and poured the drink, she placed a lid on the cup and turned toward me.

"Venti one-pump vanilla latte for..." She paused. "I love you, Carys?"

I lifted my hand and smiled. "That's me."

TWENTY

Carys

TOUCHDOWN

In the two months that followed, Deacon's and my appetite for each other remained insatiable. It was like nothing I'd ever experienced. We had sex almost every night. He'd come over after Sunny went to sleep. We'd hang out, talk, drink wine, and ultimately go at it like animals. Then he'd go back to his apartment in the morning.

Fortunately, we had a date scheduled for later this afternoon. It was a cool, crisp Saturday in September, and I couldn't wait to go out and enjoy the fall weather once the sitter arrived. Unfortunately, I'd gotten my period, so there would be no sexy times for once.

Deacon was running errands today, so he'd agreed to go to the store for me. He was supposed to be picking up super-sized tampons, among other things.

A text came in not long after he left.

Deacon: What's the difference between Super and Super Plus?

Carys: Super Plus is bigger, more absorbent. But I don't really notice a difference.

Deacon: Am I...Super Plus or Super? ;-)

Carys: Definitely Super Plus.

Deacon: So, you notice the difference then... when it comes to me?

I rolled my eyes.

Carys: Oh yes.

Deacon: Damn. I'd hate to be Regular. Or worse, Light. (Shivers) That would suck.

Shopping was always an adventure with this man. Deacon stopped texting, so I assumed he'd found what he needed and left.

A few minutes later, another text came in.

Deacon: Do you think Sunny would like this?

He'd attached a picture of himself flashing a huge smile and holding a mini toy shopping cart filled with plastic fruits and vegetables.

Carys: Hard to tell. But I think it's adorable.

Deacon: Show her the picture. See if she reacts.

I brought the phone over to where Sunny was playing. She smiled when I showed her the photo. But I suspected it wasn't the toy.

Carys: She smiled. But I'm pretty sure she's smiling at you. She's just as smitten as I am.

Deacon: I fucking love you, Carys.

My heart wanted to leap out of my chest.

Carys: I fucking love you, too.

Deacon: Not to be confused with loving to fuck you...because that I certainly do as well. But I fucking love you even more than I love to fuck you.

Since the day he'd come back from Starbucks with the coffee cup that said "I love you, Carys," our phone calls and text exchanges rarely ended without him telling me he loved me. And hearing it never got old. It had taken me probably ten minutes to notice the message written in black Sharpie that first time, but when I did, I broke out in tears. Things had only gotten better since.

Everything was perfect, aside from the fact that I still didn't understand why Deacon was so unsure of his ability to be a good partner. His actions proved otherwise. Something was missing, but I hesitated to push him for answers because we were in a good place. Still, his warnings haunted me. I sometimes worried that one day he'd wake up, realize the responsibility he'd taken on—and bolt.

At least for now, Deacon and I were masters at making the most of our time together. As soon as the sitter arrived later that afternoon, we went next door. Whenever we had alone time, we went to his apartment to have sex to make sure we got that in. Then we'd head out, grab a bite to eat, and enjoy the city. Today, rather than sex, I used the time in his apartment to pleasure him, sucking him off while I rubbed my clit until we both came together. After we were both sated, we showered and ventured out for our date.

Deacon and I decided to go to Central Park. We took a quick train ride, and then walked the rest of the way. On our walk, Deacon stopped in front of a store. He took me by the hand and led me inside. On the shelf was a football with *I Love New York* emblazoned on it.

He spun it over his finger. "Would you want to toss this around with me?"

Deacon hadn't touched a football since college. This was monumental.

"Of course I would. I'm thrilled you want to try."

He smiled and kissed my forehead. "It's time."

"This will be my first time throwing a football," I announced.

His eyebrows lifted. "Yeah?"

"I'm a complete newbie when it comes to handling any balls but yours," I teased.

"Maybe we should keep it that way." He winked.

When we got to the park, Deacon demonstrated everything I'd need to do, standing at my back and holding me close as he reached his arm around me. He tried to teach me the proper way to hold the ball.

"Put your middle finger right there at the top of the lacing." He spread my fingers apart. Then he stopped to kiss my neck.

"I thought this was a football lesson."

"Mmm. I can't help it. Anytime I'm close to you, I need to touch you—making up for all those months I held back, I guess. Now I'm addicted to you."

I smiled. My body was constantly aware of him, craving his touch every second we were together, so I was no less addicted. I'd never been in a relationship that was as sexually gratifying as it was emotionally satisfying. I'd thought I was in love with Charles before he burned me. But I'd never experienced anything remotely close to what I felt for Deacon. If this didn't work out, it would be my biggest heartbreak.

Deacon took the football from me and began to demonstrate. "When you throw the ball, it's going to roll off your fingers like this, so you get a spinning motion."

The few times I tried to replicate his technique were a disaster.

"Come here," he said. "Let me show you how to position yourself to throw." He stood behind me again, the closeness of his body warming mine. He pushed his hand between my legs from behind to separate them. The heat of his touch made my body ache for more. "You're gonna place your feet about shoulder-width apart, like this." His hand landed on my ass as he pushed down on me. "Bend your knees a little." Then his hands slid to just above my hips. "Don't move your legs, but move your torso from side to side and rotate your shoulders." He wrapped his hands around me and used them to gently twist my body.

"See that? That's how you're gonna move when you throw the ball."

"Except your erection won't be pressing against my ass, like it is now?" I laughed.

"If you want, we can make that work, too." He kissed the back of my neck. "I didn't get to fuck you today, so I'm especially worked up. Don't mind me."

"Oh, I don't mind at all."

Deacon eventually pulled himself away from me. We tossed the ball back and forth, and my heart burst with joy to see the smile on his face as he threw to me. Whenever I caught the ball, he cheered.

Finally, he tackled me to the ground and kissed my neck as we lay on the grass; that marked the end of our game. If people gave us looks, I was oblivious.

"You look especially beautiful today," he said. "Maybe because you seemed so happy when we were playing, and it brought out your natural beauty."

I cupped his gorgeous face. "Happiness is beautiful, isn't it?"

"You have so much on your plate that I sometimes forget how young you are. Today you're that young, carefree girl."

"I'm so happy we did this."

"Baby steps, right?" He grinned. "I would never have considered touching a football if you weren't with me. I always tell you this, but I will say it again... You inspire me, motivate me to want to be stronger. I feel like that more than ever now, like I need to be strong for you—and for Sunny."

Was he warming to the idea of being a father to my daughter? He'd told me he didn't want kids. I refused to get my hopes up, instead vowing to enjoy each day as it came. But I was curious about something else.

"Have you told your family about me?"

He blinked a few times, seeming surprised by my question. "My mother knows about you. I'm sure she filled my father in, although I haven't told him directly."

"Did you tell her about Sunny, that I have a child?" I braced for the answer.

"Yes. Of course. I wouldn't hide that."

As much as his assurance made me feel better, there was an air of discomfort to this conversation. "How did your mother feel about you dating someone with a child?"

"She just wants me happy. That's all she's ever wanted. My father is more of a critical person in general, and I'm sure he'd find some reason to second-guess any decision I make. He's a contrarian by nature. That's why I don't open up to him."

"What about your brother? Do you talk to him much?"

"My relationship with Alex is better now than it used to be. I was unfairly resentful toward him for many years. When I graduated from college, he was just starting his college football career, and as proud of him as I was, I wasn't in a mental place that I could be a part of his life— it meant having to face that world I'd lost. I handled it poorly."

"What's he doing now?"

"He works for a financial advisory firm in Minneapolis. We talk on the phone from time to time, but I haven't spoken to him since you and I got together. I messed up that relationship, so it's my job to mend it. I know that's something I need to work on."

THE *Anti*-BOYFRIEND

"When will you get to see your family again?"

"I'm supposed to go home for Christmas."

"Oh." That meant he wouldn't be here with us for the holidays.

"But those plans were made before we got together," he clarified. "I'd like to spend Christmas with you."

I smiled. "I'm sure your family will want to see you, but I'd love to spend the holidays with you, too."

"Maybe I'll go home for a few days and come back on Christmas Eve or something. We can work it out." Deacon turned the tables. "What about your family? You don't talk much about your mom or brother. You don't see them over the holidays?"

"My mother comes to the city about every other year. I haven't seen her since last Christmas. This year, she's going to the Caribbean with her boyfriend for the holidays. My brother, Aaron, is a photographer for a travel blog. He's in Prague right now, and I don't think he has plans to come back to the States this year. And that's it. That's the extent of my family. I love them, but we don't see each other nearly as often as I wish we would."

"I'm surprised your mother doesn't want to see her granddaughter more."

I shrugged. I couldn't disagree. "My mother's always been a little distant. It's just the way she is. She visited when Sunny was born and then last Christmas, but hasn't come to see us since."

I wanted to tell Deacon he felt more like family to me than my actual kin, but that might have been too much to admit. I was always wary about saying things that might make him feel obligated. I wanted him to be the first to

232

come to certain conclusions about us. He certainly told me he loved me enough; I just hoped his love didn't have an expiration date.

"Well, your mother doesn't know what she's missing with her granddaughter." His smile held a sad undertone. "Speaking of Sunny, do you think she's old enough to appreciate going to a farm?"

"Like with animals?"

"Yup. This guy I work with, his family owns a farm upstate. It's the type of place people pay to visit. I checked out their website. They have animals you can pet and a gift shop. You think she'd enjoy something like that?"

"Heck, if she didn't, *I'd* definitely enjoy it. But yeah, I think she would. She lights up whenever we take her for walks and she sees a dog."

"We should plan to go then. Maybe next weekend, if the weather is nice."

"That sounds great." I looked at the time. "We'd better get going. The sitter has to leave in a half-hour."

"Shit. Okay." He stood and reached out to pull me up. "This time always goes by so fast."

"It does. And I appreciate you insisting we do it every week. It's important to have this time together."

I looked a bit sheepish. "I can't help needing you all to myself sometimes."

We got coffees from a truck on the walk back to the subway. Even that felt like a luxury when it was just the two of us. Slowly, I felt like I was coming back to myself, to the person I'd been before having Sunny. I loved being a mother, but until I started taking time for myself, I hadn't realized how much I'd missed certain aspects of my life. Now it seemed I had it all.

Was it that I'd found myself again, or was it that Deacon made me feel complete?

TWENTY-ONE

Deacon

LAST WORDS

I'd rented a car for the ninety-minute drive north to Poughkeepsie, and it had been a smooth ride with no traffic. This had definitely been a good idea. I now held Sunny up as she sat atop one of the ponies at Archwood Farms. She was always a happy child, but the ponies brought out a level of excitement I'd never witnessed before.

After the pony ride, I went to fetch Carys and me a couple of coffees from the small concession building, while she took Sunny to a grassy area with a bunch of pumpkins laid out. Sunny was now walking independently. While a little wobbly, she was fully mobile.

After I ordered our drinks, the woman I knew to be one of the owners of the farm smiled at me. "Your daughter looked like she was having so much fun out there. I'm so glad you guys could come up north today."

We'd spoken to her briefly when we first arrived, but I didn't realize she'd assumed I was Sunny's father. I opened my mouth to correct her, but what came out was, "Thank you. Yeah...this was well worth the trip." Was I actually entertaining the thought of a life with Sunny?

"You know," she said. "We have something here called equine therapy. It's designed for kids with special needs. She's a little too small now, but it might be something to consider for the future."

"What does it do?" I asked.

"Well, there are many physical and cognitive benefits to horseback riding. On the physical side, it can help improve balance and coordination and gross motor skills, among other things. And cognitively, it can help improve attention, communication, and spatial awareness. Not to mention all of the social and emotional benefits."

"Do you have any information you can send me home with?"

"Sure do." She reached into a drawer and took out a pamphlet for me.

"Thanks. I appreciate it." Excited to tell Carys, I placed it in my back pocket.

As I waited for her to prepare the coffees—one cream and one sugar each—I realized that if a stranger had assumed I was Sunny's father, Sunny had probably concluded that too. *Does Sunny think I'm her dad?* Technically, I was the only man she'd ever known. How did I feel about that? Right now I didn't want to put a label on anything beyond my relationship with Carys. She was my girlfriend. I'd made that clear to her repeatedly. But her daughter didn't have a designation, aside from being special to me. Spending time with Sunny made me genuinely happy; making her smile was one of the highlights of my life. Though it was hard to admit, I knew I *did* love Sunny. But that came with things I'd sworn I'd never have—and didn't deserve to have. *One day at a time.*

The woman interrupted my thoughts when she handed me two steaming coffees. I grabbed a cardboard sleeve for each before placing the lids on.

"Can I also have one of these, too?" I asked, pointing to the pink cake pops.

"Of course."

After I paid and returned outside, I located Carys and Sunny walking in my direction. They hadn't noticed me yet, so I took a moment to appreciate the beautiful woman who belonged to me and her adorable child. Sunny nearly toppled over as she made her way forward with a heavy pumpkin in hand. When she spotted me approaching, Carys bent down to point me out to Sunny. The look on Sunny's face as she noticed me was priceless; she sped up, seeming eager to get to me and so proud to be holding that pumpkin. It was a small one, but somehow looked humongous in her little hands.

When she reached me, she held out the pumpkin. She'd wanted to give it to me. My heart clenched. I didn't deserve the pedestal this little angel had put me on. The trust she placed in me was pure and unlike anything else I'd experienced.

"What did you do?" I knelt, putting the coffees and cake pop down on the pavement before holding out my hands. "Is that for me?"

Her cheeks reddened, as if she felt shy about giving it to me. It was adorable.

I took the pumpkin in one hand and pulled her close with the other. "Thank you so much. I love it," I whispered in her ear. "And I love you, too."

I meant every word. I loved Sunny.

Carys's eyes locked on mine. Now she knew where my heart was. More and more, I'd surrendered to the fact that even if I hadn't chosen this life, it had chosen me. And I felt like the luckiest man alive most days.

As for that doubt that gnawed at me? The voice that told me I didn't deserve any of this? The voice that told me I would inevitably fail at this, just like everything else that had been important to me? I'd have to practice telling it to fuck off.

On the ride back to the city, we played some Bee Gees in the rental car and rolled the windows down on the highway.

Sunny loved the feel of the wind on her face, which triggered a fit of laughter and screams of joy. It had been an accidental discovery when I rolled the wrong window down on the way up here.

Her blond hair blew all over the place, her eyes half closed against the wind.

"She loves living on the edge," I said over the noise. "Maybe she'll grow up to be a biker chick."

Carys laughed. "Let's not wish for that. I'd worry too much."

"But if it made her happy?"

She shrugged. "I'd have to suck it up."

"Actually..." I admitted. "I don't think I could handle Sunny riding a motorcycle. I'd be worried sick."

Carys placed her hand on my knee. "Aw, that's sweet."

Those were the last words I remembered before the crash.

TWENTY-TWO

Carys

THE ONLY CONSOLATION

Two Months Later

Simone was coming by today, and it was going to be hard to put the last couple of months into words. I didn't want to talk about them, but it was time to let it all out. Today I'd rehash every painful detail. What had been like a nightmare I couldn't wake up from would now be essentially relived. In some ways, these weeks had gone by in a flash, and in others, it felt like forever since I'd seen Deacon.

Most mornings, I'd wake up, and it would take several seconds before reality set in—before it hit me all over again that Deacon was gone.

Deacon was gone.

No matter how often I went over everything in my mind, I'd never be able to wrap my head around him leaving New York. Was it a total surprise? No. He'd warned me. He'd warned me not to trust him, and I hadn't listened. Wasn't there a saying about that? When someone shows you who they are, believe them? Somehow I'd thought I'd be the person to change him, that his love for me would transcend his fears about getting involved with someone who had a child.

Something in him had snapped after the accident. He'd freaked out, and I couldn't get the man I'd had before back. An accident had ruined his football career a decade ago, so maybe it was PTSD of some kind. Whatever it was, and wherever he was now, I hoped he was getting the help he needed.

It had been more than a month since Deacon left, and I would be explaining everything to Simone for the first time. She'd been in Paris, performing in a show there, when the accident happened. Even though she'd been back for a couple of weeks, I'd been too depressed to see her. But she'd insisted on coming to check on me today.

A little while later she arrived carrying two coffees from Starbucks. It was the first time I'd had Starbucks since Deacon last brought me one. I'd stayed away from there because it reminded me of him. How would I ever look at a Starbucks cup and not remember the first time he'd told me he loved me?

Simone put the coffees down on the table and brought me into a hug. "I'm so confused, Carys. Help me understand what the hell happened while I was away."

I walked over and picked up my latte. Even the taste reminded me of him. My eyes lingered blankly on Simone's name written on the side of the cup. I felt a tear forming before it fell.

I wiped my cheek. "Jesus. I told myself I wasn't going to cry."

"Whatever it takes, you need to get it out." She looked around. "Where's Sunny?"

"She's napping."

"Okay, good. It will give us some time to talk."

We brought our coffees over to the couch. I'd previously told Simone the basics about the accident—that a car had hit us on our way home from the farm in Poughkeepsie. We were banged up and bruised, but none of us were badly injured—on the outside anyway. But I hadn't elaborated on anything that happened after. She just knew Deacon and I had broken up.

"Where do I even start?" I took a deep breath in and started to let it out. "The day of the accident was perfect. We'd taken Sunny to a farm upstate. We were like a little family. Deacon told Sunny he loved her. It was so beautiful."

"This was all before the accident?"

I nodded. "The accident happened on the way home. A man driving a truck sideswiped our rental car, pushing us into a guardrail. We'd had the window down for Sunny, so it was noisy, but I don't think that made a difference. It happened so fast. There was nothing we could have done to prevent it. I don't think Deacon felt that way, though."

She sighed. "I don't understand..."

"Neither do I, really, Simone." I shook my head. "Anyway, we all went to the emergency room as a precaution, but we were discharged pretty quickly. But Deacon just wasn't the same. He spent more and more time at his apartment, away from us. He blamed himself for what happened, said his reflexes weren't fast enough, that the wind had distracted his focus."

"But it wasn't his fault," she insisted.

"No. But he felt he should've been able to protect us. I guess if we all hadn't been buckled in, we might've died."

"But you were buckled in. Why do you think he's so hard on himself?"

I sighed. "It brought back a bad memory for him. He got into an accident in college, and it ended his football career."

She nodded. "Okay...wow."

"I tried to get him to talk about what he was feeling, but he just kept blaming himself, saying Sunny could have died, and it would've been his fault. I kept hoping things would change as the days went on, that he would snap out of it, but he never did."

"When did he leave?"

"A few weeks after the accident. One night, he came over. I went to take a shower, since he'd be able to watch Sunny for a few minutes." I closed my eyes at the memory. "When I came out, before he realized I was there, I heard him talking to her. At the end he said, 'I know you won't remember me, but I'll never forget you.'"

Simone placed her hand on her chest and her face wilted. "Oh no."

"I said, 'Deacon, what are you talking about?' And he flipped around, shocked to see me standing behind him in my towel." I hesitated. "He was crying. I'd never seen that. He just kept saying, 'I'm sorry, Carys. I'm so sorry. I can't do this. I'm so sorry.'"

Simone reached out to rub my back. "Oh my God. What did you do?"

I shook my head. "I lost it. I started screaming, 'I knew you would do this. I knew you would do this to me.' And it was the truth. He'd warned me from the beginning that he was likely going to hurt me, that it wouldn't be intentional, but it would happen. And I didn't listen. I didn't fucking listen, and it's my own damn fault."

"How did he respond when you yelled that?"

"He just stared at me. He didn't have anything to say. He tried to reach out and hold me at one point, but I wouldn't let him touch me. I told him to leave. I couldn't bear to hear anything else he had to say. It didn't matter if he wasn't going to fight for us."

"Jesus Christ, Carys. Where is he now?"

"He stuck around for a few days after that, calling me to make sure I was okay, but I wouldn't answer. I know that wasn't the mature way of handling things, but I was too hurt. He eventually texted that he was going to Minnesota for an indefinite amount of time, saying again how sorry he was."

"How can he just go to Minnesota if he has a life here?"

"He can work from anywhere. And his family is there."

"He still has his apartment next door?"

"Apparently. I haven't heard or seen anything to prove otherwise."

She shook her head. "I'm so sorry this happened."

I shrugged. "Better now than five years down the line when I was even more invested."

I was trying to come off as strong, but I felt far from it. Most nights I cried myself to sleep, praying I'd wake up to find this was a dream, with Deacon's warm body next to me. The safety I'd felt with him seemed a distant memory now. Even though he'd broken my heart, I missed him. Even more than as a lover, I missed him as a friend.

"What if he comes to his senses, returns, and begs your forgiveness?" Simone asked.

Deep down, I knew his leaving wasn't only about me and Sunny. He had his own issues, and somehow the accident had put him in a bad place—a dark place he'd been before. While I understood that, I couldn't get past my own hurt to fathom forgiving him. And even if I *could* forgive him, trust would be the bigger issue.

I squeezed my eyes shut. "It's over. Even if he came back, I can't trust someone who left me once not to do it again. It's not only me I have to worry about. It's Sunny, too. I'm better off not getting involved with anyone at this point. It's too much of a risk. Deacon was my one shot, and it failed miserably. I won't put my heart on the line like that again."

A distraught look crossed Simone's face. "That's so sad. I feel like when the wound of this has healed, you'll come around. It'll take a while, but never give up hope, Carys. You're still so young."

Would I be able to love again? It sure as hell didn't feel that way right now.

I rubbed my temples. "I don't know, Simone. I really don't."

After Simone left, I went to get Sunny up from her nap. As I changed her diaper, she said something that threw me for a loop.

"Deek."

My heart shattered. Was it my imagination? She hadn't said "Deek" since he'd left. Was she only now realizing he was gone for good? Or was the sound she made just a coincidence?

Regardless of the answer, I felt compelled to say, "Deacon is gone, honey. I'm so sorry."

I might have been reminding myself more than anything. I could only hope Sunny would begin to forget him. That was the only consolation—that she was too young to remember any of this.

Later that night, I'd just settled in on the couch to watch some TV when my phone rang. Not many people called at this hour. The noise caused me to jump, thinking it might have been Deacon.

It wasn't.

Rather than say hello, I answered, "What do you want, Charles?"

Although I'd resigned myself to letting him come around at some point, I'd been in no place to try something new since Deacon left. So every time Charles called, I still gave him some version of the same answer: I wasn't ready for him to see Sunny.

"I told you I wasn't going to give up. I'll keep calling until I get the answer I need. I would like to see my daughter."

I wasn't in the mood for this. "You don't have a right to see her, so I don't have to abide by any special timeline to give you an answer. If I let you see her, it would be out of the goodness of my heart."

"Alright. Understood. But I can't give up, Carys. I won't. I made a huge mistake in how I handled things after she was born." He expelled a long breath into the phone, sounding defeated. "And I'm sorry again that I tried to see her without your permission. As I've told you, it won't happen again."

I needed to stop prolonging the inevitable. Maybe I was feeling too weak to fight anymore, but I conceded. "You want to see her?"

"Yes," he answered immediately.

"Come tomorrow afternoon at one."

Charles let out a sigh of relief. "Thank you, Carys. Thank you."

The next day, Charles stood at the door, holding a teddy bear bigger than Sunny.

I stepped aside. "Come in."

He looked me up and down. "You look beautiful."

That was comical considering I'd done nothing to make myself up. In fact, I'd intentionally dressed in jeans and a T-shirt for this.

His eyes searched the room. "Where's Sunny?"

"She's napping. I have to get her up. I typically don't wake her until there's a reason."

When I'd told him to come at one, I hadn't thought about the fact that Sunny might be napping. But I'd opted to keep the time anyway because I wanted to get the visit over with.

"Can I go in there with you when you wake her?"

I shrugged. "Sure."

We made small talk in the living room for as long as I could stand before I decided to wake Sunny up early, against my better judgment.

Charles followed me into her room.

I lifted Sunny out of the crib. It took her several seconds to blink her eyes fully open. When she noticed Charles standing there, she had no reaction.

"Hi, beautiful girl," he said, seeming in awe of her.

Sunny continued to look at him with ambivalence. Maybe she could sense the tension.

"I'm Charles," he said. "And I'm so very sorry I haven't come by to see you sooner. More than you can ever imagine." He seemed a little choked up.

Was it genuine? Probably. Although it was still too little too late for me to forget everything he'd done—or hadn't done—up until this point. I wouldn't forget, but I would work on forgiving. I did believe he cared for her, despite everything. And I did believe he regretted how he'd handled things.

Charles followed us back out to the living room. We sat in silence as he watched Sunny play with her toys on the floor, which now included the giant, stuffed bear he'd brought.

"I asked you something once before and you dismissed it. So I'll ask again. Who was that man here with Sunny the night of the gala?" he asked suddenly.

My chest tightened. "I still don't believe that's any of your business."

"I know it's not. I'm just curious."

"He was an ex-boyfriend," I admitted.

"Ex? What happened?"

"It doesn't matter."

Charles nodded, not pushing the issue. We resumed watching Sunny together in silence. She babbled and squealed as she tried to communicate with the giant bear.

He rubbed his hands together and turned to me. "What can I do to make things better between us? I know I've lost all chance of ever having you as a lover again. But goddamnit, Carys, I need to rectify the mistakes I've made. I want to get to the point where we can be civil, friends, even. I know that may be a long shot, but a man can dream."

I shook my head. "I don't know."

He looked up at the ceiling and sighed. "Carys, when we met, I was so smitten with you. I'm not sure if you realize how badly I had it back then. I admired your beauty and elegance long before you were ever injured and working with me. My attraction to you was something I had to keep secret because I was a married man. Then when Violet and I separated, that gave me a window to finally pursue you. I never felt like I deserved you. But I loved you. I truly did—still do. There was only one thing I loved more—my children. More and more, I saw how difficult the impending divorce was on them. I started to reconsider whether I was making the right decision in leaving my family. I convinced myself getting back together with Violet was the right idea when it wasn't. I chickened out when it came to putting my needs above others. At that time, of course, I didn't know you were pregnant. By the time I did find out, I'd already made the decision to try to save my family. And then she started threatening me. I—"

"I already know why you—"

"Please, let me finish," he interrupted.

I let out an exasperated breath.

"When Violet found out about your pregnancy, she threatened to make it so I never saw Talia and Xavier again unless I abandoned you and relinquished my rights as a father to Sunny. I felt like I had to make a choice between hurting the children I knew, or the one I'd never met. My decision was a knee-jerk reaction out of fear. I'm ashamed of what I did to you. And if I have to spend the rest of my life making it up to you, I will."

I'd known Violet was against the kids finding out about Sunny but never realized she'd actually used the children to threaten Charles. Still, whether that knowledge would change things remained to be seen. "I don't know what to say. I really don't. I've completely written you off as a part of my life or Sunny's life."

"And I deserve every bit of that." He paused a moment. "I told Talia and Xavier about Sunny."

My eyes widened. "What?"

"It was against Violet's wishes, but I'm done being blackmailed."

"You always said you thought they were too young to understand."

"They are. But I came to the conclusion that the longer I kept it from them, the more of a shock it would be, and the less time they would have with their sister."

Sister? I couldn't believe he was using that term. "You do realize you're not on her birth certificate, so technically whether she's their sister is debatable."

He stared at me. "She's their flesh and blood, Carys. I have no right to keep her from them."

"What did you say to them?"

"I told them the truth, that when Mommy and Daddy were apart, I fell in love with a beautiful woman and we made a baby together. I showed them the one photo of

THE *Anti*-BOYFRIEND

Sunny I have, one Simone posted on social media. And I told them about her, about what Down syndrome is, about the mistakes I made in handling everything. And I apologized to them, just as I'm apologizing to you right now."

My mind raced. "This is too much."

"I know it is. But I had to tell you. I'm done being a disappointment to you and to myself. I needed to do what was right. My name may not be on her birth certificate, but I am her father, Carys. I will *always* be her father."

I felt sick. He didn't deserve a second chance, but Sunny had no other father figure in her life. Her biological father now wanted that role. I didn't want to make a decision she'd be upset about later.

"So what are you expecting from me?" I asked.

"It doesn't have to go from zero to a hundred. I just want you to meet me from time to time. Once a month, maybe, to start. I want her to know me, even if she thinks I'm just a friend. Eventually, I want my kids to meet her. I know I have a lot of work to do to earn your trust. And I plan to do whatever it takes."

TWENTY-THREE

Carys

NICE TO SEE YOU AGAIN

Over the next six weeks or so, Charles proved he hadn't been kidding when he'd vowed to earn my trust back. I appreciated that he was letting me call the shots on his reentrance into my life, though.

In addition to abiding by a visitation schedule, he'd also begun depositing money more regularly in my bank account. I'd never refused his occasional offerings, but now that he wasn't doing everything behind Violet's back, he'd set up a direct deposit each month. I wasn't going to complain. Sunny deserved his support.

We'd agreed on a twice-a-month visitation schedule for starters. I gave him a few hours on Saturdays. We'd take Sunny out, and she was slowly taking to him, offering occasional smiles and responses to his endless efforts to make her laugh. It was noticeably different than her immediate attachment to Deacon had been, though.

Charles hadn't insisted on using the term *dad* around her, and I was grateful. He referred to himself as Charles, and it was my strong opinion that for the foreseeable future, things should remain that way.

One chilly but sunny Saturday in January, Charles and I took Sunny to a toy store and then to get a treat. It was too cold for ice cream, but Sunny had seen the sign for the shop with the giant ice cream cone flag and wouldn't stop pointing to it.

After, we ended up in Bryant Park, and I spotted Deacon's friend Adrian at a table with a woman. We were about to walk past them. I wanted to turn around and go the other direction, but I didn't want to explain anything to Charles, so I forced myself to keep moving. I had no idea if Adrian would even look up or recognize me.

But sure enough, just as we moved past him, his eyes met mine. He squinted into the sun, holding his hand to his forehead like a visor. "Carys?"

I feigned surprise and smiled. "Hey!"

"Not sure if you recognize me. I know we only met once. I'm Deacon's friend Adrian?" He smiled.

"Of course, I recognize you. How have you been?"

"I've been good." He turned to Charles. "And you are?"

"I'm Charles." He held out his hand. "Sunny's father."

As they shook, shock registered on Adrian's face. I had an urge to explain the situation, but why? What did it matter if he drew the wrong conclusion about this? I didn't owe him—nor Deacon—any explanation.

Adrian bent to look down at Sunny in her stroller. "This must be the famous Sunny."

Sunny took to Adrian right away, flashing an amused smile as she devoured her ice cream cone. My heart raced as I wondered whether he'd bring up his MIA friend.

Instead, Adrian simply nodded once and said, "Well, it was nice to see you again."

"You, too," I said.

Relief flooded through me. Adrian likely knew the deal. There was no reason to bring up what happened. Had a part of me wanted to ask him how Deacon was doing? Yes. But ultimately, I wasn't prepared for the answer. I didn't want to hear that he was dating again or had moved on in any way. That would've been too damn painful.

"Who was that?" Charles asked as we walked away. "You seemed tense just now."

I blew out a breath. "He's a friend of my former boyfriend."

"The guy I met at your place? That boyfriend?"

"Yeah. The *anti*-boyfriend. Deacon," I said bitterly. "He was my only relationship."

"I've asked you more than once what happened, and you never answer me. I suppose I'll get the same response if I pry now?"

"I'd rather not talk about it."

"Okay. Fair enough." He placed his hand on my back. "One of these days I'll get you to tell me."

I shook my head. Normally, I could keep thoughts of Deacon at bay during the day. But Adrian had brought everything to the forefront.

"So I never mentioned what happened when I told Violet I'd spoken to the kids about Sunny," Charles said.

Not exactly a great change of subject.

"How did she take it?"

"Not well, but she didn't do anything drastic. She's not happy with me, but that's pretty normal." He shrugged. "Now that the kids know, they're insistent on meeting Sunny. They told Violet they want to see their sister soon. And she didn't exactly refuse."

"Really?"

"Yeah. She conceded."

I stopped walking for a moment. "Okay, so what does this mean?"

"It means I'd love to bring them along with me on one of our future visits, if you're open to that."

As uncomfortable as it made me, I didn't want Sunny to go through what I had, never knowing my half-siblings. I did fear for her future if anything were to happen to me. While I had every hope that Sunny would go on to live a normal life, what if she needed more support than the average person? The idea that she might have siblings to look after her if I wasn't around was quite comforting.

"That would be okay," I finally answered. "Are you sure they're ready?"

"They've gotten used to the idea of her. I think they need to meet her for it to feel real to them. They're sweet, accepting kids, and I suspect it's going to go better than I ever imagined."

"Then I'm good with it. I don't want to keep Sunny from her siblings."

Charles let out a breath. "Thank you. I'd kiss you if I could right now."

I held my palm out. "Don't even think about it."

"A man can dream." He winked. "But one step at a time."

Charles was crazy if he thought I'd ever take him back. More than the obstacle of forgiving him, I now knew I'd never really loved him. My feelings for Deacon were on an entirely different level. Regardless of how he'd ended things, what I felt for Deacon and the experience of falling in love with him couldn't be erased. Even if I wished it could.

TWENTY-FOUR

Deacon

COCKBLOCKER

"What are you looking at?" she asked.

Shit. How long had I been staring at her? I hadn't meant to make her uncomfortable. It was just... I couldn't take my eyes off her. I'd done a pretty decent job of keeping Carys out of my mind this week. Then I got to the checkout line at the supermarket where I'd been picking up groceries for my grandmother. The cashier looked like an older version of Sunny. Did she think I was staring at her because she had Down syndrome? *Shit.* That wasn't it at all.

"I'm sorry. I know I was staring at you. It's because you remind me of someone who's special to me, someone I don't get to see anymore. I didn't mean to be rude."

She rolled her eyes, and it made me chuckle, because I could see Sunny growing up to be as feisty as this girl. My chest tightened at the thought that I might never see Carys or Sunny again.

It had been three months since I'd left New York, and my life there seemed an eternity away. I still didn't know how to handle my abandoned apartment. I'd been paying my rent, which I was able to do since I was living rent-free at my grandmother's house. Gram appreciated the company and the help, and I appreciated the fact that I could be home in Minnesota without having to shack up with my parents. I didn't know how long I planned to stay here, but returning to New York wasn't an option yet.

The cashier handed me my receipt. The name on her tag read *Autumn*.

I nodded and smiled. "Have a good day, Autumn."

She mouthed, "Fuck off."

Nice.

I couldn't help smiling again. The universe was messing with me today.

One thing about living with Gram was that she could always see right through me and didn't put up with any shit. I'd refused to tell her why I'd come home to Minnesota. I'd yet to talk about the real reason with anyone in my family at all. But while the rest of them weren't prying, Gram had been insistent on getting it out of me at some point.

As I put away her groceries that afternoon, she watched me from her chair in the adjacent living room.

"I'm not as dumb as you think, you know."

My hand paused on a box of cereal I'd just put in the cupboard. "What are you getting at, Gram?"

"I know this has something to do with a woman. What else could it be?"

I resumed putting stuff away to distract from the tension I felt. "Why do you assume that?"

"Because why else would you leave the most exciting city in the world to come live with me? A broken heart is the only thing that could make someone run away and come back to the place they've been avoiding for years."

She was right about that. I'd avoided Minnesota like it was my job.

I sighed. "You're right. It does have to do with a woman. But it's not what you're probably thinking. I was the one who broke her heart, not vice versa. But I'm not ready to get into it."

My grandmother's brows drew together. "Do you plan to stay here indefinitely?"

"No." I paused. "At least I don't think so." Pointing a can of Pringles at her, I said, "Why? Are you in a rush for me to leave? I thought you liked having me here."

"While at times I like having my grown-ass grandson here, your gram needs her space once in a while."

"For what?"

She looked at me like I should have known, but it didn't compute.

"I have a friend I haven't been able to have over since you got here."

Virtually scratching my head, I still didn't get it. Until I did.

Oh.

Oh.

Well I'll be fucking damned.

"I'm messing up your game, Gram?"

Jeez. And I'd wondered where I got it from all these years.

"I'm not saying you can't stay here. But you might want to share the love with your brother one or two nights a week."

"Here I was thinking I was helping out my sweet little granny, keeping her company, doing her shopping. Now I come to find out I'm just a cockblocker." I shook my head. "Well, thanks for enlightening me."

Once I got a clue that I was intruding on my grandmother's booty calls, I hit up my brother for an alternate place to stay a few days a week.

Whereas my parents and grandmother lived in the suburbs, Alex lived in downtown Minneapolis. With my backpack hooked over my shoulder, I arrived at his building. Looking up at the high-rise, I felt a pang of longing for city life.

Well, it was less about the city and more about what I'd left behind there.

After taking the elevator up, I knocked on my brother's door.

He opened. "Hey, dude."

"Hey."

We shared a manly hug, patting each other on the back. Dropping my bag, I looked around. The furniture looked new. The place smelled great. My little bro had come a long way from the way I remembered him when I left home for California back in college. He was just under me in height, but had really grown to resemble me more with age.

"I've barely seen you since you've been home," he said. "I'm glad Gram kicked you to the curb."

"So what's the plan tonight?" I asked.

"Lindsay's coming by after work and we're all gonna go to dinner."

"Sounds good. I can't believe I've been here for three months and haven't met your girlfriend yet."

He cracked open a beer before handing it to me. "Are you okay?" he asked as he opened a bottle for himself.

"Yeah. Why?" I took a sip.

"Everyone is wondering why you're here." He let out a slight belch. "Don't get me wrong, it's not that we don't want you home. But something seems off. We've been trying to figure it out. You know you can tell me anything, right?"

So he and my parents had been talking about me. *Fucking awesome.* "Yeah. I do. And I will. Just not now."

"Okay. Well, tonight is about having fun anyway—getting your mind off things. And I've got my guitar room set up for you."

"Cool. Thanks, man. I really appreciate it. Had I known our grandmother was a freak, I would've come to stay here a long time ago."

"Worst kept secret in the world." He laughed. "But I'm glad she threw your ass out."

Alex and I kicked back on his couch with our beers for the next half-hour, taking a trip down memory lane with stories from our childhood.

The doorbell rang, interrupting our conversation.

When Alex answered the door, two women entered the apartment.

"Linds, you finally get to meet my big brother," Alex said, kissing her cheek. "I thought we were gonna have to fly to New York for this, but he came home."

Lindsay was short with long, black hair, which was interesting because Alex typically went for blondes, from what I could remember. There was a lot I didn't know about my brother now, and I regretted that.

"It's so great to meet you," she said, extending her hand to me. "You're like this mythical character no one ever gets to see. I'm so happy you're here."

"Yeah. Me, too."

She turned to her friend. "This is Hallie. I figured we'd make tonight a foursome so you didn't feel like the third wheel."

Great. This is a setup? Alex must have been in on this.

"Really nice to meet you, Deacon," she said. "You look so much like Alex."

"I'm sorry. I can't help it."

With long, brown hair and large eyes, Hallie was attractive. The blind date might have been a pleasant surprise for the old me. But under the current circumstances, it was unwelcome. Now that my brother had put me in this position, I'd have to suck it up and try to enjoy the night.

We ended up walking to a nearby, high-end steakhouse. Being in a crowded restaurant in the city felt like I'd been transported back to Manhattan.

When my phone rang in the middle of dinner, I wasn't sure if checking it would be rude. I looked down at the caller ID. *Adrian.*

I hadn't spoken to him in a couple of weeks. When I left New York, he'd been shocked that I'd broken up with

Carys and couldn't understand why I needed to come to Minnesota. I'd chosen not to tell him about the accident, and without divulging the deep-rooted reasons for my decision to leave, I'd left him understandably confused. He'd chalked my actions up to cold feet and didn't pressure me. He was convinced I'd come to my senses and return to the city any day now. He thought maybe I'd had some kind of life crisis because I'd recently turned thirty.

Not wanting to be rude during dinner, I let the call go to voicemail. But when my phone started ringing a second time, I worried maybe something was wrong. It was unlike Adrian to call two times in a row. His sister had been undergoing cancer treatments, so I worried something had happened to her. I lifted my finger, excusing myself before stepping outside for some privacy.

The phone stopped ringing before I had a chance to pick up, so I dialed him back.

It rang a few times before he answered, "Hey."

"Hey, man. What's up? Everything okay?"

"Yeah. Everything's fine."

My pulse regulated a bit. "Okay. Good. You normally don't call me two times in a row. I worried something had happened with Natalia. I'm actually out to dinner with my brother and his girlfriend. I stepped outside."

"Ah. Okay. Well, something's been bugging me, so I figured I'd try you a second time to see if I could catch you."

"What's on your mind?" I asked.

"I wasn't sure whether to tell you this, but it's been eating away at me all day."

My pulse sped up again. "What is it?"

"I ran into Carys at Bryant Park today."

My heart felt like it stopped. Literally fucking stopped. "What happened? Is she okay?"

"Yeah. It's nothing bad. But she wasn't alone. She had Sunny with her. And she was with...Sunny's father."

Sunny's father? That made no sense. Carys barely even spoke to her ex, let alone hung out with him. "Wait. How do you know it was him?"

"He introduced himself to me. It looked very casual. The little girl was eating an ice cream cone."

My heart clenched. This news stunned me into silence.

Maybe Carys had decided to let Charles be around Sunny, but it bothered me that she might've been feeling vulnerable after I left and done something she wouldn't otherwise have done. He could've taken advantage of her. Maybe it had nothing to do with me, but a mix of jealousy, anger, and confusion brewed inside.

Staring blankly out at the busy street, I had no idea how many seconds passed before I asked, "Did she say anything to you?"

"Just hello. It was just a quick, cordial exchange. I got the feeling she would've pretended not to notice me if I'd let her. But you know how it is. No one can get past my extroverted ass." When I fell silent again, he said, "You there?"

"Yeah...yeah, I'm here. Just trying to let this sink in."

"I'm sorry if it's none of my business. I just figured I'd want to know if the situation were reversed."

"I appreciate you telling me."

"I still don't get what happened, but I know how much she meant to you at one point. Hopefully she's not letting this guy manipulate her."

My head pounded. That was my fear. But this was about more than that. Hearing that she'd been out and about at the park with Sunny reminded me how much I missed them, how much I was missing out on.

"Well, I'd better get back inside."

"Yeah. Go have fun with your brother. Try not to let this ruin your night."

Fat chance. "Alright, man. Take care."

After that, it was impossible to think about anything but Carys. Whether she was moving on with her ex or not, it was inevitable that I'd lose her for good. I'd sealed that fate the day I walked out of her life.

TWENTY-FIVE

Deacon

HINDSIGHT IS TWENTY-TWENTY

Since arriving in Minnesota, I'd avoided being alone with my father. I'd gone over to my parents' for dinner but left before Dad had a chance to corner me. He hadn't said anything hurtful yet, but I dreaded encountering the version of him I remembered—the one who did nothing but criticize me. I didn't need him making me feel inadequate when I already felt pretty damn shitty since leaving Carys the way I did.

It appeared I could only hide for so long, though. I was shoveling snow outside my grandmother's house one day when I looked up to see my dad's red truck.

Sticking the shovel into the snow, I leaned on it as I watched him approach. He reached over to brush some snow off my coat, and I felt my eyes widen. It was rare my father touched me. Aside from the brief hug I'd given him when I first arrived here, there had been no other contact—no handshakes or pats on the back.

I stepped back. "What's up, Dad?"

"I figured you weren't going to come see me anytime soon, so I'd better find you."

"Yeah. I've been pretty busy helping Gram around here."

He looked down at the long path I'd cleared. "I can see that."

I resumed digging. "How's Mom?"

Cold air billowed from Dad's mouth. "She's good. She wishes you'd come by more."

My shovel scraped against the concrete. "I'll have to visit soon."

"Anyway..." he said. "I've been wanting to talk to you."

Here it is. I was about to be lectured about throwing my life away and squandering my potential by continuing to work in a field where my income was limited. Somehow he'd figure out a way to tie in my past mistakes, and I'd regret ever coming home. This was precisely what I'd been avoiding like the plague since I'd gotten here.

"So, a few weeks back, I noticed some blood in my semen," he began.

What?

"I had some tests done, and it turns out I have prostate cancer."

I froze, hanging on to the shovel for balance. I finally made eye contact with him. "Cancer?"

"I have to start radiation. They think it's small enough that they can treat it, but it's not exactly at the earliest stage. It's stage Two B, so the doctor's recommendation is treating it aggressively. But the prognosis is good."

It felt like the world around me was spinning. My father had always been the epitome of health and strength. If this could happen to him, it could happen to anyone.

"Does Alex know?"

"He does, but I specifically asked him not to mention anything. I wanted to be the one to tell you. I kept waiting for you to show up at the house, and you never did. So I needed to tell you before I start treatment in a couple of days."

A couple of days?

I sucked in a large dose of frosty air. "I'm sorry, Dad. Obviously if I had known I—"

"I know." He looked up at the sky, then back at me. "Look...I know things have not been the best between us for a long time—too long. I take full blame for that. No matter how disappointed I may have been with how things turned out, you're still my son. I should've put you before my feelings. This whole cancer thing has forced me to reflect on my life, and unfortunately, I'm seeing more mistakes than I can count."

The blame wasn't all his. "I ran away. You can't work on a relationship with someone who's not there. It's not all your fault. I made it nearly impossible."

"For a long time, I didn't feel there was anything more important in life than my career—than football. There's nothing like facing your mortality to make you realize that's bullshit."

Things were getting pretty surreal. "Hindsight is twenty-twenty, I guess."

Dad stared down at his boots and kicked at the snow. "I should've paid more attention to your pain after the accident," he said, looking up at me again. "I shouldn't have been caught up in what it meant for me. I'd only ever dreamed of you making it to the NFL. All I wanted was for you to be successful. I was devastated and didn't know how to handle it. So I shut down, and I screwed up by staying silent all these years. You probably assumed I was disappointed in you, but as the years passed, the only one I've been disappointed in is myself."

While it was validating to hear him say that, this was no time for him to be feeling guilty.

"It's okay, Dad. I don't want you worrying about all that right now. It's in the past. You need to focus on the present and getting better. Stress can do a lot of harm."

He shook his head. "I didn't realize then that success can't be measured by accolades or money. Because when you die, you can't take those things with you. In the end, all I have is my family. I need to work on mending those relationships, not only with you, but with your mother and brother. But especially with you."

"I don't know what to say, Dad. I'm in shock. This was the last thing I expected to hear."

"You don't have to say anything." He sighed. "Well, that's not true. Say you'll come to the house for dinner tonight. Say we'll get to spend some time together before I have to start this treatment shit."

Suddenly, it seemed like the least I could do. "Of course. Yeah."

My father and I had so much history, but all of that went out the window the second I realized I might lose him. Sure, his odds of survival were good, but I couldn't escape the reminder that I didn't have forever to make amends.

Over the next couple of weeks, I spent a great deal of time with my father. While he insisted we talk some about the past, it was thankfully limited. Mostly, we just worked on getting to know each other better. So some of it was stressful, but there were good moments in the mix, like late-night games of cards and, ironically, Parcheesi.

My mother, Alex, and I took turns taking my dad to his radiation appointments. He'd taken a leave of absence from his coaching job and was now considering early retirement.

During one of the treatment visits, he and I sat together in the waiting room. "Why are you here?" he suddenly asked me.

"What are you talking about? I'm here to support you."

"I didn't mean *here*. I mean, why are you in Minnesota and not back in New York? You loved living there, right? Surely you're not getting accustomed to a new life as your grandmother's servant?"

Looking down into my coffee, I chuckled.

"You can talk to me," he said. "What happened?"

Silence settled over us as I contemplated whether to tell him the truth.

"It's a long story."

"Do I look like I have somewhere to go? Talk to me."

If someone had told me a few months ago that the first person I'd open up to about Carys would be my father, I wouldn't have believed it. I downed the last of my coffee before crushing the cup and throwing it into a nearby trash can. "I broke up with someone I care about very much. I didn't know how to face her every day. So I left. It was cowardly, but I didn't feel like I had a choice. She lived right next door to me."

Over the next several minutes, I told him all about Carys, Sunny, and the accident. At least by choosing to open up to my father, I didn't have to explain how my past related to my present. He understood full well where I was coming from and why I'd freaked out.

"You know..." he said, "Fear of failure is a powerful thing. I always feared failing in my career. I definitely failed as a father, but that didn't seem to matter as much to me a decade ago. I see things in a different light now."

"I never really looked at my problem as a fear of failure," I said.

"But it is. Your fear is of failing *people*, harming people. You have to ask yourself if you really deserve a life sentence for something that happened when you were practically a kid and wasn't entirely your fault."

"You know how I feel about that."

"I know what you've made yourself believe, but it's time to stop blaming yourself."

"You were angry with me for so many years," I said. "I'm surprised you're telling me you don't think it was my fault."

"I might have been angry that it happened, but never once did I feel like you were in the wrong. That other car was going too fast, and it was a foggy night. You were momentarily distracted, trying to get where you needed to go. You weren't drunk. You weren't being reckless. Even if you hadn't been using the navigation device and your reflexes had kicked in faster, you don't know that you could have stopped what happened."

"If you felt that way, why did you act like you blamed me?"

"Because I was bitter at life. I expressed that through my treatment of you, and I'm very sorry for that, son. It wasn't fair. I'm sorry I didn't say all of this sooner."

Resting my head on the wall behind my seat, I let out a long breath. "The accident with Carys... It felt like the same nightmare all over again."

"Yes, I'm sure it did. But no one was hurt. So there had to have been more to your decision to flee New York than the accident?"

"It wasn't so much the accident as it was what the accident represented. It made me feel like I couldn't be trusted to keep them safe. And the responsibility of a child is just so...huge. Literally, her life was in my hands—not only that day, but it would've been every day thereafter. So many opportunities to fuck up."

"So you'd rather someone else raise this child you clearly care about, take care of the woman you love, because you're scared to mess up? I got news for ya, that's a good way to waste your life. And let me tell you, if you ever find yourself with a health scare like mine, you're gonna wish you had taken life by the horns and let yourself love the ones you cared about when you had the chance. It wouldn't be much fun for me to be alone right now. All I have is my family. I took your mother for granted for a long time. But she's been my rock through all this, despite some rough years together. Where would I be without her—and without you and your brother—taking turns sitting with me so I don't have to be alone?"

I turned to him. "I'm glad I can be here for you right now."

"You've paid your dues. I'd rather you go back to being there for *you*."

"I can't leave you like this."

"Sure, you can. You can keep tabs on me through Mom. I'm just a flight away if you need to come home again. Don't use me as an excuse to hide from things you haven't dealt with. You have to go back to New York eventually. You're going to have to face her sooner or later."

Would I? Or would I just give up the apartment and move somewhere else so I didn't have to see Carys on a daily basis?

"I think she might be letting her daughter's father back into her life. I don't trust him. But I feel like I don't trust myself either."

"You hit the nail on the head. You don't trust yourself. Faith in oneself is a risk. You need to accept that anything worth having is going to come with the risk of loss. Maybe the reason you haven't been able to deal with things now is because you've never dealt with the past. You ran away instead."

"How do I deal with the past now? It's been a decade."

"Maybe you need to see Becca, see how she's handling life."

My ex and I had grown apart quickly after the accident. She chose to end things, and I left town. But I'd thought about her a lot over the years. Only the more time that passed, the harder it became to make contact.

Maybe my father was right. Maybe somehow I needed to hear that she was okay.

"Thank you for the advice, Dad. I'll think about it."

That night, I searched for Becca's name on social media.

She was the first Becca Henderson to pop up, since we had a few mutual friends. I took some time to look through her photos. Her familiar face—dusted with freckles and framed by her long brown hair—took me back almost instantly. Because we weren't "friends" on here, I could only see a few images, and most of them were from years ago. One was a photo of Becca and a black lab. There were no real clues about her life now. While I'd heard through the grapevine that she still lived around here, I didn't know much else. I had no idea where her house was, as we hadn't met until we were both attending school in Iowa.

I took a deep breath and hit the friend-request button.

That would be a start. If she ignored my request, that would be the end of it. But if she accepted, maybe she'd be receptive to a conversation. I closed out of the app and opened my email to catch up on some work stuff. A few minutes later, I got a notification that Becca had accepted my friend request.

Wow.

Okay, then.

She didn't send me a message or post on my page, so I took that as my cue to make the first move. I clicked on the button on her profile to message her. I typed and deleted several times before settling on a simple message.

Hey, Becca. It's been a long time. How are things?

Then I waited anxiously for the response, hoping the answer was positive, and more than that, hoping she didn't hate me.

TWENTY-SIX

Carys

THE TEXT

This was a huge day. It would be the first time I let Charles see Sunny without me being there, too. The plan seemed innocent enough. He'd brought his kids to my apartment, and they would be hanging out for a couple of hours.

Talia and Xavier had recently met Sunny for the first time. Today was their third visit. The kids had really taken to her, and Sunny liked them. Allowing them to meet seemed to be one of the rare good decisions I'd made this past year.

So with Sunny occupied by Charles and his kids, I was off to run a couple of errands and take a breather. I had mixed feelings about leaving her alone with them, but Charles had earned back a bit of my trust in the past few months. While I wouldn't trust him with my heart again, I knew he was a responsible father to his two other kids. I had no reason to fear for Sunny's safety while in his care.

And also? Mama needed a breather. I mainly had a babysitter for when I worked, so taking an hour for myself was like a dream at this point. So when Charles had offered, I caved, though I didn't venture very far. I ran to the drugstore down the street to take my time shopping for toiletries, then stopped at a café around the corner. I'd be close by if Charles needed me to come back.

As I sipped my coffee in a cozy corner seat, I scrolled through my phone and did something I probably shouldn't have. The gaming app Deacon's company created had been installed on my phone for some time. It felt like my only connection to him. From time to time, I'd look to see what new games had been created, knowing he'd had a hand in designing them. Sometimes I'd play them. *Yes, I know that's pathetic.* But it felt like a safe way to remember Deacon without having to actually interact with him.

As I flipped through the character choices in the new game, something stopped me in my tracks. One of the main characters looked different—yet markedly familiar to me. She was beautiful, just like my Sunny, and looked as if she had Down syndrome. Her name was Autumn.

I didn't know how long ago Deacon had designed her, before our breakup or after, but this discovery made my heart feel heavier than it had in a while.

A few nights later, Sharon arrived to babysit. Sick to my stomach from nerves, I'd just gotten dressed and ready to venture out on my first official date since getting my heart broken. I'd decided to accept a casual dinner invitation from a guy I'd met online. If I didn't push myself to move on from Deacon, I never would. Maybe at some point it would feel natural and not forced, but it certainly didn't yet. *Fake it till you make it.*

"You look gorgeous, Carys," Sharon told me. "Are you meeting this guy somewhere safe?"

"Yeah. Of course. Taking an Uber to the restaurant and Ubering straight home."

"Good." She smiled. "Don't worry about Sunny and me. You have a good time."

At almost two, Sunny was starting to say more words, pointing to things a lot and saying "that." A new speech therapist came to the house twice a week to work with her on language, and I did my best to repeat the words I believed she was trying to say whenever the opportunity presented itself. Sunny and I had also learned sign language to help her communicate until she was able to sound out more words.

"Mama will be back, okay?"

My girl reached her arms out to me and started to cry. "No, Mama."

She'd become more attached to me than ever lately, maybe the result of the greater awareness that came with growing into a toddler.

Guilt followed me out the door as I made my way into the car waiting outside. During the ride, I looked out the window, which was covered in raindrops. A sadness that seemed to match the dreary weather came over me. I should've been happy about going on this date. But I missed Deacon, longed to be in his arms, and knew that would never happen again. Grief definitely comes in waves, and mine always seem to hit at the most inopportune times.

Once at the restaurant, I discovered that my date, Peter, had secured a candlelit table in the corner.

He stood as I approached, and his eyes went wide. "Carys, you're even more beautiful in person." He practically drooled. "Wow."

"Thank you."

Peter was handsome—not drop-dead gorgeous like Deacon, but attractive enough. *Enough.* Would that be the story of my life now? Attractive *enough*. Good *enough*. At this point, if you were decent looking and a decent person, you had a shot with me. Because that meant you were a safe distraction, something I'd desperately needed since Deacon walked out of my life.

I knew from our online interactions that Peter worked with kids who had special needs, but I hadn't realized until our conversation got going tonight that some of his students had Down syndrome. What were the chances? That left us with no lack of things to talk about during dinner. I picked his brain throughout our meal—so much so that I almost felt sorry for the guy.

"If you ever want to come visit the classroom and see some of the things we do, I'd be happy to be your tour guide," he said. "Actually, even better, I can take you down to the integrated preschool. That's not my classroom, but you could take a look at some of the ways Sunny might be learning when she eventually starts school."

"You know what? I may just take you up on that. The preschool years aren't too far away, and I should start thinking about my options."

I was starting to think I might have met this guy just to light a fire under my ass in terms of planning for Sunny's education.

"If you don't mind my asking..." Peter suddenly said. "You mentioned this was only your second date with someone you met online. I assume you haven't been in a relationship since Sunny was born?"

I wished he hadn't asked that, but I answered honestly. "No. I was in a serious relationship for several months. We started out as friends, and it evolved into something more."

"I see. What happened?"

I'd nearly cried on the way here. Talking about what happened with Deacon would put me over the edge. "I'd rather not go into it. Let's just say he freaked out and moved back to Minnesota. He was a good man, but not the one for me, I guess."

"Fair enough." Peter nodded and changed the subject.

We spent the next hour talking about much lighter subjects. I discovered Peter had grown up not far from where I did in Wayne, New Jersey. We'd never crossed paths, maybe because he was seven years older. But we had a blast recalling some of the old haunts we'd both frequented, including my favorite diner.

Peter came across as kind and attentive, and dare I say, I was actually enjoying the date. That is, until a text turned my evening on its axis.

No. It rocked my world.

Sharon: Everything's fine, Carys. But I wanted to give you a heads up. Deacon came by tonight looking for you. It seems he's back in New York.

TWENTY-SEVEN

Deacon

FROM THE GROUND UP

What the fuck did you expect, Deacon?

You disappeared for four months, came back unannounced, and didn't think there would be repercussions?

Carys had Sharon here babysitting. She was out. Sharon didn't divulge where Carys was, but I put two and two together.

Fuck. I felt nauseous.

Originally, I was going to call her, give her some warning. But I decided it would be better to just jump into the fire. There was so much I needed to say to her, but that wasn't going to be happening tonight.

Pacing in my apartment for over an hour, I listened intently for any sign that she'd come home. When I heard her door unlatch from the hallway, and muffled conversation through the wall, I knew she'd returned.

My pulse raced as I debated whether or not to go over there. I wasn't sure if she'd text me once she found out I'd come by earlier. Maybe it was better if I waited until morning to bombard her.

One thing was for sure: I wouldn't be sleeping for shit tonight.

Carys never texted or called. Not that she should've. But I'd braced myself for a "what the fuck are you doing back?" message.

Dragging myself out of bed, I got dressed before walking to the kitchen and making some coffee. Watching the java drip down into the carafe, I could feel my stomach in knots. My heart was in my throat as I geared myself up to face her. I didn't know where to begin, or if she'd even listen.

I sipped my coffee alone at the table, running everything through my head, but knowing none of it was going to come out the right way. When I'd had two full cups—enough to make me jittery—I forced myself up.

Adrenaline pumped through me as I walked next door.

My knock was reluctant, lighter than it used to be, representative of the shame I felt for having hurt her, for having left.

The stoic look on her face when she opened told me she'd been expecting me.

Despite my nerves, my body came alive with an awareness it hadn't felt in too damn long, because *holy shit* I'd nearly forgotten how beautiful she was. Only now, her eyes emanated pain and confusion instead of happiness as she looked at me. And I deserved every bit of it. I never wanted to leave her again, and knew I wouldn't—willingly, at least; I just had no clue how to convince her of that.

We stood in silence for the longest time, staring at each other until I finally mustered the courage to say, "Hello."

"Hi," she whispered.

I cleared my throat. "Can I come in?"

She nodded and moved out of the way.

Now we were back to staring at each other, only from a different spot.

"You look beautiful."

She didn't say anything, and that was all the hint I needed to understand how difficult this exchange was going to be.

Carys wore a fitted black turtleneck. Something told me she'd selected that particular shirt—one that covered her neck as protectively as armor—for the visit she likely knew I'd pay her today.

Sunny was playing on the floor. *Oh my God. Sunny.* I had to do a double-take. She'd gotten so much bigger. Her blond hair had grown and was tied up in a little wispy ponytail. When she finally looked up and saw me, she made brief eye contact and looked back down at her toys, as if I were a stranger.

My chest felt tight.

Did she not remember me? It had only been four months. Depending on how you looked at it, that could be a short time or a lifetime. I bet in almost-toddler years it was more the latter.

I walked over and knelt down. "Hey, Sunny. I missed you."

She looked up, handed me one of her toys, and babbled, but she didn't seem as excited as I'd hoped. I couldn't blame her, but it still hurt not to be greeted by that infectious smile I loved so much.

I put two little plastic people inside the toy car she'd given me, then wheeled it toward her.

When I turned around to face Carys, she had her arms crossed over her chest. If she could have covered her entire head with that turtleneck, she might have considered it.

I had my work cut out for me and could only pray I wasn't too late. Standing, I walked over to her. "I came by last night. You weren't here."

"I know."

"I figured Sharon told you."

"She did."

I couldn't fucking help myself. "You were out with someone?"

"Yes. I was on a date."

Dread filled me as adrenaline pumped through my veins. "With Charles?"

Her eyes narrowed. "Charles? No. Why would you think that?"

"Adrian told me he saw you together a while back, so I thought maybe…"

"No. I've been lonely, but not desperate. Although Charles has been making an effort to get to know Sunny for some time now."

"Are you good with that? He didn't force his way—"

"It's been fine. It's been my choice."

I nodded, looking down at my feet. "So you're seeing someone…"

She hesitated before answering. "It was a first date. He was really nice, but once Sharon texted me that you were back, I found it hard to focus."

Relief washed over me. I'd been about to apologize for ruining her night, but *fuck that*. I was thrilled I'd intercepted it. Now that she was standing right in front of me, I couldn't imagine how I'd ever let her go in the first place, couldn't fathom the idea of this woman I cared so deeply about in someone else's arms.

Her tone turned colder. "Why did you come back?"

Taking a deep breath in, I said, "Because it was time. I have a lot I need to explain, but I can't blame you if you're not ready to hear it."

"Just yesterday I thought I'd never see you again, so forgive me if I don't really know what to make of this, Deacon."

"I know I have no right to your immediate attention. You're in the driver's seat, Carys. If you're not in the mood to do this now, just let me know when we can talk. But we *need* to talk. Take all of the time you need to let the fact that I'm back set in. I'm here, and I'm not going anywhere again."

Her lip trembled. "And I'm supposed to believe that?"

"You don't have to believe it. You don't have to trust me, especially when I haven't given you a reason to. But it's the truth."

When she started to cry, it nearly undid me. I wanted so badly to hold her. But I knew doing so would be crossing a line.

She wiped her eyes. "I need some time before we do this—before we talk."

"I understand."

I'd often imagined this moment, the day I came back. It hadn't been as painful in my warped mind. Right now,

I'd stepped into an alternate universe, one where instead of making Carys smile, I caused her pain. And one where Sunny didn't recognize me. I was going to have to rebuild our relationship from the ground up—if Carys would even let me.

TWENTY-EIGHT

Carys

JUST COFFEE

Despite saying he'd give me time to ready myself, Deacon texted me a few days later to ask if I would be willing to meet him during my lunch break on one of the days I worked in the office. I said yes. We needed to have the conversation away from Sunny.

I chose Friday, but instead of a lunch meet-up, I opted to have the sitter stay late so I could meet Deacon after work. I didn't know how I'd feel after our talk, or how long the meeting would last, so I didn't want to have to go back to the office.

Deacon was waiting in a corner seat at Starbucks when I arrived. It was my first time in here since before he'd left for Minnesota. He looked painfully handsome, dressed in all black. He fidgeted with his hands as his eyes wandered the room. His mouth curved into a hesitant smile when he spotted me. He stood.

When I approached, I could tell he wasn't sure what to do, whether to hug me or not. He leaned in and gave me a peck on the cheek. My nipples stiffened as soon as his mouth touched my skin, reminding me how much control he had over my body. I couldn't let my strong physical attraction to him overpower my judgment.

"Sorry I'm a few minutes late," I said as I sat across from him.

"I'm sorry if I pushed things by asking for this meeting sooner rather than later. I just couldn't wait any longer."

"It's probably better that you pushed it, because I don't think I'll ever be ready."

He nodded. "I know." He pointed toward the counter and stood. "Let me get your usual."

My stomach growled as he walked to the register, not from hunger but from nerves.

He returned and handed me my drink. "Here you go. One pump, just how you like it."

I looked down at his name in black marker on the side of the cup, then back up at him.

When our eyes locked, he grinned slightly. My instinct was to smile back, but I wouldn't let myself.

"Thank you for the coffee."

"Of course."

Deacon's demeanor was a bit different from the last time I'd seen him right after he returned. His eye contact was more direct; he seemed determined to get through to me today.

He cleared his throat. "I know we don't have an infinite amount of time, so I'm just gonna start."

Staying silent, I took a sip of my drink.

"First off, I'll never be able to apologize enough for the way I freaked out after our accident. Leaving the way I did was not the answer. It felt like I was doing you a favor at the time, but I see things much differently now." He let out a long exhale. "The accident... It brought back some difficult memories for me, and I didn't handle it well." He shut his eyes. "There was something I hadn't told you, and that omission was part of why my reaction probably didn't make sense to you."

My heart sank. I'd always suspected there was something he hadn't said.

He took a deep breath. "When the accident happened back in college, my girlfriend at the time, Becca, was injured, too. She was ultimately okay—I told you that before. But...I didn't tell you she was pregnant." He swallowed.

I felt my eyes widen.

"She was four months along, and the impact of the crash was too much. She lost the baby."

Sadness rushed through my body. "I'm sorry. So sorry, Deacon."

He nodded and stared down at his cup. "So while the loss of my football career was devastating, it was compounded by knowing I hadn't been able to stop the accident that killed my unborn child. It was so much more than football. And I'm sorry for never telling you that part. I was very ashamed."

I reached across the table for his hand. He looped his fingers with mine.

"After the accident—understandably—Becca became depressed. Between that and my own depression, our relationship couldn't survive. We were so young to begin with." He squeezed my hand. "Anyway, we broke up, and soon after, I moved away to go to college out of state. And that was it."

He would've had a child around ten years old now. I let go of his hand. Touching him felt too intense at the moment.

Deacon ran his fingers through his hair. "I ran away from everything back then, Carys. I hadn't dealt with any of it until recently. It wasn't until I met you that I started allowing myself to even reflect on those days." He began to shred a napkin. "But then *our* accident, coming home from the farm..." He shut his eyes tightly for a moment. "It threw me back to that place I'd been a decade ago. I couldn't protect the two people I cared about most in this world—it scared the fuck out of me. And I panicked, overcome by the fear that I was destined to hurt the people I love."

I looked away. "Well, that certainly explains things a little more, but I don't understand why you couldn't have told me this then, why we couldn't have worked it out together."

He nodded silently. "I don't fully have the answer to why I reacted the way I did, why I couldn't sit down and tell you the story like I am now. I felt ashamed and a little shell-shocked, and I think running is my pattern. That's how I handled the first accident, and my impulse was to do the same again. I know that was terrible, but I've realized that all this time, I hadn't dealt with anything that happened back in college. I'd only buried it. It took being back in Minnesota, facing the people I believed I'd disappointed so badly, to start that process. Unfortunately, I also hurt and disappointed *you*."

"What happened in Minnesota?"

"A lot happened. I don't have to tell you about it all now, but—"

"Tell me," I interrupted. "We're here now. Tell me everything."

Deacon went on to recount his father's cancer diagnosis and how he'd connected again with his dad and his entire family. But I was most surprised by what he saved for last.

"Before I came back to New York, I decided to look Becca up on social media. I hadn't seen her since leaving home ten years ago. My father convinced me it was important to get some closure there, since a lot of my guilt came from hurting her."

A sudden wave of jealousy hit me. It was perhaps the strongest emotion I'd felt since this conversation started.

Did he rekindle something with Becca while he was away? "What happened?" I asked.

"Well, I found her profile online. We chatted for a bit and decided to meet for lunch."

As angry as I was at Deacon for leaving, and as sad as I was to learn he'd lost a baby, nothing gripped me as powerfully as my jealousy over his reconnecting with someone he likely once loved.

"We met at this restaurant near her house. I told her we didn't have to talk about the past if she didn't want to, but she was open to it. And it wasn't anything like I'd expected—and dreaded."

"Did you love her?"

"I thought I did. But honestly, I'm not sure if it was love. I was so young. I didn't know what I wanted. When we found out she was pregnant, we had planned to stay together because of the baby, but then everything fell apart."

Swallowing the lump in my throat, I asked, "What did Becca say when you met with her?"

He blew out a long breath. "She said she was pretty devastated that first year, not only about losing the baby, but about losing me. But in the end, she came to the conclusion that everything happens for a reason. She saw a therapist—something I've never done but probably should. A year after the accident, Becca went back to school. A couple of years ago, she met her current fiancé. They live together in the next town over from my parents with their dog."

I exhaled. "So she's happy."

"Yeah, and my takeaway is that all these years I'd believed she must hate me and blame me for everything. But that was a reflection of my feelings toward myself. I know now that lack of communication can lead to years of needless suffering. Maybe I *wanted* to suffer because I felt I deserved it, but I certainly didn't have to. And I don't want to repeat that mistake, though I've already caused *you* needless suffering, too. I know that."

We sat in silence for a bit until he took my hand again and looked into my eyes.

"Leaving the way I did was a huge mistake. I'm not justifying it, only trying to explain what I was thinking at the time and let you know that I grew a lot while I was away. I don't know where your head is, Carys, or whether you can ever learn to trust me again. But I need you to know that I see things more clearly now. I'm not going anywhere. Even if you choose not to give me another chance, I'm not leaving again. I'll be here for you no matter what—if not as your lover, then as your friend."

I sighed, feeling so many things all at once. "I don't know what to say. I haven't processed you coming back, let alone all of this. I'm not sure I can trust you not to leave again. That's not something I want to go through a second time—or a third time, actually. I'd rather be alone."

"I understand," he said after a moment. "Can I ask you one favor?"

"Okay…"

"Will you let me bring you coffee again? No commitments. No promises. Just coffee a few times a week."

It seemed like a simple thing, but it was letting him back into my life. Would I be better off not seeing him while I thought things through? He had just poured his heart out to me, though… And I did have a different perspective on why he left. In the end, the pained look in his eyes made it impossible to say no.

"Okay. Just coffee."

His expression transformed. "Thank you. It's more than just coffee to me. Thank you for not shutting me out, even though I probably deserve it."

After we finished our drinks, Deacon and I left the café separately. I made the excuse that I needed to stop at the store so I could walk back to the apartment alone.

That night, sleep evaded me as a million thoughts floated through my mind, including an internal debate about trusting Deacon again, and images of a beautiful baby with his eyes who never came to be.

TWENTY-NINE

Deacon

HOW DEEP IS YOUR LOVE?

You've heard the saying that *life is not a sprint, it's a marathon*? Well, earning Carys's trust back was more like a slow wade through an ocean. But it was worth it, even if not getting to reach out and touch her was downright painful. A month-and-a-half after I returned to New York, my relationship with Carys was slowly improving.

One afternoon, as we sat in her living room drinking the coffees I'd brought over, I presented her with something I'd made back in Minnesota.

I took it out of the small bag. "I forgot to give this to you. It's for Sunny. I made it while I was home."

Carys smiled as she examined the pink hat. "You crocheted this?"

"Yup. My grandmother was trying to get me out of her house, where I stayed half the time. She wanted to invite dirty old men over without my being there, but that's a story for another day." I laughed. "Anyway, she commissioned me to help her make hats and scarves, just like the old days, figuring it would make me want to leave. I'm not sure it will fit. Might be too big."

"Well, there's only one way to find out." Carys walked over to where Sunny was playing with her toys. She placed it on her head. "It's perfect."

It did seem to fit, but unfortunately, Sunny hated it. She took it off almost immediately and threw it on the ground. That's about how I'd been doing with Sunny since I returned. She'd offer me some smiles, and things were a little better, but it wasn't the same as before. She didn't cling to me. She didn't adore me like she used to. I was determined to get back there.

"Maybe the material wasn't comfortable on her head," I said. "It can be a little scratchy."

Carys's expression softened. "It's the thought that counts. Thank you for making it."

"There wasn't a moment I was away that I wasn't thinking about you," I said.

"Were you with anyone?" she asked.

The way she'd unleashed that question made me think it had been weighing on her mind, just waiting to come out.

"No!" I rushed to reassure her. "No, I wasn't. I haven't touched anyone since you. I thought that was understood. I'm glad you asked, if you were doubting that."

Carys's face was red, and she let out a deep breath. It made my heart come alive, and gave me confidence that she hadn't totally written us off.

She changed the subject. "How's your dad?"

"He's good. He hasn't had any negative reaction from the radiation. I think he's going to beat this."

"I'm glad." She smiled.

There was a knock at the door.

"Are you expecting someone?" I asked.

"It's Charles. I told him he could come over to see Sunny today."

Shit. I'd managed to avoid Sunny's father until now, other than that night months ago when I'd kicked him out of here. But he was coming around regularly now, so I suppose it was time I got used to him.

Carys went to the door, and I stood up from the couch. Charles looked equally surprised to see me.

"You haven't formally met Deacon," she said.

He held out his hand. "Deacon. Long time no see. Although I believe you told me your name was *Dick* the last time we met."

We shook.

"Just doin' my job," I said.

"I appreciate that you were diligent in protecting my daughter that day."

When she spotted him, Sunny ran to Charles and tugged on his leg.

He lifted her. "Hi, beautiful girl."

That stung. But he'd been here when I hadn't. And the months I was gone were enough to undo the bond I'd had with Sunny—allowing space for him to form one.

Charles sat on the floor and played with Sunny, while Carys and I watched. We finished our coffees in silence. It was a strange dynamic.

I took the time to reflect on my future with Carys. Maybe there was no way to erase the hurt I'd caused. Maybe I could only work to mask it. Either way, I hadn't figured out how to do that yet, how to make her happy when she was still so guarded toward me.

After about forty-five minutes, Charles kissed Sunny's head and looked over at me. "You mind taking a walk with me, Deacon?"

I turned to Carys who shrugged.

"Sure."

Charles and I exited the apartment together.

"Two fuckboys…"

"Did you hear something?" Charles said. "Did someone say…*fuckboys*?"

Mrs. Winsbanger's door moved.

I nodded for him to follow me down the hall. "That's our crazy neighbor. She likes to spy on everyone and has the mouth of a truck driver."

Charles started to laugh, and I followed suit. As nuts as Mrs. Winsbanger was, she'd broken the ice a little.

We said nothing else to each other until we made it outside the building.

Charles slid his hands into his pockets as we walked. "I don't need to tell you the story of what happened with Carys and me," he said. "I'm sure you know what I did, how I abandoned her when she needed me the most."

I nodded, letting him continue.

"It's been a challenge getting her to trust me enough to be around Sunny, but we've finally arrived at a good place. I didn't deserve a second chance, but she gave it to me anyway."

As much as I never liked this guy, his words gave me a shred of hope for my own situation.

"I'm not going to lie to you, Deacon. If Carys would have me back, I would love to be with her. She's beautiful and kind, and something you can't begin to understand, because you weren't around in those days—she's so very talented."

"I wish I had known her then."

"My point is...despite my feelings for her, there's no future there. She doesn't love me the way she loves you."

My heart began to accelerate as we weaved through people on the sidewalk. "How do you know she loves me?"

"When you were away, she wouldn't talk about you for a long time. But she finally told me what happened. It's clear to me that her feelings still run deep. She's just afraid of getting hurt again. Unfortunately, I started the trend. If you fuck up a second time, that would make three times she's had her heart broken. That can't happen."

I raised my voice. "That's *not* gonna happen."

"Only you can prove that. If I thought I had a shot with her, I'd be giving you no advice right now. I envy the fuck out of you for even standing a chance. So don't waste this opportunity."

I raised my eyebrow. "I'm surprised to be getting such encouragement from the enemy."

He chuckled. "The first time I met you, I didn't like you. You pushed me away and wouldn't let me see my daughter. But here's the thing, I respected the hell out of you for it. You were protecting Sunny that night—something I wasn't able to do at the time. That should've been my job as her father, not yours. It takes a strong man to be a good father to his own kids, but it takes a special kind of man to be a father to someone else's." He stopped walking to look me in the eyes. "If you want Carys, if you want a life with her and Sunny, then prove it. Do whatever it takes, and don't fuck up again."

"I don't plan to." This guy really surprised me. Maybe I didn't hate him so much after all.

Charles nodded. "I'd rather see her with someone I know is a decent person than some asshole from the Internet. But just know that I'll be around, too. I'm Sunny's father. And I'm earning my way back in. I'd be willing to share that role if you earn the right to it, too."

"Understood."

I would've never imagined that Carys's deadbeat ex could inspire a new determination in me to stay the course, to fight for what I wanted. But maybe the greatest lessons come from those who've been there, who've lost things they can never get back.

Later that afternoon, when I'd gone back to my apartment, I noticed a bright pink postcard slipped under my door. There was an elephant on the front and it read *Sunny Turns 2*.

My chest constricted. Her birthday party would be held at the YMCA in a couple of weeks.

Two. Where did the time go?

This invitation meant everything. Carys wanted me there, despite her reservations. This elephant meant there was still hope.

The gym at the YMCA was all decked out in pink. A bouncy house in the shape of a castle had been set up, along with a ball pit and obstacle course made out of soft objects.

Charles sat with his teenage son in a corner of the gym. Carys's friend Simone, whom I'd only met once, was jumping with a girl I assumed was Charles's daughter, based on the resemblance.

Also in the mix were several toddlers and their parents, people I figured Carys knew from her Mommy and Me class.

Carys stood next to the refreshment table with an older woman. She hadn't seen me yet. Pink and gray balloons surrounded her. The cake on the table had a big elephant on it—and of course there was me: the *biggest* elephant in the room, the man who'd broken Carys's heart. Many of the people here likely knew the story and would be sizing me up today.

I placed the giant bag containing Sunny's gift on a table with the other presents.

Carys finally noticed me and waved for me to come over.

"Deacon, this is my boss, Cynthia."

Ah. I should've known.

"Cynthia... This is my friend Deacon."

Friend. Ouch.

Cynthia was probably in her late fifties. She had her brown hair up in a twist and exuded elegance, just how I might picture someone who ran a ballet.

I extended my hand. "Cynthia, it's a pleasure to meet you."

"You, as well." She smiled, not seeming to give off any funny signals; that made me think Carys had never talked about me with her.

Sensing a vibe, perhaps, Cynthia excused herself under the guise of wanting some punch, leaving Carys and me alone.

"I'm glad you could make it," she said.

"Wild horses couldn't have kept me away. Or wild elephants." I smiled.

"You look nice," she said, touching my arm as her cheeks turned pink.

I was unsure of a lot of things when it came to Carys lately, but I knew I still had an effect on her physically. But instead of feeling smug about that, it made me sad and frustrated, because I wanted her so badly. I always told myself I would know when the time was right to make a move. It hadn't come yet.

"This was a really great idea—to have the party here," I said.

"Well, I knew the apartment wasn't an option, and I wanted it somewhere she could have a good time."

"Mission accomplished." My eyes wandered over to Sunny, swimming around in the ball pit. "Look at that face."

Carys smiled over at her daughter, and I took that moment to stare at her gorgeous profile.

"My baby is so happy around other kids. And they're all too young to notice or care that she looks different. It's a beautiful age."

I shook my head. "She was six months old when I met her. Where the hell did a year and a half go?" Of course, that reminded me I'd been gone for four months of that time. I swallowed. "Can I help you with anything?"

"No. This place is great. They have everything covered. They bring in the pizza and cake and clean everything up."

"Well, if you need help packing those gifts into the car, I'm your man. I'll be here till the end." My eyes seared into hers. I wasn't just referring to today.

"I'll keep that in mind."

Carys wore a pink dress with thin straps and a flared skirt. The skin on her neck was slightly blotchy. I knew that happened when she was nervous.

"You look beautiful in pink. Well, you look beautiful in everything. So fucking beautiful."

She moved her hair behind her ear. "Thank you."

Perhaps my gaze lingered a little too long, because she excused herself to go talk to one of the other parents.

I spent the remainder of the afternoon watching Sunny having a blast and stealing glances at Carys. I wondered how this day would have been different if I hadn't left. Carys might have been leaning against my chest as I wrapped my arms around her and watched Sunny play. Sunny might have been closer to me than she was to Charles. I reminded myself that I couldn't be here for them the way I was now if I hadn't freaked out, hadn't gone home, hadn't made peace with my demons. I knew now that I would never hurt them again.

When Sunny opened her presents, I waited anxiously for her to get to mine.

Eventually, Carys handed her the large bag I'd brought and opened the card. "It's from Deacon, Sunny. What is it? Let's see!" she said.

Sunny seemed more mesmerized by the pink tissue paper than anything else.

Carys helped Sunny remove a furry, gray elephant from the bag. I'd figured if she liked elephants, I couldn't go wrong with a big, stuffed one.

"If you push on the chest, it plays a song," I said.

Carys pressed her hand to the center of the elephant, and her mouth dropped open when the song began: "How

Deep is Your Love" by the Bee Gees. I had no clue if Sunny would even recognize it.

It was a pleasant surprise when Sunny hugged the elephant to her and flashed a huge smile—the biggest one I'd contributed to since I'd been back. Her eyes turned to slits as the beautiful grin spread even wider across her face. Carys had admitted that she'd stopped playing the Bee Gees album for Sunny after I left, so I knew she hadn't heard that song in a long time. Whether she remembered it from before or not, she was sure as hell connecting to it now. Maybe one day she'd connect to me again, too.

Charles and his kids presented their gift next: a gigantic stack of children's books. Charles began reading off the titles, one of which was *Monkey Bandit and the Naughty Ball*.

Carys, standing next to me, leaned in and whispered, "Monkey balls."

Holy shit. I started to crack up, elated that she remembered the day Mrs. Winsbanger had called me that. I'd never forget that day, our first coffee together. It all started with monkey balls, and at this moment, monkey balls gave me hope that all was not lost.

THIRTY

Carys

NAUGHTY GIRL

The months since Deacon's return had reminded me a lot of the early days of our relationship. He was there when I needed him but didn't cross any boundaries. I knew he was being careful not to make assumptions about my readiness to let him back into my life.

It all felt a little like déjà vu because Deacon had reverted back to being a good friend I desperately wanted to have sex with. But I hadn't let myself *go there* yet. I kept waiting to feel a hundred-percent sure he would never hurt me again. But is it ever possible to be absolutely certain?

One Saturday afternoon, Sharon called to tell me she had the day free if I wanted her to come spend a few hours with Sunny. She said she figured I might appreciate some time to myself. Never one to refuse unexpected help, I thanked her and said I would love to take her up on that.

She arrived about an hour later. As I kissed Sunny goodbye and headed out the door, I realized I had absolutely nowhere to be. I didn't want to *go* anywhere. I wanted to see Deacon. I wanted to be *alone* with Deacon, something that—very strategically on my part—hadn't happened since he'd come back.

But how would I make that happen without sending the wrong message? Did I care about the consequences anymore? My body was more than ready, but my mind wasn't there yet.

I stood in front of his door, frozen, for probably five minutes.

"Naughty girl...going to get the boom-boom from Fuckboy."

I turned around to see Mrs. Winsbanger's door suddenly close.

Shit.

If she was onto me, surely Deacon would see right through this little spur-of-the-moment visit, too?

Nevertheless, I sighed and decided to knock.

Deacon opened the door with a white towel wrapped around his waist. Water dripped down his bare chest. *Holy shit*. I'd nearly forgotten how hot this man's body was.

"What's up, beautiful? This is a nice surprise."

My eyes traveled down his torso. "I'm sorry to interrupt."

"You're not interrupting. I just took a quick shower after the gym. I'm glad you're here."

Barely able to get the words out, I said, "I, uh, got an unexpected call from Sharon. She had some time today and offered to babysit. So I was wondering if you wanted to hang out."

I couldn't break my eyes away from his amazing chest, hard and glistening. He was even more ripped than I remembered. Deacon had mentioned working out more lately, perhaps to get out some of the sexual frustration.

"I would absolutely love to spend time with you." He stepped out of the way. "Come in. Please."

We faced each other in the middle of his living room, the proximity of his body wreaking havoc on me.

He smiled knowingly.

Yup. He was onto me. "What?" I asked.

His mouth curved into a smirk. "I like the way you're looking at me right now."

"I'm trying not to."

"I know you've worked really hard not to be alone with me up until this point. I get it. But...what do you want, Carys?" His eyes brimmed with intensity. "Because I'm pretty sure it's the same fucking thing I want right now."

The utter need in his voice matched the feeling in my loins. He pressed his chest into me, and I buried my face in his hard pecs.

"Apparently, I'm obvious," I said, speaking into his skin. "Even Mrs. Winsbanger called me out for coming over here to have sex with you."

His laughter shook against me. "Mrs. Winsbanger thinks everyone is having sex twenty-four-seven."

I looked up to meet his glassy eyes. "I want you," I whispered.

He nodded. "But you're scared."

"Yes."

He pulled back to look into my eyes, placing his big, rough hands around my face. "Please don't be scared of me anymore."

My breathing quickened. "I'm sorry."

Deacon placed a firm kiss on my forehead. "Don't you dare apologize."

He kissed down to my nose, and then my mouth. I opened for him as his tongue slipped inside. *Damn.* It was good to taste him again.

His nails dug into my side, his voice filled with need. "It's been a long fucking time for both of us. If you want me right now, it doesn't have to mean shit, Carys. Just use me. Fucking use me. Let me make you feel good. I promise it doesn't have to be anything more than sex yet, if you don't want it to. And yes, I would say just about anything to have you. Because I need it. But I promise I won't hurt you."

Closing my eyes, I nodded, so desperate for him.

The next thing I knew, I felt his hand under my dress and between my legs, shifting my drenched panties to the side and slipping his fingers in. The sound that escaped me signified a long hunger, finally satisfied.

Burying his fingers inside me, he moved in and out as I tightened the muscles between my legs. His lips enveloped mine as he continued to fuck me with his hand. My body went wild. Unable to pull his hair hard enough, I was practically climbing him. As soon as he pulled his fingers out and pressed his erection against me, I knew I was done for. There was no turning back.

"Carys, I'm gonna fuck you so damn hard. Do you want that?"

"Yes," I panted.

I ripped the towel off of him. His erect cock glistened at the tip, and I couldn't wait to feel him inside of me.

Deacon undid the zipper at the back of my dress and pulled the frock over my head. He lifted me off the ground and wrapped my legs around his waist, entering me in one hard thrust. It burned for a few seconds before the euphoria set in. He was bare inside of me with no barrier, something I'd never experienced with him before.

"Fuck. I forgot how damn good this feels," he said, pumping in and out of me.

Deacon's teeth sank gently into the side of my neck as he began to fuck me hard, holding me up with his hands under my ass. There was something so carnal about biting my neck. This felt different from any other time we'd had sex.

He suddenly pulled out. "I have to get a condom."

As much as I didn't want to stop, I knew that was the right decision.

He put me down gently, and I marveled at his sculpted ass as he ran to his bedroom. He returned with the rubber in hand, ripping the package before slipping the condom over his thick shaft.

"I want to take you on the floor, down on this rug, because Sharon doesn't need to hear how hard I'm gonna fuck you right now. I would fucking break the bed."

I quivered with excitement and lowered myself to the floor. As soon as my back hit the soft, shag rug, Deacon was inside of me again, penetrating me hard and fast. The weight of his body was overwhelming. How I'd missed having him over me like this. His lips locked on mine as we refused to come up for air, our hands intertwined. Every part of me felt connected to him as he rammed into me.

"I love you, Carys," he said softly. "I'm sorry. I know I said this was just sex, but I fucking love you, and I need you to know it while I'm inside you. I love you so much. Don't say it back. That's not what this is about."

As much as I'd tried to convince myself this was only sex, the second he said those words, my muscles pulsated even harder. The thought of fucking him had thrilled me, but the knowledge that he was making love to me put me over the edge. Because the truth was, I loved this man so much, and no amount of fear or mistrust could erase that. I would *always* love Deacon.

He snapped me out of my thoughts when he lifted my ass, sliding me toward him before throwing my legs over his shoulders.

He thrust into me hard for a few seconds from that position before his body shook and he groaned in pleasure. The feel of Deacon's hot cum filling the condom prompted my own release. It was the most intense orgasm of my life.

As he came, he kept repeating, "I love you. I love you, Carys. I love you. I love you. I love you."

With the wind knocked out of me, my body lay limp against Deacon's floor as he hovered above, still inside me.

He lowered himself to kiss my neck. "Are you okay?"

I smiled. "Yes."

He cupped my cheek before taking my mouth with his again.

Then he pulled out and stood up, showcasing his gloriously naked body, the full condom tip hanging from his cock.

He ventured to the bathroom to dispose of it, then returned to the rug. He wrapped his arms around me from behind, pulling my body into his.

I turned to meet his face. "Do you mind if I take a shower?"

He drew me in closer. "Of course not. But on one condition."

"What?"

"You let me take you to our favorite diner for lunch."

I beamed. "That sounds good."

I sat up and was just about to head to the bathroom when he wrapped his arm around my waist. "Come here," he said, pulling me back for another kiss.

After he finally let me go, I took a long shower, relishing the masculine smell of his body wash. My insides ached in the best possible way.

Once out, I took my clothes into his room to change, where I noticed an open book face down on his desk. *Down Syndrome Parenting 101*. Another book sat next to it. *The Everything Sign Language Book*.

While I'd been stuck in limbo over whether to trust Deacon again, he'd been moving forward—learning and preparing for a life with us, whenever I was ready.

A week later, Deacon and I hadn't spent a night apart since that day at his apartment.

One afternoon he offered to go on a Target run for me since Sunny wasn't feeling well. She almost never got sick, but today she had a small fever.

One of the things on my lengthy, handwritten list was children's pain reliever, since I was running out.

Deacon sent a text from the store.

Deacon: Is the generic brand really as good as the name brand?

Carys: It's supposed to be the same thing.

The dots moved around.

Deacon: Okay.

A few minutes later, he sent another message.

Deacon: Not gonna risk it. Getting the name brand.

I smiled. The sweet and caring side beneath that masculine exterior never ceased to amaze me.

Carys: Okay.

Several minutes went by before he reached out again.

Deacon: What's organic penis?

Carys: Huh?

He sent a photo of my handwriting.

Carys: That says organic peaches. Sorry for my chicken scratch.

Deacon: I was gonna say... ;-) Mine is totally organic, by the way. But got it. Peaches. Organic.

He followed that with five peach emojis.

Deacon: Ironically, the peach emoji represents ass. So you can imagine where my mind is going right now.

Next, he texted an eggplant emoji and a peach.

Carys: That reminds me, get an eggplant, too. Gonna try to make eggplant lasagna tomorrow.

Deacon: Yes, ma'am.

The texts stopped for a while. Then I received a photo of a black, lace thong draped over his hand.

Deacon: After all that talk of eggplants and peaches, I walked by the ladies' underwear section, saw this, and pictured you in it, bent over in front of me. Now I'm fucking hard in the middle of Target.

Deacon: I need to get in line, but it's not safe to leave this aisle at the moment.

Deacon: Shit! An old lady is looking for granny panties across from me, and I'm hiding in place with a stiffy.

I doubled over in laughter.

Deacon: I shit you not, I think the old lady just farted.

THE Anti-BOYFRIEND

Deacon: Fuck my life.

Deacon: That's it. I'm moving out of here. I've got the cart in front of me to hide my junk. And thanks to her, I'm not that hard anymore anyway.

Carys: Will you just come home before you get into trouble? LOL

Deacon: Heading home. With the thong. You. Me. Tonight. It's on.

I sighed. We'd had our ups and downs, but I really did love this man.

Deacon: By the way, you're a size small in shirts, right?

Carys: Yes. Why?

Deacon: I got you something.

Carys: Uh-oh. Let me guess. Low-cut neckline?

He sent a photo of a plain, white, fitted T-shirt with a simple message on the front: *I Heart My Boyfriend*.

My face hurt from smiling.

Carys: You know, before we got together, I used to refer to you as the "Anti-Boyfriend."

Deacon: Oh really? Well, the "Anti-Boyfriend" found the one.

I sighed.

Carys: Hurry back.

One more text came in about five minutes later.

Deacon: Picked you up a coffee from the Starbucks in here.

He sent a photo of the cup, which had a message written in black marker. At first, I thought it said, *Carys Like Paris*. But then I looked closer and realized he was getting me back for the peaches mistake earlier.
Carys Likes Penis.

EPILOGUE

Deacon

Getting Carys to fully believe in me didn't happen as quickly as I'd hoped. And there was no formal discussion or announcement when things had finally crossed the barrier of trust. Our being back together happened slowly and organically. I spent every day for months showing her I wasn't going anywhere, and taking the time to learn how to be a good partner to her and a father to Sunny. Because I'd put in the work, I finally reaped the rewards.

In the five years since Carys entered my life, I'd learned many things, including the following, in no particular order.

One: You can't prove yourself with words, only actions.

Two: You can't choose who you love. It never mattered what I told myself about not getting into a relationship with Carys. From the moment we connected, I was destined to lose the battle with my brain.

Three: Full freedom can't be achieved until you forgive yourself. I finally sought therapy for my fear of failure and harming others and learned how important self-compassion was to my recovery.

Four: It's not all about you, Deacon. There were things in life far more important than myself. Sunny taught me that. When you have children, they come first, always.

And finally, I learned blood doesn't make you family. Sunny is my daughter, and it doesn't matter that I didn't technically make her. The only caveat? I had to share the father role with Charles. She called neither one of us Dad. I was Deek and he was Cha-Cha. But we both believed we were her father, neither of us willing to give that designation to the other. So we accepted that Sunny would have two fathers, each checking and balancing the other and holding each other accountable.

My daughter is a trip. She recently learned to twerk, thanks to Charles's daughter, Talia. At five and a half, Sunny's speech was still a work in progress. While Carys and I could understand almost everything she said, it wasn't always clear to others. But we'd been told that with continued therapy, her speech would improve as she got older. She'd be able to meet all the same milestones as a typical kid, just on her own schedule. No one knew exactly what the future would bring for Sunny in terms of living independently, but I had high hopes that she would achieve whatever she set her sights on. I'd be there cheering her on until the day I died.

Of course, it wouldn't have been possible for me to fall in love with Sunny if I hadn't fallen in love with her mother first. A couple of years ago, Carys and I left Sunny behind with Charles for the first time and flew to Vegas to get married. It was four glorious days of having my beautiful ballerina all to myself. Soon after we got back, we moved to the suburbs of New Jersey so we could have a yard.

Now we were typical suburbanites, spending our Saturday morning at our kid's soccer game. Not only had I never foreseen myself as a dad, but I certainly never imagined my grand return to sports would be as a soccer coach for a bunch of rugrats. Sunny's school offered an integrated sports program, so the kids with special needs played right alongside the others. I figured rather than having to force myself to stay on the sidelines, I'd coach the team—you know, in case Sunny ever needed me.

But you know what? Most of the time, she didn't. And I was learning to let her fall sometimes. That was hard.

I waved to Charles, sitting in the stands with his two kids. They showed up for each and every one of Sunny's games. When we moved, we'd intentionally bought a place close to Charles, since he often helped out with Sunny.

Our daughter was a joy to watch on the field. She loved being around other kids, and they'd often help lead her in the right direction. She didn't always follow the rules of the game, and had only made one goal the entire season, with the help of one of her peers, but she always had a smile on her face. With Sunny, it was never about the destination. It was the journey. If she fell while running, she always picked herself up and kept going. People could definitely learn a few things from my little girl.

When today's game finally ended, Sunny ran to Carys, who'd been watching from a blanket on the grass. Charles and his kids came over to give her high fives.

A couple of parents interrupted me on my way to my family, so it took me a while to join them.

When I finally broke free and got to Carys, I said, "Ready to head home?"

She nodded and tugged on one of Sunny's two blond braids. "You're going to need the longest bath, girl. Let's get you home and scrub you down."

I leaned in to whisper in Carys's ear, "Did you say *rub* down? I could use a rub down later."

She shook her head, and I stole a quick kiss before wrapping my arm around her. We walked back toward the car.

Sunny looked up at me and made her hand into a fist while mimicking licking a cone, which was sign language for ice cream. The ice cream truck was parked at the edge of the parking lot.

"You need to have lunch first," I told her.

She jumped up and down. "Peez, Deek!"

I sighed and reached for my wallet.

"You're such a sucker." Carys laughed.

After we got Sunny her frozen treat, we resumed the long walk to the car, which was parked at the far end of the lot in a shady spot under a tree.

"I was so proud of Sunny today," Carys said. "I'm glad I never pushed the ballet thing, because it's clear she's much more interested in sports."

Carys now held a part-time position as an instructor for a local dance school. She'd tried enrolling Sunny in some classes there, but all our daughter did was fidget with her tutu and make silly faces at me. She had no interest, but she was always excited for her soccer practice and games.

"Well, if Sunny's going to be a tomboy, maybe I can get this one to dance with me." Carys kissed the top of our baby boy's head.

"If he wants to dance instead of playing sports, that's his choice," I said.

Jack had been sleeping in the carrier on Carys's chest the entire game. He was six months old now—exactly the age Sunny was when I met Carys. We'd waited to have a baby so we could give Sunny as much attention as possible in her toddler years. Then when Carys found out she was pregnant, she decided to leave her PR gig to devote more time to the kids and not commute into the city. Our boy evened out our little family of four. And I was much better equipped to change diapers this time around.

We got to the car, and Carys got Jack into his car seat while I fastened Sunny's seatbelt as she continued to eat her ice cream.

As we drove through the parking lot, Sunny yelled, "Monkey bah!"

Carys and I turned to each other.

"Did she just say monkey balls?" Carys asked. "Who taught you that, Sunny?"

Sunny pointed to her left. "Monkey bah!"

I realized she was pointing to the playground. *Monkey bars*. "Monkey *bars*!" I said.

"Oh!" Carys started to laugh. "For a second, I thought you taught her that." Carys turned around. "No playground today, honey. We don't have time. Maybe next weekend."

As we traveled down the tree-lined road, I could see Carys smiling over at me.

"What are you smiling at, beautiful?"

"When I met you, I couldn't have imagined the stud next door would end up my husband, and we'd be living in the suburbs with two kids."

"And that I'd be coaching soccer. Not exactly playing the field in the same way anymore." I chuckled and reached for her hand. "But you know, it all makes sense now."

"What does?"

"Everything had to happen the way it did. Could you imagine if I'd gone on to play for the NFL? I would've never met you. I probably would've gotten myself into some kind of messed-up shit. I guarantee you I wouldn't be this content. All those years I thought losing that career was the worst thing that ever happened to me. But my second act? This? I'd take it any day over that other life."

Carys squeezed my hand. "When you said that, you reminded me of something. Did I ever tell you how I came up with Sunny's name?"

"No."

"I was all alone in the hospital after I had her. The entire pregnancy had been scary with so many unknowns, and on top of that, I'd just learned my baby had Down's. Fear had nearly crippled me." She stared out the window a moment. "The day before, I'd given birth to her in a blur with a ton of drugs. After everything I'd been through, for the first time, it was just me and Sunny. She looked up at me, probably wondering where the hell she was. I looked out the hospital room window and saw the sun coming up. I just kept looking at that sunrise over the city and back at her little face. She'd just been through the hell of birth, yet she was so peaceful. She was alive and content in my arms. And I realized I wasn't alone at all anymore. I had everything I needed. *Sunny.* The light that emerges from darkness."

"That's beautiful," I said, feeling a lump in my throat. "I've always loved her name. But now I love it even more."

In the rearview mirror, I glanced back at Sunny, whose ice cream cone was now melted all over her face.

The light that emerges from darkness. "You know how you felt when you saw the sun that day, Carys? Pretty sure that's exactly what I felt the first time I looked into your eyes."

OTHER BOOKS
by Penelope Ward

RoomHate

Neighbor Dearest

The Day He Came Back

Just One Year

When August Ends

Love Online

Gentleman Nine

Drunk Dial

Mack Daddy

Stepbrother Dearest

Jaded and Tyed (A novelette)

Sins of Sevin

Jake Undone (Jake #1)

Jake Understood (Jake #2)

My Skylar

Gemini

My Favorite Souvenir (Co-written with Vi Keeland)

Dirty Letters (Co-written with Vi Keeland)

Hate Notes (Co-written with Vi Keeland)

Rebel Heir (Co-written with Vi Keeland)

Rebel Heart (Co-written with Vi Keeland)

British Bedmate (Co-written with Vi Keeland)

Mister Moneybags (Co-written with Vi Keeland)

Playboy Pilot (Co-written with Vi Keeland)
Stuck-Up Suit (Co-written with Vi Keeland)
Cocky Bastard (Co-written with Vi Keeland)

ACKNOWLEDGEMENTS

This book was written during a really challenging year for all of us. In these unprecedented times, I'm so happy to be able to help provide an escape for you. I consider myself the luckiest gal in the world to have readers all over the world who continue to support and promote my books. Your enthusiasm and hunger for my stories is what motivates me every day. And to all of the book bloggers who work tirelessly to support me, please know how much I appreciate you.

To Vi – Forever my partner in crime. Hopefully you don't get tired of me singing your praises. Each year our friendship becomes more invaluable to me. I couldn't do any of this without you. The best part of this career has been our collaborations and getting to work with my friend each and every day.

To Julie – My late-night watch dog. Thank you for your friendship and for always inspiring me with your amazing writing and attitude.

To Luna –Thank you for being there day in and day out and especially this year for being such an inspiration. The best is yet to come.

To Erika –Thank you for always brightening my days with your daily check-ins and virtual smiles. It will always be an E thing!

To Cheri – An amazing friend and supporter. Thanks for always looking out. Can't wait 'til the day we can all get together again.

To my Facebook reader group, Penelope's Peeps – I adore you all. You are my home and favorite place to be.

To my agent extraordinaire, Kimberly Brower – Thank you for everything you do and for believing in me long before you were my agent, back when you were a blogger and I was a first-time author.

To my editor Jessica Royer Ocken – It's always a pleasure working with you. I look forward to many more experiences to come.

To Elaine of Allusion Book Formatting and Publishing – Thank you for being the best proofreader, formatter, and friend a girl could ask for.

To my assistant Brooke – Thank you for your hard work in handling all of the things Vi and I can't seem to ever get to. We appreciate you so much!

To Kylie and Jo at Give Me Books – You guys are amazing! Thank you for your tireless promotional work.

To Letitia of RBA Designs – My awesome cover designer. This cover is one of my favorites that you've designed. Thank you for always working with me until the finished product is exactly perfect.

To my husband – Thank you for always taking on so much more than you should have to so that I am able to write. I love you so much.

To the best parents in the world – I'm so lucky to have you! Thank you for everything you have ever done for me and for always being there.

Last but not least, to my daughter and son – Mommy loves you. You are my motivation and inspiration!

ABOUT THE AUTHOR

Penelope Ward is a *New York Times, USA Today* and *#1 Wall Street Journal* bestselling author.

She grew up in Boston with five older brothers and spent most of her twenties as a television news anchor. Penelope resides in Rhode Island with her husband, son and beautiful daughter with autism.

With over 1.5 million books sold, she is a twenty-time *New York Times* bestseller and the author of over twenty novels.

Penelope's books have been translated into over a dozen languages and can be found in bookstores around the world.

Subscribe to Penelope's newsletter here:
http://bit.ly/1X725rj

Made in United States
North Haven, CT
09 July 2022

21130104R00198